ALSO BY EDWARD J. DELANEY

Broken Irish
Warp and Weft
The Drowning and Other Stories

FOLLOW THE SUN

Requests for permission to make copies of any part of the work should be sent to:
  Turtle Point Press
  info@turtlepointpress.com

Library of Congress Cataloging-in-Publication Data is available from the publisher upon request

Cover photograph by Emerald Bailey
Design by Jakob Vala

Hardcover ISBN: 978-1-885983-55-8
Paperback ISBN: 978-1-885983-51-0
Ebook ISBN: 978-1-885983-56-5

Printed in the United States of America

EDWARD J. DELANEY

FOLLOW THE SUN

TURTLE POINT PRESS
BROOKLYN, NEW YORK

PART ONE

THE FUNERAL FOR A MISSING MAN BECOMES REDUCED to objects. Small proxies, a collection of artifacts. In lieu of a body, just left-behind things. Things judged dear to the departed, or emblematic of his quicksilver existence, as all our existences are ultimately mercurial. The table, where the eye looks for a casket, is set up with his childhood photos and the chosen props: the mildewed leather baseball glove, the football cleats, all the equipment of lost youth. The brass sextant, ceremonial and that day left behind, ironic perhaps for a man disappeared into the sea. Some rust-tinged tools, as if the place setting of a simple life. As present in the moment are the objects not offered: the needles and pipes and plastic bags, all those defeated soldiers of a decades-long war. How ironic, then, that his beloved sea has claimed him after he'd thought he'd looked behind at all his demons.

The funeral parlor, filled with his own kind, of two kinds: the remnants of his family and old friends, and to the other side, the thick-handed lobstermen rubbing their weathered faces, itching to cast off even as they account for another loss among them. Small murmurs in the back rows about another, a man swept off a deck down by Cape May. They sit in leather jackets and mended trousers and look warily at those here who are not among their ranks.

3

Their boats fill the harbor today. The lobsters are granted stay. A man is gone, but a table of effects remain as scant touchstones of a full existence. And over it hangs that fog of indistinct death, and possibly of murder, but by whom, and to whom, unknown.

1.

THE BUGS INVADE QUINN BOYLE'S MIND IN THE NIGHT, strangely, now that he's finally clean. Or maybe because he is. It's been almost three years from the spider's bite of that last needle, nearly two years off the prison bit, and a dozen months since he finally felt he had mastered it. But the bugs are a nightly reality, crawling up into his head.

When he worked on that first boat, he'd laughed when they called the lobsters that. *The bugs.* He laughed hard at nearly anything back then, seventeen years old and looking at all the world as a joke. He laughed hard before the fatigue of life wiped it from his face.

Bugs. In that diminution, he came to see, lay the illusion of control, a presumption of rendering them manageable. Always, they came out of the ocean fighting, tail-fisted in the back of the bedrooms of the stainless-wire pots, slashing into light and air they'd never known. Pulled free and sorted by the thick-gloved human hand, that unfamiliar rival. Rubber-banded into submission, and then dropped into the churning hold tank. The broken and undersized got probation, flipped back over the side like an afterthought. The strong ones were the doomed.

Down in that bristling hold, the lobsters could shimmer like dark coins. When you were still out there, on open water, they never stopped being the enemy, cutting through gloves, pinching, snapping, and making you earn every victory.

Back home was when they truly got in your head. Back at the dock, someone had to ease down into the tank and begin pulling them out. In that darkness, you began the filling of the plastic crates the seafood wholesalers brought out. Someone had to descend into that foaming fray. Down into a purgatory of a thousand claws reaching brainlessly to seize what they could: they strained at your boots, your orange waterproofs, the hang of your slicker. Some, always, worked off their bands, wrenching free again to inflict their surprises. The big claws could catch you as hard as a human bite. The bugs were all instinct and no proper thought, and he's been down there a thousand times without ever being used to it. When he was able to convince some green kid to come out and work with him (as he was conscripted as a teenaged dropout with a pregnant girlfriend), he risked losing that guy by sending him down too quickly.

But: better to lose them on shore, of their own volition. He's seen two men lost from boats at sea in his twenty-five years of work. The first one was on someone else's boat, and Quinn was just glad it wasn't him. The second was off Quinn's own stern. The wife of that man is still calling Quinn a murderer, and loudly, especially when she's had enough drinks. Twice, Quinn himself has gone into the far ocean, mouth filling with brine and boots leaden with water, and somehow he has lived. But the ingrained fright of being down in the bughouse is what comes to his head when he cries out from his bed, on the stillness of dry land.

He's running straight west, plotting behind the setting sun, that long funnel into familiar port. The hold churns with the new haul, and the work has been hard. The shoulders throb, the neck, the leathered hands. But on his charts, he knows where he is. The soles of his arthritic feet are more sensitive of depths than the sonar's digital paint-palette of soundings. The two kids working for him are sleeping now in the cabin, exhausted, but he'd never tell them out loud where they are right now. He knows precisely those spots where each man was lost; as the boat churns on he intuits those lost souls, deep below, staring up at him with cold, white eyes from frigid depths. When he passes this haunting patch of water, fifty miles east northeast off Nantucket, he sometimes does feel like a murderer. Botelho, he thinks, duly notes this from his grave at thirteen unlucky fathoms.

Robbie Boyle, the older brother by a year, is waiting over a mug of draft beer. He's cut out of work for a couple of hours to meet Quinn at Jack's Bar. Leaving the office early to receive Quinn is widely understood, extending far enough to amount to community service: Quinn spent a lot of years making trouble, those first hours back ashore.

Down at the docks, the boat is in and the bugs are coming out. Quinn will come through the door, sustained by cash payment and dry-land coffee, both of which have allowed him to remain awake into his third day. Caffeine is a poor substitute for cocaine, but Quinn is also just off probation, finally. Robbie only sees him the nights he's just back.

Robbie's forty-three and he's been at *The Record* twenty-one years. He's spent that seeming eternity writing for the sports section that once wrote stories about him, and about Quinn, when they played all the sports: football, hockey, baseball. Both of them had been very good in that small-town way. There was a time Robbie dreamed of being in the press box at Fenway Park, or at the Boston Garden, covering the big leagues. But his skills were never polished enough, and his ambition never burned sufficiently hot. Tonight he must eventually leave this bar and venture out to cover a boys' basketball game, and he's feeling the vise of obligations.

Somebody whose name he can't recall wanders past, asking him if he's waiting for Quinn. He nods. When they meet, Robbie tends to watch Quinn closely, doing the talking even as Quinn rarely talks back in those first landed hours. It's an oiling of his re-entry into the world. Robbie promised him this two years ago, up at the federal correctional. Maybe the time in prison saved Quinn's life on two accounts, Robbie has observed. Quinn got clean, and then grudgingly into a safer vessel to replace the one seized by the Coast Guard. The newer boat, sadly, is just a shell of affectless fiberglass, nominally seaworthy. The engine needs an overhaul, and until such time threatens to quit two hundred miles out at sea. And Robbie prays Quinn hasn't let the insurance payments get behind. The Hell of lapsed Catholicism doesn't compare to that of lapsed coverage.

The door bangs open and there Quinn stands. He's a big man now, bearded with flecks of gray, two hundred and fifty pounds or more, bulky in the neck and shoulders and heavy in the gut. He outweighs Robbie by sixty pounds, and is likely twice as strong. In his heroin days he'd been somewhat thinner, possessing the deceptive aura of apparent health. Quinn moves far more slowly coming in off the ocean. He slides up wordlessly onto his stool, nods to Peggy behind the bar, and takes his first seventy-five-cent draft.

"So how was the run?" Robbie says.

Quinn shrugs. "More bugs, money about the same. The prices have been dropping. The more we all bring in, the more the prices drop. I'm always chasing it."

"At least you're not losing money."

"But I was hoping for better."

Despite being the younger brother, Quinn's face seems irredeemably aged. His cheeks and nose and neck are spidered with keratosis; fresh off the water, the smell of salt and sweat billow off him.

"When are you going back out again?"

"Jesus, Rob, I just got in."

"I'm just asking."

"Sunday, maybe, Monday. I need to give these kids I got working for me a chance to rest up, but also not too long to reconsider."

"Are they any good?"

"As good as any I can get. So no, not very good."

"So can't you get somebody else?"

"Who?" Quinn said, tightening. "From where?"

"There must be somebody who needs the work."

"It's always harder to get guys . . ."

The "since" in that sentence is implied. "Since" Botelho went under. "Since" the arrest and the prison time that resulted. Quinn has been making a living depending on raw kids who too often quit after their first run, to be found at the bar later telling girls about their lobsterman days. And if they're any good at all, and they decide to keep at it, they end up on another boat.

Quinn's fatigue looks sea-deep, and his soul seems as callused as his roughened hands, which fold onto themselves thickly, broken and then healed in many places. He knocks back the first beer and raises his hand for another. There is no celebration here. He's back in, from another of a thousand trips out to the edge of the depths.

Quinn takes his fresh beer, bolts it, and passes the emptied glass right back to Peg, the bartender. She pours a refill, and says, "You'll need to slow down after a reasonable number."

"Who is this girl?" Quinn says generally. "And what's this supposedly reasonable number?"

"You know who I am," she says. "And I know who you are."

"Beer can't even dent me, kid. It's just a little help getting off to dreamland."

Peg looks at Robbie, waiting.

"He's fine, really," Robbie says, although in all these years he's never been completely sure.

2.

THE HIGH-SCHOOL GYM IS OVERWARM, AND THE NOISE more frank than the bar's murmurs and lamentations. Robbie has dropped Quinn off at his sagging house of rental rooms. He's always surprised by his brother's somber affect, so changed from what he once knew. No goodbyes in the moment; just Quinn, succumbing to exhaustion, out of the car and shuffling up the front steps.

This high-school basketball game unfolding before Robbie is a late-season contest of middling consequences, two teams tied in the lower standings, a regional rivalry of debatable intensity. The game has the trappings of all meaningless high-school struggles. The thumps of a dozen balls purl on the floor as the players warm up, trying to style. Their spins and leaps won't be replicated in the game itself; they're aspirational. The stands are half-full, mothers gabbing in clusters and a smattering of students.

The scorer's horn sounds. The milk-pale players furiously take their last warm-up shots. Then everyone stands to face the flag that's thumbtacked on the far wall of the gym, where the fading championship banners hang in various states of age. The teams Robbie and Quinn played on—*Football, Sectional Champs, 1988; Hockey, Holiday Tournament Champions, 1987*—are at least fresher

11

than the moldering felt pennants of his father and uncles—*1955 County League Champions; 1954 Co-Champs*. They're all dead now, those second-gen Irishmen, done in by heavy smoking, joyful drinking, muscular cars and, by their own accounts, too-demanding women. Robbie, standing with his hand on his heart as the anthem plays through the tinny PA system, never fails to be saddened about how long ago all these moments have become.

On that level, at least, he and his brother had been very good. There was, besides that, a fundamental clarity in the structure of the games. He'd had a childhood of plumbed chalk-dust lines and careful measures. In-bounds and out-of-bounds; offsides and onsides; balls and strikes. It was only after the sports ended that things had gotten blurry.

Below the banners are the bleachers, with clusters of students in their hoodies and their jeans. It slowly comes to him that there is, among them, a familial face.

Robbie sees Tina, up there, looking at him from afar. His niece, Quinn's second daughter, from what was always resented as a forced marriage. She's in the high rows of bleachers, and he can tell by the tilt of her moon-round face she's checking him out. He hasn't seen her in a while; the quick mental math reveals the shock that she must be a senior in high school now. If someone had mentioned her name, he'd have conjured a twelve-year-old.

He neither waves nor nods; the family ties are tangled ropes; certain gestures can be read as aggressive. The ref blows the whistle to start, and Robbie turns his attention to the tip-off, between a couple of six-foot-one centers, boys pale as the moon.

The scorer, an old man who doubles as the high-school janitor, turns to him and holds the stare.

"What?" Robbie says.

"Take a breath mint or something, pal. You smell like a goddamned brewery."

Tina watches her uncle, tapping at his laptop. She's the younger daughter of Quinn Boyle. There is a sister she hasn't seen in three years. The nine-year age gap between them is informed by the chronic troubles of her parents, the marriage that could never possibly succeed. Tina doesn't begrudge anyone, though; she's never known much different. It may be oddly constitutional, to be the calm child of raging parents. But when she sees Robbie tonight from her spot high in the bleachers, she thinks maybe his is the branch of family genetics she shares.

She hasn't much seen her father in her adolescence. Tina last saw Quinn ghost by the window of Buddy's Diner in the gray rain, down the sidewalk with his hands in pockets and head tucked down, heading for his boat. She hadn't consciously looked up from her waitressing; it was more registering a presence, like a frigid draft through a shut door. The broad window of the restaurant looked out on the slope of street down toward the harbor. She knew it was her father, without seeing his face, with his back to her. He looked as if he was limping. She could tell, as well, that he'd be heading back out on the water, imminently. Small memories of girlhood, of him helming the boat out of the harbor, of her standing with her mother on the dock, waving. It felt like happy times to a girl so small. This was at the tail end of things. She was too young to wonder about the men who were on the couch when her father was at sea, the men who sat with their feet on the coffee table drinking their beer as she was taken by her mother's hand and put in bed. The music would play from the living room, loudly, as she fell asleep. Then her father would come home, and things would go silent. The laughter she heard as a child was in her father's absence, from other men, and sometimes from behind her mother's bedroom door. In time, Quinn's absence became permanent, but the men still came and went.

She didn't know other people lived differently. Maybe a lot of them she knew didn't.

"Hey, *Boyle* . . ." The voice is tight in Robbie's ear, the touch upon his person insistent. Before he turns, he tries to place it. The second tap comes harder still on his shoulder, nearly a poke. "*Boyle* . . ."

He turns and is patently unsurprised. It's Williams, father of the Hawks' undersized point guard, Billy, who at five feet, two inches would not often be mistaken for a basketball player.

"Jeff. I'm covering the game here."

"I'm sure you are," Williams says. He's his son's father, a pugnacious man not far over five six himself.

"I want to talk to you man-to-man," Williams says.

"It's not still about the preview, is it, Jeff?'

"Yeah, it's about the *preview.*"

The crowd lets off a tepid cheer, and he checks back to see the Hawks have just scored, by whom he does not know.

"Ryan Blake," the scorer says. But even he is watching the better action here, Robbie and another pissed-off parent, from sidewise view.

"Jeff, there's nothing to say," Robbie says, dampening his voice. "I wrote that preview in November, and you're still worked up about it?"

"You shit on my kid!" Williams shouts. Glancing back at the court, Robbie can see Billy Williams, his basketball shorts nearly brushing his ankles, looking over at them as he brings the ball up to half-court.

Robbie has come to the conclusion that covering high-school sports is a career in which you say less and less until, mute, you die or retire. In the Winter Sports Preview just before Thanksgiving, he had called Williams's son "short."

14

Billy Williams should be a key contributor. A magician with the ball who distributes well from the point, his only liability may be that he's a bit short to provide solid defense.

Robbie turns to Williams. "I only shit on your son if saying he's short is shitting on him."

"Don't give me that," Williams says. "You knew what you were doing."

Indeed, he did. That a parent is now up in his face at the end of a disappointing season, barking about a December sentence, is clear: Robbie was right all along. Billy, a perfectly good kid, has been useless on defense, a liability, and proof positive that some people will simply not get beyond their limitation, height-wise or otherwise.

"You embarrassed my son," Williams says, more angry.

"Sports are in a public arena, Jeff."

"He's just a goddamned kid."

"If you want to be praised, you have to deal with some criticism."

Now, Robbie's prophecy fulfilled, Williams says to him, "You probably cost my kid a scholarship."

"Oh, please!"

"What is that supposed to mean?"

"It means his weak defense cost him the scholarship," Robbie says, and behind him another rise from the crowd. The scorer, in his version of intervention, says, "Billy just scored. Williams, you're missing it."

Williams turns, perplexed. "How?"

"Drive and a layup," the scorer says.

Williams, at cross-purposes, points his stubby finger at Robbie. "This isn't over," he says.

"It never is," Robbie says. He's just waiting for the clock to run down the quarter, and the one after that, and finally to grant him one more small release.

3.

ON THIS MORNING, AS ON ALL MORNINGS, ROBBIE shuffles on achy legs to the bathroom. He feels as if he's walking on circus stilts: the plastic folding chair at the scorer's table granted him no favor. But his post-divorce apartment is small enough to make for brief journeys, in this case back to the kitchen, and thinking only of shaking the grogginess. Winter sports season is the toughest: night games, then at the office later than that, then at the bar later than that. He closed Jack's last night with the copy editors, feeling as if he'd just gotten there.

The knock now at his door is too soft to be Quinn's, whom he assumes to still be sleeping long hours over in his flop. The second knock is even softer now, apologetic if a knock on a door can be so. He opens up a crack, and sees it's Tina, his niece.

"Hang on a minute," he calls through.

"Okay," comes her voice, so softened it's nearly a wraith.

He goes to the bedroom and pulls on his pants and zips up. Back to the door, she's still standing there with the same face when he opens it.

"What's wrong?" he says.

"Nothing, at least not urgently," she says, as he motions her inside.

"You keep the place clean," she says.

"That's such a surprise?"

"I guess I don't expect that from men. How's your daughter?"

"Sarah . . ."

"Right, I knew that. How old is she now?"

"She's seven now. She's good, very good. She'll be staying with me next weekend."

They stand, looking at each other in an awkward interlude.

"So what can I do for you?" he says, knowing it's come out sounding all wrong.

"It's about my dad."

"What else could it have been?" he says.

"My mom's been trying to get the money from him."

"I need to stay out of their issues," Robbie says.

"I'm completely aware."

He turns to the counter to retrieve his coffee. "So what do you need from me, then?"

"This is even more awkward than I thought it would be."

Robbie motions for her to sit.

"I think you know I graduate high school in June," she says.

"Of course," he says, still surprised.

"I want to go to school in the fall. Just community college. I just need a little money. A loan. Just a little to make it work."

"So why aren't you talking to him?" Robbie says.

"When have I ever been able to talk to him?"

"He's getting better."

"I haven't really talked to him since before he went to prison. That was sort of the end of things. I was only wondering if you might say something."

"I'll try."

"Meaning you really won't?"

"Meaning I'll try."

17

"My mother says she could get him thrown in jail."

"Your mother knows that would only cost her more money. She pays a lawyer to stick him in jail, he loses the new boat, that's the end of any more money."

"I'm just saying," she says.

"He's trying, honey," Robbie says. "The man is working his ass off, trust me on that, but the money just isn't coming in. The going rate on lobster is what it is. And trust me that he isn't living it up, either. He's just getting by."

"Family Court has a formula."

"Family Court doesn't go a hundred miles out into the ocean, in the winter, trying to survive. Family Court doesn't control the market price for lobster."

She appears to sit in her own thoughts now.

"You should talk to your father," Robbie says. "Just to talk."

Tina pushes off from the kitchen table, and stands.

"That's something I'd have to work up to," she says.

4.

QUINN STANDS AT HIS BATHROOM SINK AND COUGHS, a deep liquid hacking that barely dislodges the muck and makes the heart leap as if from starting blocks. It's early afternoon now; his lungs feel full of water. He tests the leaden resistance of the legs, the burn in back and the shoulders; his seaward timetable is usually set by their sluggish recovery, and only secondarily by the weather. He isn't hung over; beer does nothing at all to him anymore. Not after all the harder stuff, the heroin and coke and speed that he calibrated as if a technician, dialing in his ups and downs. Those were the days of deciding, pharmacologically, when to work sixty-six straight hours, then when to sleep like a dead man. When to punch the needle through the skin and let the happiness roll in like a fog, misting the landscape of his troubles. The heroin had seemed like love when he had first come to it. When he tried to get out it was yet another bad match, something to shut up, to put at bay.

He has no food, no coffee or milk or orange juice, so he drinks from the kitchen faucet with the cup of his hand. He'll dress and go to find food, soon. But the envelope, as yet unsealed, lies on the counter, with the familiar handwriting, *Quinn* in that loopy, overdone hand that already speaks to him like indictment.

It's not a letter as much as a balance sheet.

Quinn—
Balance on missed child support is 4,000
Interest is now about 7,000
That's $11,000.
WTF?

—G

Interest! Gina's usurious rates, set independent of any jurisdiction. She hasn't gone to court on it, and she clearly thinks he should be thankful. But after standing at the docks last night receiving his payout, he knew that he was screwed, after the catch-up mechanical work on the boat, paying the inept crew, and buying fuel and supplies. He will pay the money out for his daughter, all of it. He just doesn't know when.

He knows he won't sleep more and if he can't sleep he may has well get back out there, if he can rope a crew. That's the hardest part, finding guys too young or too down on their fortunes to pass on the obvious misery this living tends to be. The absence of the drugs not only means he can't mask the fatigue, neither can he mask the reality. It's been two years like this.

He came off heroin in the most inadvisable way, his way. He was trying to be a man about it. He simply got on his boat absent the required substance, and pushed headlong out toward the horizon. Heroin had become not just the way to come home; he had for some time brought his kit out to sea, unable to concentrate without the fix. He was burning through his profits and the needle tracks were becoming obvious on his arms. So, one day, he simply fled his abuses, putting himself in the middle of two powerful-but-opposing negatives: to not go forward without his fix, and then to not succumb and turn the boat around without a hold full of bugs. But he had still loaded up the coke, on the premise of one battle at a time.

He started puking two hours out, to the consternation of his two-man crew. They were new, and understandably worried about sailing with an apparently seasick skipper. The cramps bent him over, and the shits kept him running below. Out fifty miles, the bad waters came up with the winds and he felt he could barely stand. But the work went on and on.

He tried to think only of finding some peace. That was the new preoccupation for him, as he pushed forty. He'd been in hand-to-hand combat with Peace since he was a kid. Now he was ready to taste it, to take it on as a new substance of choice, to be consumed and ridden. He'd pretty well screwed up almost everything, starting at fifteen. His last year of high school he was "the kid who had a kid," as his father dolefully lectured him nightly about the responsibilities he had, up to now, continued to mostly evade.

Peace, he thought as he leaned over the rail, ready to puke up those last strings of bile he'd not already heaved. He clung to the side as the boat steered itself, East-Southeast into the darkening sky, toward the Great South Channel.

The older of the new guys, João, started in on it.

"I hope you're ready to work as hard as we are," he said. "I need the money. I don't need a skipper who can't pull his load."

"I'll pull my load," Quinn had barked over the grind of the diesel.

"I got kids to feed," he said. "If you can't do the work, give me and the boy equal bigger shares."

"Is that what this is, then?" Quinn said, more sharply. "Negotiating shares a half-day out of port? Because you don't do that."

"You look like shit."

"I'm just getting prepped," Quinn said.

"I didn't know I was signing on to a jackpot," João said.

"You'll do just fine," Quinn said over his shoulder.

Quinn had done his farewell mainline the night before the trip. He was sleeping on the boat in those days; the spent needle went off the back as they cast off, held since morning for this bit of concealed ceremony, something approximating baptismal waters. And he had been ebullient the first few hours, both riding the dregs of the last of the smack, yet too easily allowing himself the sense of celebration of being off it. The new guy had been all smiles, sensing fun. Quinn asked, "Why did you want to work on lobster boats?"

"Beats sitting at home listening to the bitch run her mouth," the new guy said, grinning.

As Quinn came down, it all came down. After he'd wrung himself out for hours with the vomiting, they began to bait and set the pots. He was instantly without strength. It was now twelve hours since the last rush, and the cravings came in on schedule, as precise as a train into a station. Quinn was overcome with the need. João and the kid were going hard, and Quinn's own legs were cramping in a way he'd never known. He was suffering, but João was unrelenting.

"I'm not doing all the work," he shouted, and bitterly. "I'm starting to think maybe I was had."

The work, once out there, was always rote, mindless and mechanical. At the open stern the traps slid off one by one, roped into a long train. The job was like working on the edge of a tall building with no rail. Skill meant marking the edges nearly subconsciously, the industrious dance made leaden by withdrawal. He snuck to the cabin and snorted some more cocaine, filling the ache with the wrong medicine.

By late afternoon, this wasn't turning out to be a good run. Better than half the pots were coming up empty, and a lot of throw-backs, and the cold rain in sheets. Quinn was in full agony, knowing that turning now, toward land and a fix and insolvency, was pure futility. He had the kid "notching the eggers"—the law said that any fertile female, egg-laden on the underside, be knife-cut with a V to denote its status, before being thrown back. The kid was only getting the hang of it, slowing it all.

"Waste of my damned time," João was saying from the stern.

"I didn't guarantee the bugs would jump right into the traps," Quinn said, "and you ought to know it."

Soon enough, the younger one had faded completely. Stamina was earned over time. Sixteen hours in and he began to wobble, not used to the sleepless stretches the work demanded.

"Go under and crash for an hour," Quinn said. "I'll come and get you."

In the middle of the night, the big lights made the deck like a tiny arena of their failing. Quinn and João kept on with the work, no longer speaking, backs to one another. Somewhere in there, Quinn began to rally, letting the work try to be the cure, letting it be the anesthetic. He kept on, pulling and sorting, getting from one moment to another. Then he turned and saw that João was gone.

He didn't have any idea of how long it had been. He stood, looking. Past the open stern was only the wake fading into the darkness behind the trundling boat. No one was there. He went below and found the kid sleeping hard, and shook him. The kid startled, scanning as if he had no idea.

"Where's the other guy?" Quinn said.

"Who?"

He went back up top and looked fore and aft. The guy was just gone, and the boat was only so big. Quinn looked at his watch. It was past four in the morning, with the first hint of light at the horizon. Out beyond the boat, the waters rolled dark and relentless.

He got on the radio in the wheelhouse, and quickly had the Coast Guard. He already knew it was going to be a search for a body, and likely a useless one. They weren't wearing life jackets, as they hindered the work. Off the radio, he unfolded the paperwork on the chart table, and looked at the handwriting. Botelho was the guy's last name. He hadn't remembered that. The Coast Guard radio man said there was a boat not far away, and coming at him full throttle.

Under the bunk were the bags of cocaine. His bank; his assurance of unbroken chemical relief. He was frantic with what to do with it. The prospects of a double withdrawal were just too daunting. He was expecting the Coast Guard ship to be coming up on him imminently, somewhere in the rising dawn. Quinn opened the first bag, went in with his finger, and snorted hard. He was thinking at that moment to just hide them away. There would be no pretense for a vessel search. He immediately knew he was fooling himself, of course. But he needed the powder that badly.

He tends to find himself back out there a lot, the engines cut and the wind gusting and the rains coming down. The young guy, afraid to let go of the rail and crying to go home. It was only when that white Coast Guard ship was in sight with the gray light of a shrouded rising sun that he panicked fully. Abruptly, he went underneath, pulled out the bags, and began to dump them on the lee side, hoping no one was on him with their binoculars. Which, of course, they were.

And, as always, he brings his head up now, surprised to find himself not back on that boat's deck but in the ongoing present.

When Botelho disappeared from the deck of Quinn's boat, it had changed Quinn's life in ways that were probably for the better, but felt much worse. Prison time allowed him to fight through withdrawal, a state-funded version of a rehab getaway. Had he instead come back from that run with an intact crew and a hold full of bugs, he'd have surely succumbed to the needle by nightfall: maybe, finally, too much. There was always going to be that time.

In the county jail in those next days, they could have begun to wean him with methadone and let him sweat through the days in an infirmary bed, had he ever asked. But he told no one. He still stubbornly held that this was a personal battle. By the time he went to court with his plea bargain signed, he had the strange thought he might live to forty after all.

"Guilty," he'd said, almost stepping on the judge's words in the rush to get it out.

Federal prison bit wasn't so bad, either; he was surrounded pretty much by guys like he worked with every day in the lobster business. He went to a medium-security facility in upstate New York. Ray Brook. It was mainly just uneventful for him. The first few nights, at "orientation," he'd been in a cell three down from a guy coming off something; the guy kept screaming into the night that he needed his fix. Then, one night, the noise stopped. At chow, someone said, "He hanged himself." Someone else said, "Bullshit, he got taken to rehab." Either way, things got quiet then. There were occasional fights, but nobody came near him. The work had made him too big to mess with. He didn't make conversation, didn't take exceptions, felt no need to pose or preen, and quietly counted down the weeks. Some guys, they were still trying to prove something, or maybe disprove something. Quinn took it only as a quiet recusal from many things.

He goes back to that at moments like this, lying sober on his small bed in the middle of the night. Quinn has awakened again after sleeping through the day and then the evening; it's closing time for the bars as he awakens from his stretch, and he has nothing to do. Below his window he can hear the hoots of the drunks coming out to the street; he misses none of it. Instead he lies here and fights the urge to think about things he'd rather not. The way he did in that silent interlude of prison, although that interlude is what invades his thoughts.

His public defender told him that if he pleaded guilty to straight possession they'd drop the distribution charge.

"But I wasn't distributing," Quinn said. In conference, the defender wondered aloud if, given the amount of powder found, and the amount estimated to have been dumped, if he had the constitution of a plow horse. Yes, Quinn apparently did. The defender waited until he was sure that wasn't an effort at humor, then began talking about a one-year probation and mandatory drug counseling. The defender didn't know he was coming off heroin. The anxiety and down moods that came with it, and Quinn's struggles to keep it together while voluntarily off smack and forcibly off coke, led to certain conclusions in town. Mainly, that he had killed Botelho. He was, to most, visibly stewing in his own guilt. The theory was relentlessly peddled by Botelho's woman. The key piece of evidence seemed to be, at the moment Botelho evaporated, the convenient absence of the kid who had crewed with them. The new guy had truthfully noted that Quinn and Botelho had been at odds before the man disappeared. About pay.

Fact was, Quinn still had no idea what had happened. The traps were all in the water, so he wasn't pulled over by an outgoing line; the sea was moderate that night, so he wasn't taken by a rogue wave. How he could have gone over was something Quinn rolled over in his head, constantly. He must have just slipped, which no one was ever going to believe. He must have had an absent moment, when he took that one step where nothing firm rose up to meet his boot.

The search for the body, working on a too-generous 900-square-mile grid, had been the usual pointless exercise. Botelho was not a dolphin, and the currents didn't move that fast, and his life vest was still on the nail in the wheelhouse. Quinn sat in his small cell before bail, and waited for someone to tell him what was going on, which no one did. In those first days back on land, he stalked the small space as an animal would, and slept without realizing it. He'd lie on the bunk staring at the ceiling, and in a blink he was in a dark room. The mere notion of any drug-running was a joke. You didn't buy product on land and take it that far out to sea. But that much presumed powder (the primary evidence was the size of the bags from which it had been dumped) and a vanished man (and the imprecise claims he must have just fallen off the backside) meant something had to be made to stick.

Quinn understood that. He wanted it done fast. They'd already seized his crumbling boat as part of the initial distribution charge; he was ready to let it go, and try for a new boat and new escape, back Out There. On a Monday morning, he was driven by Robbie to the federal courthouse in Providence. There seemed now a distance from the matter of Botelho's disappearance, for which no evidence existed. He went into federal court and blurted his guilty plea on possession. The judge, a middle-aged woman, looked at him narrowly over the tops of her reading glasses. His clothes were soaked through with flop sweat, and he was long unshaven. She seemed to come to certain conclusions. Thirty-six months in federal prison, twelve months to serve, is what had turned out to be on her mind.

"Jesus," Robbie said aloud from the back of the courtroom. They remanded Quinn right then, another surprise. As the handcuffs and shackles went on him, he said to Robbie, "Winters are slow anyway. Three years means a year, and twelve months means six. I'll be ready to work by next spring." It didn't even bother Quinn that much. It was no better or worse than anything else, he thought.

5.

SHE'D SAID HELLO AS HE SAT UPON HIS STOOL, MIND-
lessly watching a women's college basketball game on the big TV
over the bar. She was sidling up for drinks for herself and her
girlfriends, over in the corner. And in the way it happens when
there's some attraction, she's now sitting here while her girlfriends keep a wary eye from their table. Jean seems okay, as far
as he can tell. She's tall, with blond hair that may be holding off
the gray with some chemical intervention. Fortyish, he guesses.
The talk has been tame enough, and he's made that mistake that
happens when you're starting to like someone, which is to foolishly confide one's most assailable opinions.

"When I was young, girls playing sports seemed stupid to me,"
Robbie says, to her narrowing gaze.

"Is that so?"

"But let me continue."

"Go on."

"So now I have a daughter. Seven years old. And what I'd love
is for her to play every sport she can. Hockey, even. I see the utility now of any of that. It would be the only thing I'd ever imagine
we'd have in common. Except she's shown no interest at all."

"No boys?" Jean says.

"No. Just the one girl. My brother has two girls, too. Our older sister—she lives down South now—has a girl. The name seems to end there."

"What's the name?"

"Boyle."

"Don't worry, I think there are plenty of those left. How old is the niece?"

"Senior in high school. I just saw her today."

"That's nice, for a family to be close enough to see each other so much," Jean says. He lets it lie there.

"You?" he says. "Kids?"

"A daughter, too. She's thirteen."

"And where is she?"

"Home, I hope!" Jean says. "It's been a little bit of an adjustment. But this is where the company sent me and that's why I'm here."

"And the father?"

"He didn't leave me in the classic sense, just an hour at a time. We almost never saw him. When we packed the rental truck, he showed up to talk me out of it, but seemed half-hearted. He also had a girl in the car. He said she worked for him and he was driving her home. He owns a restaurant. That's a tough business, where monogamy is concerned."

He supposes it is; he's listening but also confounded about why she apparently likes him. He'd abandoned all hope after the divorce from M.; she'd weakened him, and his faith in himself. In the office he'd often tell the younger guys, "Marriage—a contract for idiots!" That played as a punch line, but he was dead serious.

"Do you know her?" Jean is saying.

"Huh?" Robbie realizes how far adrift his unmoored mind has gone. "Who?"

"The woman shouting at you from over there."

"I didn't hear her."

"So you didn't hear her screaming 'Hey, asshole'? Everybody else did . . ."

He turns, and looks. Oh. It's Botelho's widow, clearly drunk, her eyes ablaze.

"Yeah, that's right," the woman is yelling, "the brother who helped cover up the murder, right over there!"

"Well, I really should run," Jean says.

"And who could blame you?" Robbie says.

"Nice meeting you," Jean says, standing. "And good luck with all that about a murder . . ."

Nothing like the mention of murder to scare a woman off! Probably better off; for a man without a woman, Robbie seems well-weighted with woman problems. Walking home, he ponders not just the specter of M., but also the prodigal return of a girlfriend he'd thought he'd not see again.

Dawn is back up from Florida, to Robbie's mixed regret. She'd been in Orlando trying to do the real-estate turn, but the recession has apparently driven her back. She's had scant success in a place where half the houses are in foreclosure. Dawn, forever the victim of bad timing, such as when connecting with a man who has just come out of a marriage vowing never to marry again. She was the rebound relationship, unfortunately for her.

He's followed her fortunes indirectly, via that ethereal network of small-town talk and well-meant reports. He'd hoped, badly, she'd succeed. He regrets she hasn't, both because he actually likes Dawn, a lot, but as well because her departure from town seemed like a healthy denouement for both of them. It seemed, in fact, like pure relief. There were too many cold nights with them ending up in bed, even when they long knew it couldn't possibly work out. Yet his memories of being in bed with her are happy. It was by daylight that it all got too complicated.

The thing that most appealed to him about Dawn was that she was the antithesis of his ex-wife. A high compliment, to be sure. He'd gotten married on what felt like the too-younger side, although much older than Quinn had. M. never stopped treating him as a boy—the way he watched M.'s mother treat her father, until that old boy's heart gave out with a massive infarction. M. had quickly taken the air out of their marriage with what might have been called, in another era, henpecking. As the years went on, her disappointment in his failure to move beyond his local sportswriting job, and the pay that came with it, was palpable. Used cars and forestalled luxuries. She ran up the credit cards as if he had already succeeded, to punish him that he had not. He punished her in turn by letting go of any ambition at all. Coming out of that mess, he met Dawn, which felt like oxygen again. She laughed hard, they had real fun, and he came to have deep affection for her. He just couldn't marry her.

Then he heard she was back, from one of the secretaries at the paper who knew them both. A kind of "brace yourself" sideways warning, because coming home disappointed was never easy. A few weeks after that, he heard Dawn was back at the bar at The Wharf, a place he then frequented much less frequently. But then there he was, at the bar of The Wharf.

Why was he here? He knew why: the whole thing always had the opposing forces. It needed to be done. He'd watched the door even as he'd fought the urge to flee. He leaned back over his beer, trying ineffectively to convince himself once more he didn't come to see Dawn. The Celtics were on the big screen above the bar, playing the Nets, and he focused in on that, just as ineffectively.

"Well, let's get this done with," she said from behind him.

"Hey, look at you!" he said.

He'd not have recognized her. The hair was cut so severely short it almost seemed applied. It seemed lacquered down with some kind of hair product and the smallness of her head was the shock. Her mane, shorn. She was deeply tanned, baked in a way he suspected came from extending it in the local tanning parlor. But he had to admit it was good to see her. She pushed her cold cheek at him, the awkward kiss, and he could feel the shaky vibe.

"Your hair looks great," he said.

"Yeah, well, things happen," she said. "I assume you heard I was back."

"I think I had."

"Come on, you knew," she said. "I made sure you would, so this wouldn't be an ambush."

"Thanks. Are you back for good?"

"Oh, God, I hope not! I was trying to sell real estate in a place where every other house seemed to be abandoned. That doesn't mean I'm giving up."

"Good for you."

She was dressed smartly, if not warmly. In their times together, she tended toward jeans and sweaters, but tonight she was bedecked as the tropical real-estate woman she had tried to be. Silk blouse, pencil skirt, jangling jewelry up and down. And that perfume he always liked, but the name of which he could never remember at Christmas.

"And you're still at the paper."

"Of course. Where else would I be?"

She was smiling in a way, with the tan, that spoke of some gained perspective. She'd been places, as he had never, something he wouldn't have expected.

"Don't you ever want to even try to do something different?" she said.

"Such as?"

"Such as moving to Florida, even if it doesn't work out. To have an experience!"

33

"But there's Sarah."

Dawn, childless, backed off a little at the mention of the daughter. "And how is she?"

"Great. As always."

"You know, she could come visit you somewhere else."

"Dawn, I can't move to Florida."

"I'm not talking about Florida. I'm not even talking about me. I'm talking about you."

"Florida is too far away."

"Try Connecticut. Try New Hampshire. You can't aspire for something better? You can't try to move up a little before it's too late?"

Her phone was going in her bag, and she looked at it and looked over to her sister, sitting in a booth with her phone to her ear.

"I'll be right over," she said in that direction, then turned back to Robbie. The exasperation was now patently noticeable.

"I'm not talking about you and me," she said. "For good or for bad I just had an experience where everything was exciting. I want that for you, because I know it's what you really want."

"I do?"

"Robbie, you're stuck and you don't even know it," she said, turning away, her scent still enveloping him.

6.

THE PUCK'S ON YOUR STICK; NOW TURN UP ICE. THE PIV-
ot and quick look. See who's open. The wide white expanse, the
fresh layer. The wheeling of players, peripherally, planets in orbit.
The bite of blades into the sheet, the churn of legs. The air, cold.
The low thunder of everyone surging, skates pounding the ice and
echoing from a rink's low girders. Your hands are soft in the thick
gloves, feeling the puck through the length of the stick. The mo-
ment seems attenuated. The faces seem familiar. Keep moving,
keep moving.

Quinn opens his eyes. Another of his limited slate of recurring
dreams, again and again. In this dream he's still in high school,
on the ice, but in it he's also a middle-aged man. He sometimes
wonders why he goes back to it so constantly. But he knows it
was the best time he had, and so brief. His frequent and painful
return to the happy past.

His dreams are all backward-looking now, and that's a vague
worry. The grind of the work doesn't forge hopeful visions. He
feels old. He feels spent. The radial ache in his shoulders when
he falls back on his mattress makes him wonder: *How do I keep*
on? The seduction of physical work is about not thinking of any
future, not to anticipate the worn years and insistent aches. In a

body sagging with fatigue, the mind doubles back to the crystalline moments of furious youth, which you didn't bother to note at the time because you thought you couldn't possibly run out of them.

The end of winter hangs on. The snow still dusts the ground and the skies hang flat and compressing on the mirror-gray harbor. The pleasure boats stand in hibernation on their cradles, shrink-wrapped in white polyethylene sheaths and lined down the dirt road of the storage barn, a herd of eyeless beasts awaiting their spring molting.

The only sound off the harbor is the waterline thrum of diesel work engines, the egress of the commercial fleet, barnacled hulks slipping out toward the far sky. March has a dour taste to the workingman, be it rubber-clad fishermen on the water or the flannel-wrapped roofers up in cold winds, or the road crews working into the early darkness of the winter day.

Quinn has no taste at all for lobster. He hasn't eaten one in twenty years. He generally eschews fish, the way an office type avoids seeing coworkers off-hours. They're enemy combatants. With the bugs, he's been cut and clamped so many times that to enter a restaurant on that rare occasion, and to see them docile in a bubbling water tank, elicits a strange melancholy, and possibly even fraternity.

Restaurants no more, anyway. He'd gone underground after his release, but he knew Botelho's wife was resolutely on the case. She was manic to have her say. He could have told her how it was: that they had the life vests per regulations, but the regulations didn't say you had to be wearing one. That it was easy to get too blasé walking along the open stern as the trawl let out with the big polyball floats and the ground lines and ganglion whooshing wetly by your ankles. An article of faith, out there, was that the ones who lived were the smart ones, and the others simply attrition. That people misstep, all the time, but it's worse with forty liquid fathoms beneath you.

Then there was that night he saw her. This was in Jack's Bar, when he'd only begun to venture there, tired of drinking alone on the new boat, and tired of avoiding Robbie as he had in those early months out of prison. She was with an old man who had the roughened look of someone only now at rest from a life of work. Quinn found a stool down on the lee side of the cash register and looked down into his beer mug; when he looked up, he saw her, the face a hard mask of pure hatred. He would never have recognized her, but the face was what told him what he needed. She was blinking furiously, and her face reddened; she had the tough look of someone who'd been trading shots since birth.

This was the night she said nothing, before the rants and drunken keening, before she arrived at a point where going after him gave her the same pump as the drinks would, and became her tailored act, the endless victim. But it was this night, knowing that reaction across the bar might have been the one genuine moment between them, that he felt truly awful. He was being haunted by proxy.

Two more first-timers on board for this run, predictably. Quinn pretty much knew it when he was casting off, but these guys are even worse than he'd expected. They'd come down to the docks that morning, looking for work. He'd said, "Okay, get on."

The two of them, eighteen or nineteen at best, looked at each other.

"Right now?" one of them said.

"Get on and off we go," Quinn said. "We can still beat the day."

The other one laughed. "Seriously?"

"I thought you wanted to work."

"I got plans tonight."

Quinn leaned against the gunwale. "So when do you want to go? Because I'm ready now. I have paperwork you can sign."

"What are you going to pay us?"

"The shares split six ways," Quinn said. "One share for the boat, one for the fuel, two for me as the owner and deck boss, one each for you as stern men. That's if we go right now. If we kill half the day while you decide, then you two split one share and I take one more for wasted time."

Quinn looked at them in a hard squint. "But if you have such big plans . . ."

"We'll go," the first one said, reaching for his phone. "Just let me call my house and let them know."

"You can call home when we're out on the water. We need to get right to work." Quinn knew better than to let anybody talk them out of this before they cast off.

That was at eight in the morning; now it's near midnight and the first of two hundred traps are coming up, and these boys are already fading fast. They have no strength, no stamina, and clearly no real work ethic. Quinn is doubling their output, even one-on-two, and he's getting second thoughts about the shares. But this is the crew he gets now, reduced to scraping for warm bodies willing to board his dubious vessel.

One of them simply stops, and sits, and takes out cigarettes.

"You need to get back to work," Quinn shouts.

"I can't anymore," the kid says.

"Yes, you can," Quinn says, yet more ominously.

This, uncountable times. Condemned to raw beginners who've bought the idea that lobstering is easy money. It only looks like that when you're back on land, getting handed cash, or when you're in the bar, watching it slip away. These two are getting their sea trial. First time out is always shit, bumbling over the traps and missing knots. Quinn keeps an eye on them, always, the same way Chuck Joyce watched him on his first run, all the years ago.

The connection between his father and Chuck Joyce had the usual indistinct ligature surrounding many of Dad's acquaintances. This was with Gina pregnant and school already bottomed out. He'd kept his grades just high enough to limp through junior-year sports. But when baseball ended and the report card dropped through the mail slot, his changed life was instantly upon him. Even then, he was surprised at how events pulled him along.

There had been the short spell in which Gina, who had first tried to ignore that she was pregnant, had kept her mouth shut and considered her options. But her mother was immediately on to something—preternaturally, it seemed, but maybe just not fooled by what was going on. It was as if her nascent maternity was wafting in the air. Decisions then were made. One of them was for Quinn to be forbidden to see Gina until he was working.

The old man had his own ideas. Furious on all accounts, he brought Quinn down to the docks, where Chuck Joyce sat on his cedar-planked Jonesport, the *Cassie Lee*.

"Need some help down here?" the old man had called to him, sounding too rehearsed.

"I might," Chuck had called back. "If this one's not a pussy."

Quinn never figured the connection, or if there was a human Cassie Lee. But he began the work with Chuck, his apparent purgatory for cleansing all manner of sins. He was supposed to be making money to support the new baby, and that meant going out on as many runs as Chuck could muster. The *Cassie Lee* was a short boat, drafted for inshore work, but Chuck seemed intent on driving her far past what was logically safe for a light craft with a tight cabin. The *Cassie* had a narrow beam and that meant it could move fast to open water. But once the work began, she got tippy. The dance of the work on a rolling deck struck Quinn as nearly a new sport to try out for, and he took to it. He was, quickly enough, fast and efficient; the more facile parts of the work became quickly mastered skills. He learned the nuances: banding a lobster's claws, you don't hold it upside down, which makes the lobster nervous; nervous lobsters drop claws, and a one-claw lobster is a cull, and a cull is wasted money. Tie your buoy hitch not quite right. Missed routes change the knots, into cow hitches, clove hitches, and buntline hitches, all of which looked much the same but won't always hold the pot on your snood, nor your snood to your trapline. A pot lost because of a bad knot shears fifty dollars off your take-home. Quinn also learned, quickly enough, that Chuck was cheating him.

The matter of shares was always a tricky one, with many junctures of potential malfeasance. Handshake deals could be interpreted far more broadly than the U.S. Constitution. The dealings were done word-of-mouth; when you went out on a boat being told you get one share of six, but then were told back on land that it had been a one-of-eight that had been negotiated, it was your word against another's. And he learned that when you stood there watching a wholesaler count out the money into the boat owner's hand, that there were often side agreements between them that held back other money. There was, in all that, complex kickbacks that could serve to further devalue the stern men. Quinn at sixteen was already a regular at the bars near the waterline, and the guys from other boats sat and explained to him how he was getting royally screwed by Joyce, who apparently was notorious. Quinn, still the hothead at that young age, got increasingly furious, even though his fellow-men (laughing at full throat at his teapot redness) reminded him it was the way all the first-timers broke in. Quinn the teenager couldn't imagine Chuck Joyce's life, of upkeep on a boat and small margins and pushy ex-wives and maybe some bad personal habits that had become too hard to shake. Quinn just wanted his money.

There was a two-day run to the South Channel that went very badly. All manner of rotten luck was visited upon them. Every string of traps seemed to come up with berried hens (which had to be notched and tossed back, the real time-killer), with shorts (some so small he could measure against his hand to know they had to go back), or with pistols (which, clawless, would take three or four molts to regrow the missing limbs). Then there were the traps that came up with nothing, one after another, so many empty bedrooms Joyce took up his binoculars and began to scan the horizon for poachers.

"What in the hell is going on?" he said generally.

The number of legal bugs in the live tank was woeful. They came into port bone-tired and frustrated. Quinn had a payment scheduled for Gina that Friday, the payments set up between his parents and hers, and he knew he wasn't going to make it. He could see that Joyce was likewise in a black mood. When Joyce finally said, "I might have to cut back your share," Quinn blew up.

"How do you cut back the share? I worked every bit as hard as you."

"If you don't like it, you can quit," Joyce said, casting his eyes out on the open water.

"You can't even look me in the eye," Quinn said. "Make good on the share you agreed to, and I'll quit after that."

"Sorry," Joyce said, more quietly.

Quinn got in close to him, trying to make Joyce look at him.

"I get my money," Quinn said, nearly growling.

Joyce, who was past the age of fifty back then, laughed. "Or *what*?"

41

When Quinn grabbed Joyce's suspender to try to make his point, it felt instant that he was being slammed to the deck. Joyce had him by the throat and cracked Quinn's head down hard enough that he was out, for how long he didn't know. When he came around, he first thought he was on the ice, laid out in a hockey game. But the sky was gray, the wind hard upon him, and Joyce sullen at the wheelhouse. They didn't speak another word, three hours in. Joyce held back any money at all, on account of being assaulted. Mutiny was serious business, he intoned. Quinn's father made the payment to Gina's family and told Quinn it was time for him to move out. That Monday, he was on a new boat, a harder man now.

Quinn looks up from his memories and sees two soft boys on his own deck, struggling to do anything right. He could threaten them, or scream, but he can see it will do no good. Even baiting, an easy job, somehow seemed difficult for them as they sat with buckets of salted herring and filled the pouches. The trouble seemed less any physical shortcoming, but rather a wholesale inability to concentrate on anything for more than three seconds. He'd been told once that a lobster's brain was the size of a grasshopper's and not really a brain at all; these guys seemed worse than that.

Now, as the trapline winches up and it's a time for some strength, these two boys have none at all. Quinn knows now about Joyce's accumulated strength, something seeded over years and gained without conscious thought. If Quinn is going to come home with any profit, he'll need to be the one doing the bulk of the work. He looks at them sitting tired on the gunwale, and he says, "I might have to cut back your shares."

The taller one looks at him, but he's clearly spent.

"Whatever," he says.

The other one says nothing at all.

7.

WHEN HE'D GOTTEN OUT OF COLLEGE AND WAS HIRED at the local paper, Robbie drew what was known in that business as the "lobster shift," the 11 p.m. to 6 a.m. yawner, sitting in a dark newsroom with the police scanners, listening for anything at all out of the static crackle. He always found himself nervous about what might happen in those dark hours, but in the silence he learned the true measure of his boring town. The occasional closing-time fight at a local bar, or a car driven off the curve on Middle Highway and into the woods, or the full-lunged domestic disturbance in the depths of the hours.

He did his hitch in the wee hours, and in time was granted his request to shift to the sports department, where he spent his first year taking phone-ins from coaches, to fill the agate columns of minor schools playing minor sports, still thinking then of how he'd soon enough make it to the Fenway Park press box, writing for some big metro newspaper. He has the occasional pang of nostalgia for all his thwarted ambitions. He's not ashamed that he once aspired, even as he does no more.

Again, he cools it barside, awaiting his brother and another round of medicinal drinking. He spotted Quinn's boat coming in by the breakwater as he sat at the window desk in the sports department, the third-floor long view like a widow's walk. There's a game later he'll need to cover, but he sits now, happy for the respite.

And there's Jean, the woman from the other night. She looks over and he gives her a nod, and surprisingly she's on her feet, approaching.

"Happy happy hour," she says. "You seem to spend a lot of time in bars."

"But you're here enough to notice. I'm waiting for my brother, again. He just got in."

"From where?"

"Out there," Robbie says. "He's a lobsterman."

"I hear they're trouble."

"At least three-quarters of them. But about that murder thing, it was a guy falling off his boat. The guy's own fault."

"I know, I already asked around on that."

"Yeah," Robbie says. "Most people in this town know the story."

She isn't backing off, to his surprise.

"Care to join us?" she says. "I'm with some friends."

"If you stay here instead, I'll buy the drinks."

Jean slides onto the stool. "Fair enough," she says.

She orders a glass of wine from Peg, who notes that their selection is rather limited, "red or white, but I think we're out of white." But when the glass is put in front of her, Jean doesn't touch it anyway.

"How's the sports writing?" she says.

"Same as always. And you? Did I ask you what you do?"

"You didn't. Medical records. They transferred me up to manage the office up here."

"Do you like it?"

"I like the pay, is what I like."

The door kicks open and it's Quinn, who comes shuffling over, bringing in the usual ocean gloom, and stands by Robbie at the bar.

"Jean, my brother, Quinn," he says.

"You remembered my name," she says.

"And how close are you two?" Quinn says, shaking her extended hand.

"This is our second date," Jean says, to Quinn's puzzlement.

"Kidding," Jean says. "Just saying hello."

"We'll do a real date sometime," Robbie says.

"Is that a declaration or an invitation?" Jean says. She digs her card out of her bag, hands it to him, and says, "Use the cell phone number." And she's off to her friends.

"And how did it go?" Robbie says, but already knowing.

"Not good," Quinn says. "So bad, in fact, that you're buying the beer today."

Quinn is looking off at something, and now Robbie can see what it is. Freddy Santoro, who sits in the corner booth, chain-smoking as he has since they were all in high school. It's a surprise to see him: he's waiting to go on trial on a trafficking rap far more serious than anything Quinn ever got himself into. Santoro looks over, raising his head as if he's about to say something, but Quinn looks away. He nods to Peg for a draft and waits for people to show up.

Robbie is aware of the outlines of Santoro's story, more from dock gossip than from *The Record*, where Santoro's troubles were reported briefly and without undue excitement. It involved a massive amount of hash oil packaged in plastic shampoo bottles, more than a hundred pounds, at a thousand dollars a pound of street value, in watertight boxes under the false bottom of the deck. The boat was not Santoro's but didn't seem to be anyone else's. Santoro was the only person on the boat, a cabin cruiser that had been leased in Florida using a false front company. The boat had been boarded a few miles from the harbor, where he was sometimes employed running a shuttle skiff for day sailors to get to their boats. And Santoro wasn't talking; always a nervous type, he'd spent a lot of nervous months in which the feds had tried to turn him. Whereas Quinn's indiscretion was incidental to the lobstering, the amount of product and the matter of the boat made Santoro's fishing (the stated purpose) mere camouflage to the true commerce. There had to have been some big hitters in the shadows of this deal, and even Freddie Santoro knew to say nothing.

Santoro's family, the parents and two sisters, have all put up their meager houses as surety for the bonding; even with that, there was some surprise when the judge granted bail. The Honorable Judge Milton Paiva, known across Rhode Island as "Not Guilty Miltie" for his forgiving ways. Santoro has kept on, but the fight seems all gone. In the next week or so, the rumors have it, he'll go into the courthouse, likely plead to a reduced count, and hope the trial judge, Nevins, a harder soul than Miltie, isn't going to slam him for not giving up the others.

It was in those days after the arrest that Santoro had seemed to again home in on Quinn. Robbie knew it was a tension that went back to muddy football fields of high school, to fights in the schoolyard, and to rivalries over girls, most of whose names were long forgotten.

One night here, after the arrest, Santoro had been drunk and smoking and he had an audience, and he began shouting across the bar, asking Quinn how many blowjobs he'd given in his time in prison. Santoro seemed first to be thinking he wouldn't be going to prison, and then once he did realize he would, he seemed terrified.

Santoro had squawked at Quinn until it had become obvious it wasn't ending without a fight, or an attempted one.

"Did you take it from behind in there?" Santoro had barked.

"Not the way you will," Quinn finally shouted back. "You'll be in the joint so long your ass will be like the Ted Williams Tunnel."

Santoro had leapt up as if he'd only been waiting for the cursory provocations.

Quinn stood up; Robbie knew how much strength his brother had from the years of the work, but still aimed to talk him into backing off. You never knew, with guys like Santoro, what kind of hardware they had in their pockets.

"Don't let him take you down with him," Robbie said. "Why should you end up in a jail cell tonight?"

"It's his game," Quinn said.

"He's drunker than shit," Robbie said. "Why bother?"

Quinn had nodded, and let Robbie turn him toward the exit. "See you some other time, you pussy," Santoro shouted in his presumed victory.

Now, tonight, Robbie sees Santoro getting up and edging toward them.

"Here he comes," Robbie says.

"It's all right."

"He looks hammered."

"So I would assume."

Now Santoro's against Quinn, leaning in hard.

"You didn't even say hello," Santoro says. He's always got an aggressive way about him, and Quinn long ago came to the conclusion he doesn't always know it.

"I guess I'll soon be saying goodbye," Quinn says.

"Not funny," Santoro says.

"I thought you'd laugh. How long you think you'll be in for?"

"It's either going to be a long time or a real long time. But they were talking worse if I didn't plead. Like, basically life."

"They wouldn't give you life," Quinn says. "That's how they scare chickenshits into pleading guilty."

"But they said twenty years. So that's basically life, I mean, given I don't take very good care of myself."

"That's rough," Robbie says, wedging into the conversation to avert another standoff.

"So I hear you need a sternman," Santoro says to Quinn.

"Yeah, you know anybody?"

"I'm talking about me . . ."

"I thought you were going to prison."

"I have about a week left. Look, I need the money. Every bit I can get. My lawyer isn't cheap. I don't want them going after my parents."

"You should have gotten a public defender, like I did."

"I thought this guy was going to get me off," Santoro says. "He was talking probation or a year in minimum security, so I kept paying him. Look, any money I can hustle right now, I need real bad."

"And it's worth getting one share from me?"

"I was thinking two."

"And how's that?"

"I'll do two guys' work. I can do better than any two guys you're able to sucker on the boat these days. Seriously, I hear about what's going on. I know it's been bad, since the Botelho thing. I want to get out there and make a killing. I have a lot of motivation."

"This last run wasn't so good."

"So let's get right back out there. You have an unlucky boat, but I need money bad. For my parents. I'll make that work. Two shares is more than I can make any other way with the time I have left."

"I don't know, man."

"Look, let me go. I'm about to be stuck in a damned cage for at least eight or nine years, and I want to get out on the water, one more time. I want to be able to be out on the ocean, so I can remember it when I'm in a cell. You should understand what I'm saying."

"You can't just remember all the other times?"

"I want to go out like a goddamned demon. Working hard, using my muscles. I want to be thinking about what I'm doing while I'm out there. I regret now I didn't think about it enough."

"It's work, Freddy. You're not supposed to think about it."

"You do when you go to prison."

"I did go to prison."

"A few months, Quinn! That was a vacation!"

"Well, lucky me."

Santoro is getting worked up. "I can't believe you're even having to think about it. I'll make you money, and you know it."

"A couple of weeks ago you were calling me out."

"This is business," Santoro says.

"I'll think about it," Quinn says.

"Jesus Christ," Santoro says. "You don't think you owe me something?"

"I said I'll think about it. Come down to the boat at four tomorrow morning. If I haven't gotten a better crew, you're in."

Santoro goes off, head shaking.

"Quinn, you must be able to find someone else," Robbie says.

"It's gotten a lot harder, Rob. Yeah, the guy is a pain in the ass, but it sounds like he's got a reason to work."

"Why not work inshore, by yourself?"

"That's what everybody does, and it shows in their yields. There's even less money hugging the shore. I need more. I got Gina on me about the child support."

"You should keep looking. Get a couple of guys you can depend on, and maybe they'll stick."

"Well," Quinn says, "I now have high motivation to find these hypothetical guys."

8.

OF COURSE THE PREMISE OF INCARCERATION IS TO wrench away all things one holds dear; Quinn was given to ponder what that might have actually been, as Freddy Santoro will soon do. On that night of his arrest, Quinn was brought off the Coast Guard cutter Monomo, and handed over to Federal agents at Woods Hole. He had conceded the Christine to impoundment, and presumed he had a better-than-even shot at prison. When by dawn they bunked him down in that solitary cell at the Wyatt Detention Center, awaiting federal charges, he presumed it. By the time the lights went out, he'd largely resolved he clearly needed to be punished for Botelho's disappearance. He'd been in the throes—shaking, hallucinating, witnessing the starburst against his own retinas. He should have been more watchful; that was the unspoken agreement you made on a boat, even with your worst enemy. He'd let his own shit cost him the few seconds of awareness when it would have mattered. Prison, for that moment, was the best place he could hide.

But what he had lost was a murkier proposition. His boat, on its last shreds of usefulness? He'd nearly expected it to crumble beneath him. It was more caulk than timber. His good name, which he'd begun to destroy so young? Not likely. His ability to move freely in the world? His work had taken that away, mostly.

His marriage was long over, and that had been both merciful and too late coming. He'd let it ride out, on habit and denial, and now he'd come to regret that.

The only thing he really lost was his high. His coke and heroin and alcohol, all the things that had made all those other things remotely tolerable. That first night on that thin prison mattress, he rode the sleeplessness and anxiety, breathing slowly, stretching, and getting on the floor to punch out some pushups. It was like going into training against a physical opponent. He'd always approached the world like an athlete, and now he fell back into the reassuring routines. He did sit-ups until he was exhausted and then lay on the concrete floor breathing. One of the night guards came by and said, "Are you all right?"

"Can't sleep."

"Don't you have your arraignment in the morning?"

He did. Hours later he came into the courtroom and there was Robbie, to his regret. Quinn didn't know why he didn't want to see his brother, he just didn't.

He was being bailed out without having asked. He would have just as soon stayed put behind those bars. His spell of freedom until he pleaded guilty and reported to federal prison was the worst punishment, aware from minute to minute of his screaming urge for a needle. The prospect of this journey alone, only facing strangers, had its merit. By the afternoon, back in his room in a full withdrawal sweat, having met an affectless lawyer who would defend him, he was clear on the true indictment. He realized that out on the water, far offshore, they were still looking for Botelho, the costly effort to be humane, no matter how logically pointless.

The man was dead minutes after he went off the stern. Quinn sweated into his mattress, and shook in near-convulsions, and wished himself locked in a cell instead. He wondered if he could revoke his own bail. And for the first time in a long time, he wondered how he'd come to all this.

In his recovery from heroin, Quinn had been left with an unsettling rime, an infection of a self-awareness he had never thought could be harbored by his DNA. Regret. Shame. In his clear-mindedness, his memory had become sharp, and serrated, and unbidden. He went back to moments that probably only he remembered, things that at age eighteen or twenty-five or thirty were just fleeting moments but had somehow gone dormant in himself, to flare up constantly and unforgivingly. He remembered one night in his early adulthood going behind a bar he'd just been ejected from, and with his buddies looking on he'd shoved his fingers down his throat and vomited all over the hood of the bartender's car. His friends were howling, and in the moment he'd felt heroic. He was giving them a damned performance. He had a wife and baby at home and he didn't much care. Now, when memories like that intrude, he only feels the dull ache of having been a fool, so foolish he didn't even see how obvious it was. That is the person he showed the world, at least his small world, and now he avoids the world altogether. The 4 a.m. walks to the docks are at least enshrouded in silence, and he can move through this town unseen, and in many ways, he hopes, forgotten.

That life had begun on the boats he'd joined after Chuck Joyce's. Quinn was learning then that some lobstermen he knew were straight arrows, but most not so much, in varying degrees. Some deck bosses he knew went home after every run to good wives and clean children, made their house payments and maintained their pickup trucks. He saw, in time, that most of these were inshore men. The ones he knew who went out to the Banks, the ones who took too-small boats to too-distant waters, were the ones who were pulled to the risk, and the risk wasn't limited to putting traps in the water.

It was a time when coke was everywhere. It was coming in cheap and plentiful, and some of the guys he knew were doubling as sellers. Everything was a joke to Quinn in those days. He didn't know how to treat anything otherwise. He met the world with that still-white smile, and aqueous blue eyes. It was kid stuff, a goof. They had figured out how to beat the disapproving world of adults.

Cocaine, he found, had many levels of magic. It wasn't just the high itself; it was the entrée it offered. The powder was getting them into parties to which they'd otherwise not have ever been invited; there was a girls' college a couple of towns over where Quinn and his buddies would allow themselves to believe it was they whom the girls were interested in, and not the goods. They'd stand in the corner at parties, beer in their hands, watching the good-looking ones dance, after they'd snorted in a back bedroom. None of the girls seemed overly interested in them, and the others guys—the college boys from the university and the boyfriends shipped in from hometowns—knew why they were actually there, and seemed unduly scared. He was eighteen and Gina was living at the family home with the baby; after being ejected from the family home, Quinn was sleeping on the floor of an apartment three older guys shared as they alternately went out on the runs. Nobody was ever present at the same time, it seemed, so he moved onto the couch and began kicking in some money. He was making the payments to Gina's parents. When one of the guys asked him if he'd run some bags up to some buyers at a college in Boston, and that he'd get some "commission grams" for it, there seemed no reason to say no.

He bought a bus ticket to Boston, with tight-packed bags of the blow under his coat. And when he walked the halls of the dormitory, at Northeastern, he felt wholly on another planet. He felt like a man among children. Boys lay on their dorm bunks listening to records and drinking weak beer. They seemed as children seem, untouched by true experience. When he knocked on the appointed door, the boy who opened it pulled him in and fanned cash across his small desk. In all, it was simply transactional.

He bought a cheap car, three hundred for a '79 Buick Regal with busted suspension. Now he could alternate work on the boats, but with city drop-offs here and there as a favor, and that favor got him work on the boats, where the money was; he and his buddies were also throwing that cash around much too easily. Kids their ages were pulling minimum wage at McDonald's while he was hauling in man money. They were closing every bar they went to, and raging through the night until they met their boats, hours before dawn, to load bait. When he began using a chunk of his coke to simply keep going, he'd made that crucial turn.

The life plan had always seemed foregone. He was going to marry Gina, although nobody had ever asked him how he felt about that. She was going to finish high school while her mother minded the baby and Quinn put some money away. One afternoon the old man came down to the docks with Robbie—who was back from his first semester at Stonehill College—looking to patch some of the damage between them.

"You should get another job," his father said. "This isn't going to be good work for a married man."

"What other job?" Quinn said.

"There are lots of jobs," the old man said. "This one was just to toughen you up."

But he was already too far gone. Land looked different when it was only a thread of horizon, and in the work he could expunge from his mind for those hours all these things that clawed at him.

The more coke he did, the more that time became something that purged from him all the frustrations that had come at him too early.

Robbie, the older brother, stood there, abashed.

"So did you make the hockey team up there?"

"No."

"Why the hell not?"

"I'm not fast enough."

"Oh, come *on*."

"What do you care? It's my problem, not yours."

"Cut it out, you two," the old man croaked.

They all went quiet again. The old man looked like he was waiting for some kind of an answer.

"What is it, then?" Quinn said.

"You need to find a real job and then marry that girl."

Quinn thought about that. He didn't want to do either of those things, in truth. But there was the baby, his daughter he'd hardly seen.

"Look, I'll marry her," he finally said. "But I'm not getting some other job."

That was it. There was something inescapable about the daily grip of his work. To cast the baited pots into deep water and pull them back to discover within them the salt-slick prize, the glistening bugs snapping angry in their entrapment. To pull from the sea the hard currency of true sustenance, the same miracle that made him feel distant fraternity to some Midwestern farmer pulling growing things from sour dirt. It was a marvel, and it made you wonder about the fraud of any other work people could do. It was almost enough to make you forget you were losing money each time you touched that simple miracle.

Robbie's visitation days with his daughter, Sarah, come crosshatched with both thrill and dread. He's never felt like a very good father, with his twice-monthly contact. But that's what the ex, M., had demanded in divorce court. She sat with her new boyfriend, who she had lined up for his job. Robbie, in turn, had just wanted it to be over, but now regrets his willingness to fold so easily. Sarah was little more than a baby then; the assumption was that as she got older, they'd spend more time together. That has yet to happen. His own work schedule thwarts such change. When Sarah comes weekends with her backpack, dropped off in the mall-parking-lot switchover by her mother with no words exchanged, he feels as if he has to introduce himself all over again. She comes at him, always, with a smile that makes him bereft at all he has missed. The mystery of why things fail so badly arrive with her. But, at least, Sarah gets in the car each time as if this is a familiar corner of her large universe.

In the car, seat belt fastened, she says, "What's for dinner?"

"Mac and cheese," he says, to her predictable delight. Having dinners her mother does not abide is one of the small pleasures he can afford her. Their relationship involves mostly eating at franchise restaurants and watching the DVDs Sarah brings in her backpack. She is entranced by endless loops of princesses and fairies and 3D animals. The fatherly indulgences he sponsors are both bribery and distance, as he has no other ideas what to do with her. He remembers as a child that his sister was largely his mother's ward, he and Quinn their father's. It seemed a natural order of things. So he spends his weekends with Sarah mostly trying to figure out how to kill the time, a series of long jumps from breakfast to lunch, lunch to dinner, dinner to bedtime.

"Do you ever think about playing a sport?" he says, hopefully.
"Not really."
"You want to play catch?"
"I don't really like that."
"Want to go the park and kick a ball around?"
"No."

56

"Oh." Which leaves him out of ideas.

He doesn't cover games on the weekends that she comes over, and so it would probably seem odd to take her to one. He brought her to the Red Sox one Saturday afternoon last summer, but she folded under the noise of the crowd, and they left the ballpark with her sobbing on his shoulder.

"I wish Coco was here," she says.

"Is that one of your toys?"

"No, Daddy, she's my *friend*."

"You have a friend named Coco?" he says, to which her face goes sour.

"She's a toy, but she's my friend."

One of the provisions of the divorce was that Sarah was not allowed to be around Quinn. He was in his worst addiction at the time, and it was another fight Robbie didn't choose to make. He never mentions Quinn, and Sarah seems to have no memory of him. There's less and less about the family that she knows. Dad is gone and Ma is down at the nursing home, her mind seeming erased of all but the very oldest memories. His sister, Margaret, moved to North Carolina years ago; between she and Robbie and Social Security and Medicaid they manage the payments for their mother. They were as tight a family as any, he thought, but now it's been reduced to him, and Quinn, and the duty Robbie feels toward him. And he's only slowly admitting to himself he's become so weary of Quinn. He carries enough weight, as he sees it, without his brother entering the room. When Quinn messed up, Robbie knew Quinn would pay for his sins. What he didn't realize was how much Quinn's sins would exact a toll on Robbie himself.

He looks up and his daughter is staring at him.

"I want to watch my DVD," Sarah says. He furtively wishes the marriage had lasted long enough for a second child, so at least they could occupy each other. A DVD makes a poor sibling.

By the time the DVD is ten minutes in, Sarah's already fallen asleep in front of the television. He hopes this is the most awkward phase to bridge, a man and his second-grade daughter. He's hanging on, as always, hoping things will get better.

He sits for a bit, then goes into the bedroom. The business card Jean had given him is on the dresser, where he'd laid it out that night when he'd come home.

9.

TINA HEARS THE RAKE OF HER MOTHER'S VOICE THROUGH thin doors. Time, or day, or situation: no idea. Just darkness; just her mother's bellow, come in drunk again on cheap wine, needing attention.

"Tina!" Gina shouts, as if calling down a mineshaft.

"I got work in the morning!" Tina shouts back, rolling her pillow over her head.

Tina hears the leaden footsteps, the endless rub of shoulder gliding along wall as Gina tries to stay on her feet. And now the shadow in the doorway, framed by light, somehow insistent. Now the breathing, drink-heavy and humid.

"I saw him," Gina says, "but he didn't see me."

"Who did you see?"

"Your father."

"So what?" Tina says, rolling over toward the wall, trying to make a point.

"I don't even think he knew it was me."

Tina is silent, but her mother knows she's awake.

"He's got the money to drink beer," she says, "but not the money for us."

Tina says nothing.

"And I'm broke trying to support you."

Bullshit, Tina is thinking. Gina is in her forties now, and bristling with grievances. She only works sporadically, and they both know they're getting the usual array of support: AFDC checks, food stamps, an EBT card, and a Section 8 apartment, all for the purported purpose of providing for the child. *Me*, Tina thinks, *the dependent minor*. But Gina cashes out the food stamps with a cooperative package-store owner, and has a convenience store where the Pakistani owner will give her cartons of cigarettes and ring it up as milk and eggs and bread at twice the listed price.

That's the place Gina's gotten to, on wiles and rationalizations. Tina doesn't know past history, but she's seen her mother mixed up with such a gallery of unfortunate men that Tina wonders how life might be if she just got a job, stopped drinking, and shut the hell up.

"Are you even listening to me?"

Tina looks at the clock. It's a quarter past three in the morning. The bars all close at one.

"Ma, I gotta sleep."

"Your father doesn't give a shit about you."

"I know. You told me already."

"You should ask him for that money."

"I will."

"He's fucked everything up. I mean like, forever."

"Okay, okay."

Then there's another voice. A man.

"Gina?" he calls from what sounds to be the kitchen, a voice similarly drink-sodden. "Are there any clean glasses?"

Tina awakens again in the darkness, as if by phantom noise. The apartment is quiet. She has no idea if her mother's still home, or come and gone. Her clock reads four thirty and she sits up in bed. She doesn't remember a dream, but feels as if she's been knocked roughly from sleep. Some revelation. Some intuition. She doesn't know quite what it is. But she feels convinced, right now, that it's time to go see her father and have it out.

It's been so many years. She needs for him to help her, but maybe the help could be mutual. Maybe there's something she could do for him. She's never heard of a girl working a lobster boat. Maybe something else, though.

She dresses quickly, only rubbing a palmful of tap water on her face. Out the door pulling on her coat. It's cold in the mornings, still. She shivers and then quickens her pace to warm herself. The streets are quiet, but from inside houses she passes, dogs hear her steps and begin the howling chorus. Turning at the bottom of the street and onto Main, she passes empty shops and a few diners open for the earliest risers and latest drinkers. Men in plaid coats sit over their coffee. As she moves, she inventories, trying to see if he's among them. But no. She pushes on to the docks.

The boats are loading up under blued floodlights. She's not sure which one is his. It's a new boat, she knows, after the old one was seized. She has no idea, however, what this boat would look like.

Some fishermen come walking from the near shadows, and she asks if they know Quinn Boyle.

"He's around here somewhere," one says.

She walks along the seawall, sighting down the long docks. A half dozen boats are getting ready, tired men moving slowly, the endless routines. The pots, wire boxes in high-visibility yellows and oranges, stack on the afts in risen walls that seem to likewise cage in their owners.

One boat is just pulling off to open water, its engines surging as it moves to gather speed. Now she sees in the weak light that it's him. She cannot mistake the imprint of his shape and movement, as little as she ever knew him. There he goes, out to sea, once again. Just missed. She could shout but he'd never hear it, wouldn't probably know her now if he saw her. Then he turns his head; for that fraction he seems to lock on her from across the water. She'd like to think that, but who can say. The boat swings to the starboard and she sees the name hand-painted on the stern. *Christine II*. Her given name, the name no one calls her by. Her mother had christened her Tina somewhere along the way, the cute contrivance of "Gina and Tina," like matching outfits in a yellowed Easter photo.

She watches the boat, her namesake, as it escapes out past the breakwater. She's determined to follow it to the horizon. She has the time and even as she shivers she doesn't waver. In time, somewhere out there in its tininess, it disappears from her sight, lost amid the broad, gray palette of the morning ocean. She stays anyway, until she guesses it has slipped across the other edge of this constricted world she knows. All she can hope now is that he has a good catch, for both of them.

10.

FOUR DAYS AFTERWARD, AND ANOTHER MORNING SUN reds Robbie's eyelids and he clamps them more tightly, trying not to awaken. He feels the chill and tightens his arms around himself. Drifting, as on still water, he tries to descend back. But he can feel the insistence of his bladder now, each discomfort rising like a piece in an orchestra to wake him.

He opens his eyes, expecting his bedroom. In fact, he's in his car, in the middle of an empty parking lot. The keys are in the ignition and he starts the car reflexively, pushing up the heater controls. The dashboard clock reads 5:12.

He thinks backwards two hours. Of rising from Jean's bed in her condo, telling her he had to go. He was still thinking of that awkwardness with Dawn, of her seeing them out and obviously together, and the unexpected hurt in Dawn's face. It complicated the night he was having with Jean, who had asked and been told about M., had been asked and had told about her own ex, and had been cheery and chatty until she said to him, "That's not your ex-wife right over there, is it?" And he looked across the restaurant and there was Dawn, locked in on them from a table with her two girlfriends, who seemed to be trying to draw her back into the conversation.

"That one's hard to explain," he'd said, to which she said, "I hate it when there's a hard-to-explain one."

He could have thumbnailed Dawn as a high-strung ex-girl-friend, and he supposed she is, by most definitions. He felt, though, as if his time with Dawn was a long chain of insistence and surrender, when he thought he might settle into something that was just what it was, with no expectations, a state he then found endlessly impossible. He had thought of Dawn as a Fri-day-night date while she was trying to get him to meet her fam-ily. He had finally begun to think of himself as resolutely single, or more accurately alone, when she was already talking about themselves as a couple. He kept trying to slow her down, to posi-tion her to explain. Finally, when it was impossible, he told her so, and she'd tearily decamped to Florida.

So why was he feeling so guilty, sitting with Jean at a cheap Italian restaurant? The date had seemed train-wrecked with Dawn's presence, but they'd eaten and had drinks, and when Jean invited him back to her place, he didn't see the harm in it.

As the car's heater warms him now, he thinks backward six hours. He'd met Jean for the date at Jack's, as he'd waited for Quinn. But even before she arrived, he was telling himself that Quinn re-ally didn't need him anymore. Getting Jean out on a weeknight seemed a good first effort; it made the wait feel different.

And he thinks a few hours before that, when he'd checked his phone and had seen no one had called. Quinn didn't have the money for a satellite phone for the boat, only an archaic ship-shore radio; he did have a cheap cell phone he could use when he got close enough to land. The first call always went to the wholesaler, to meet him with the refrigerator truck to unload; the second call was to Robbie, to give him an ETA of the bar time. No calls came, and he put it out of his mind as he followed Jean home in his car.

He thinks of how they made love, very gently, and how as he and Jean lay together afterward, the music ran out. Jean got out of bed in the dark and opened her iPad to find something new to play. Robbie, under the sheet, watched her naked and bathed in the screen's blue light, her breasts and collarbone and long neck as perfectly rendered against the darkness as marble under a master's hands—exquisite and noble. Then, as quickly, he told himself that he wouldn't allow himself to do that to another woman in his life.

Then it was Robbie startling awake, past four in the morning, in an unfamiliar bed. Jean sleeping next to him. He took his phone from his pants on the floor and checked it. No messages. Quinn had made long runs and had late arrivals when the work was going well, but now Robbie was thinking this seemed awfully late.

He dressed quietly and when he sat on the bed to put on his shoes, Jean stirred a bit.

"I have to go," he said. "I'll call you tomorrow." She'd mumbled but didn't seem to be hearing him.

Down at the docks, Quinn's boat still not in its slip. The time was creeping toward three-thirty. He knew that people would start showing up for work by four. He'd wait; maybe he could find out what was going on. Up the hill a bit, there was the church parking lot, broad and empty, and higher ground. He steered his car up there to have a clear sight line across the harbor and the breakwater, and instantly lapsed into sleep.

And now he is awake again, at a bit after five. The dock seems as placid as before. A light day of work; whoever has chosen to go out has already loaded and launched. He puts the car in gear and rolls down the hill and parks and gets out. He walks along the boats until he sees a man mending his traps.

"Have you seen Quinn come in?" he says.

"Not yet," the lobsterman says.

He looks out across the breakwater. The seas are still and the skies are cloudless. There's been no rough weather.

Waiting on a boat isn't like waiting for a man to emerge from a prison, where the date is determined and the time must be passed with patience, but also with calculation. Waiting for a boat is like waiting for something to happen imminently, when it then does not. He's gone to find Quinn before. The last time he failed to show he was in the hands of the Coast Guard, with his boat being towed behind and legal storms ahead.

Waiting for a boat is different. It's a thousand false sightings and a rising anxiety in which you tell yourself you're overreacting. But then it turns out, sometimes, you're not. You wait all morning debating what you should do. You first find the harbormaster, who has nothing to tell you, and cannot raise a voice from the crackle of the radio. Then to the Coast Guard, who ask you if you're making an official report. You first say no, and hang up. Then you call back and say yes, and then you wait to hear back from them. When they call you back late in the afternoon, they sound more somber. They tell you that they still can't raise the boat on the radio, after constant effort, and they can't find a signal from a distress beacon, and that the boats they've contacted "out there" haven't seen the *Christine II* but think they might have remembered a few buoys from the boat, bobbing untended. When you arrive at the Coast Guard station they're waiting for you, and you answer their questions. They ask you if you know who was sterning for him and you can't tell them, because you don't know. Kids off barstools, usually. They tell you that you can wait, or you can go home and they'll call you.

So what you do is drive up to the bar with your heart banging away. When you get there, you first take the hopeful look for your brother, hoping somehow he's turned up, hoping he's slaking his sea thirst with his first cold one. But you never really expected that. So then you begin your search for Santoro. He isn't there, either; nobody's seen him. So you keep asking. By eleven, you're at his parents' little house over on the backside of town, asking them where he is. And they stand foggy on their little stoop and tell you he went out on somebody's boat for one last run, and they don't know where he is, either.

The search begins at the next dawn, small planes and some fast Coast Guard cutters, doggedly trawling the grid. For two full days you sit in your apartment, waiting for a call. But it's on the kitchen radio you hear, Tuesday night as the last light leaches away outside your window, that the search has been suspended.

PART TWO

11.

IT'S BEEN A YEAR SINCE. SHE PREFERS TO BE CALLED Christine now. Not *Tina*. She'd almost rather be called Christine III, next after the boat that ferried her name into the unknown. Christine the First was the impounded boat; that would have once made her Christine Before That, back then; as a baby, as a little girl, before she was rechristened "Tina" out of her mother's spite, and became the frustrated human being that name always seemed glommed to.

She's glad, at least, that she got to see the boat going out that last time. That's more than a year ago now.

The harbormen might have declared that "Christine" turned out to be a bad-luck name. She imagines the lettering having been painted on that stern with at least a little bit of hope. Her father didn't reach out to her in any other way. All the competing stories and mixed loyalties. And maybe he, like she, had a fear of being turned away.

What if she'd caught up with him that last morning, and they'd talked? She wonders if it would have made what happened after that much more difficult for her to live with. The uncertainty of how it might have turned out allows her to make up her own favored version of the story.

They'd all waited, far past what made any sense. He'd survived a lot, after all. Would it have been all that surprising for another boat to have suddenly come upon him as he was treading water, waving for help? He just seemed that way. Unsinkable, if only by force of habit.

When that didn't happen, she went on to the next phase: waking up at night with a million competing visions of how the boat went down, how they hit the water, what it was like for him to finally give up hope in those last seconds. But she imagines he'd lost all hope long before the boat went down, and that may be the most painful thing of all to realize.

There was a mock funeral, because there was no body. There were no real friends, either, hadn't been in a long time. The lobstermen turned out if only out of respect. Robbie had made the rounds at all the bars and diners and fish stores, and what he'd mostly found was people who just didn't want to come. They may have had good reasons: superstition of men who live their lives on the decks of boats, or people who harbor the old resentments, or maybe just an unwillingness to see what your own future might be.

She wasn't angry; people have their decisions to make. Her mother wouldn't shut up about the fact that he left no life insurance, even though the divorce decree said he was supposed to. With that missing vessel went the end of Gina's illusion of back child support, of a fat cash payout (which in theory was supposed to be earmarked for Christine, but whatever). Quinn's ship went out and Gina's ship did not come in. And Christine was summarily announced as more of a liability than ever because of it. But Christine suspected Gina was mostly mad at Christine having any grief at all. Christine wouldn't share it with her, but she knew Gina could tell it was there.

Gina called Christine's older sister after the search was terminated, and told her what had happened. The call was short.

72

Heather, long departed. Heather with no interest in coming back for whatever empty ceremonies were in store. Christine didn't know her life. Heather had her own take on what she'd grown up in. She was, after all, the shameful product of this teenage pregnancy. Christine was at the other end, the part where they were still trying to keep it together and have some kind of normal. *Why did they even have me?* she sometimes wondered. There must have been circumstances.

It wasn't so hard to think of Quinn and Gina as teenagers, even as they got older, because Christine never really witnessed them acting like adults. She'd look at the pictures of them from when they were young: good-looking, not a surprise, because something must have been going on that they were in so much trouble so young. Blond, tan, white smiles; they couldn't stay away from each other. And both beautiful enough to hold their selfishness. They'd looked harsh as adults, all worn out. Gina had never stopped partying; Quinn had never stopped anything.

Summer passed, and with it Christine's dwindled, foolish hopes, the secret wish for her father to somehow have survived. In her first class at the community college, Intro to Lit, the professor read a poem aloud, and she prepared to be thoroughly unimpressed. But when he got to the part that said . . .

Good men, the last wave by, crying how bright
Their frail deeds might have danced in a green bay

. . . that was when she finally sobbed. Her classmates stared at her. She finally blurted, "It's a really long story." The professor couldn't hide being pleased, finally, by any kind of response to the words. So that was her true memorial service, basically, a freshman breaking down on her second week at school over a *poem.* They sent her to counseling. She tried unsuccessfully to explain to them that she was moved by the beauty of the lines. They sent her to a doctor. He said, "Think about Paxil."

What she thought about were the little connections to a man she'd really never gotten to know. By the time she was old enough to understand the architecture of her family, he was gone. Gina was endlessly repeating what she heard, about his drug problems, about women he was with, about how he must have had better things to do than to see little Tina. But he always sent a birthday card. She presumed it must have been something that stuck in his head to do. Maybe it was her grandmother in the background, when her brain wasn't scrambled, insisting that he do it. The card had the usual awkward, misspelled sentiments— *I hope you have a really great year now that your 8*—but it was the writing itself Tina studied, as if it would tell her something about him. She took out a book at the public library, on handwriting analysis. She learned the terms, and tried to interpret, from the crabbed scratches from her father's pen, what kind of man he was. These cards came from someone whose hands were probably aching from days of work, or maybe unsteady from whatever substance abuse he was involved in. But like a junior graphologist, she created the picture of him she wanted to see: the slant of his words, the book indicated, signaled friendly approach, and warmth of heart (and not just a drunken lean as pen contacted paper). The heavy pressure, making ridges along the card stock, was a clear signal of the commitment to his sentiments (and not the awkward push as he wrote in a boat rocking in the harbor waves). The full loops in his lower zone spoke of intention and thoughts of a future. She pinned those cards to the bulletin board above her nightstand, and she studied them. She put paper on her small desk and on a few occasions tried to imitate the writing with her own hand, trying to replicate his *garlands* and *arcades*, trying to feel what he felt. It was all she

74

really had to work with, so she worked it hard, even as Gina went on and on about how he really didn't give a shit about anybody.

Memories of her father were always as thin as the inked lines of his words. It seemed to be only the hardest of those ones that stayed with her. As she tried to pull back something to remember him by, she understood it had been she who had cut the tie, and he who had allowed it too easily.

This had been the time when Quinn was still taking her out one day a week. She was six or seven, the divorce still fresh. She, decked in her best dress and with her toys in her backpack for moral support, waiting on the front steps for him to show. Gina sat in the kitchen in her stained bathrobe, hung over and smoking cigarettes, with a man whose name Tina didn't know, a man sitting shirtless and barefoot in his fish-smelling jeans.

The truck came rattling up the way, the metal reverb of a loose muffler when he stopped. Quinn looked over at her with what felt like the same fear she had. He swung the passenger door open, its hinges groaning, and she stepped onto a floorboard covered in coffee cups and sandwich wrappers. He stomped on the gas pedal and they were off.

The first stop was her grandparents', where they all sat awkwardly while Tina was served toast. Her grandfather gruffly asked about her life, and she gave them a story with enough holes for them to see how she was protecting Gina. It felt natural at that age, to do that. She talked about school, and they all smiled knowingly when she said she didn't like it. A family trait, no doubt. After a period of silence, her grandmother smiled and asked her what she wanted for Christmas.

"It's October," Tina said.

After that, she and Quinn got back in his old pickup and took on the long stretch of hours before they could eat lunch. He more or less just drove around.

"Can I see where you live?" she said.

"That probably wouldn't be a good idea right now," he said.

She didn't like being around his boat, because of the stink. She didn't like going out to the water, and that pretty much dead-ended his ideas for activities. They drove up a narrow street above the harbor, and he said, "I have to run in here. I'll be right out."

He went up the steps of an old house, and in. Tina locked the truck's doors and turned the dial on the old AM radio until she found any music at all. She was relieved to be alone in the truck, but felt less so when he didn't come right back out. It seemed a while. She took out a picture book she had in her pack and tried to get interested in that. There was a tap on the side window. She looked up and it was a face that startled her, red-faced and wild-bearded, a man with eyes that seemed to be rotating in their sockets.

"Hey, do you know what time it is?" he said.

She was frozen.

"I need the time."

She said, "It's about eleven o'clock."

"What?"

"*Eleven*," she said.

"I can't hear you," he said, even though she could hear him. He tried the door handle.

"Unlock the door so I can hear you," he said.

She couldn't move, or speak. He came around the front of the truck and to the driver's side. He tried the door, then again, trying to force it. The lock held, and he walked around the truck again, trying to find entrance. Tina was openly crying now, and that didn't seem to back him off.

She was in that glass capsule and he was circling inward. He seemed angry now, but then he turned his head—the sound of a vehicle on the street down the block.

"I just need to know what time it is," he said, as if the offended party, and stalked off.

It was a long time before her father keyed the door and slid onto the seat. She'd wiped her face with her sleeves until it was raw, and he could see.

"What's the matter with you?" he said.

"Nothing . . ."

"I wasn't that long," he said. She burst into tears again.

"Do you want to talk about something?" he said.

"*No.*"

"Oh, Jesus Christ," he said.

He was supposed to drop her back home at six, but when he did, after a seeming eternity, it was more like four, to Gina's irritation. It was the last visitation he'd make. Her relief was palpable and forever guilt-inducing.

In her last days of senior year, after enough weeks had crawled by to make it foregone that her father was dead, she had sat numbly with her girlfriends at lunchtime, knowing they were no longer close. Her friends were obsessing about vodka and weed and partying. She had vowed to have nothing to do with her parents' selfish addictions. This particular form of teenage rebellion was lost on most of her friends.

Now, in further defiance and with the enabling of the Financial Aid Office at the community college, she'd wheedled a student loan she knew she probably couldn't pay back. She used some of it to move in with some girls she'd graduated high school with, but didn't know especially well. That left Gina to her own empty nights. Gina seemed stunned, and victimized, that Christine was reacting as she was to the death of her father.

Christine now worked more shifts at Buddy's, a little diner near Town Hall. She'd started there one day a week the summer before, and Buddy had liked her well enough. She also began, slowly, to pick up on a near-silent subtext. People were talking about what happened, still. Everybody had their theories, apparently. The fact that people disliked Santoro as much as they did accounted, she thought, for a nearly even split on the question of whose fault it must have been. But she was hearing this second-hand, from a fellow waitress or a roommate and once or twice from Gina, who predictably cast Quinn as the party at fault. Who had sunk whom, in the end?

12.

OVER THE SUMMER AFTER HER FATHER WAS LOST, Christine found herself constantly going down to the docks and looking across the open sea past the breakwater. She supposed that when the ocean was your grave, the people who cared about you could find you right at the water's edge. She also found herself looking, more often, for her uncle. It was only after Quinn was lost that she felt that familial pull. When they'd all sat together, mourning, it was the first time in a long time she'd felt as if she belonged to something real.

Being out of high school amplified her uncertainties. On graduation day, Gina, turned up shaky but sober, with her camera and her low-cut dress, pinked in her early summer sunburn. She shouted out her woo-hoos when Christine went on the stage to get the diploma, so loud Christine could hear that cigarette-wrecked voice above the courtesy applause from the other parents. But like it or not, school had been a binding for her that she was terrified of severing. It had always been something just to go to.

A few days after, she took on the rent of a shared apartment, and took the loan, and enrolled for the fall. The balance loomed above the summer like the August thunderclouds. She waitressed as many shifts as she could and still implored Buddy for more hours. On one of those mid-June Saturday afternoons, Robbie came in with Sarah, asking if it was too late to get pancakes.

"It's never too late here," Christine said, as her cousin gave her the tight hug around the hips.

"I'm glad you came by," Christine said to her.

"We wanted to see if you'd ever like to come over and hang out," Robbie said. "Sarah's been asking." Sarah, next to him, nodding and grinning, a smile-in-progress with two adult teeth just pushing up into place.

"Yeah, I'd like to," Christine said. "I'll be there." Robbie had told her once that he never knew exactly what to do with Sarah, and Christine guessed he needed her help. She was fine on that. This was family. After work that day she went to Robbie's. The three of them did nothing more than sit in front of the television. Sarah slumped against Christine as her own sister never had.

That Quinn had left no will had surprised no one; what was there? He left no life insurance, no vehicle, no furniture, and no possessions other than dirty laundry and a thin mattress laid on the floor. Robbie had gone up to his rented room and gathered what was there, but it wasn't anything worth keeping. Everything that mattered had gone down with him.

She asked if there was maybe an old coat he'd left, but Robbie said he'd already thrown it all away.

"Why did you do that?" Christine said, too sharply, and he'd looked at her with some surprise.

"I should have asked you first," he said. "I got used to being the only person he was connected to anymore."

This was the part of the summer when she began feeling generally angry. Part of the process, people said. She was angry she wasn't grieving someone she'd loved, but someone she never got a chance to love. She went moody in the middle of the July, and sat off by herself more. But she'd go up to her uncle's apartment whenever Sarah was there, and then Sarah began coming more than just twice a month.

Robbie was covering Legion baseball for the paper, and Christine went out to see some of the games, with some of the boys she knew from school playing on one team or another. Jared Kelly came over after the game, as she was starting to walk home, he said, "Is Mr. Boyle from *The Record* your dad?"

"Kind of, yeah," she said.

By August, it seemed that the disappearance of Quinn Boyle and this other man Santoro had already become local history, and consequently distanced, and less real. It was as if you could talk about them like characters in a movie you'd seen. Christine didn't remember exactly when she started to realize what people were saying, until it came together all at once.

There was a man she didn't know in the restaurant, and obviously he didn't know her. He was just going on about it.

"They both had a reason to disappear," he said. "They'd known each other for years. They were up to their ears in bullshit. One was a drug runner and the other one had already been in prison for possession."

Christine was at the counter, picking up an order for another table, but was locked in now. The guy had theories about South America, theories about drug cartels, and theories about Quinn Boyle and Freddy Santoro laughing all the way to wherever they had gone.

The men he was with didn't know Christine, either, otherwise they would have waved him off. She could feel her face burning.

"Why don't you keep your fucking theories to yourself," someone said, although Christine quickly realized that someone was
actually herself.

The man turned around and looked at her. "Why don't you
just serve the fucking toast?" he said. She took the plates in hand
and put them in front of the wrong customers, nearly dropping
the food in their laps, and then went into the ladies' room and
locked herself in a stall. Once you start crying, she had found,
you really had no control of it. When she came back out, there
was her boss, Buddy, telling her she was fired.

Robbie went back there the next day, to talk to Buddy. Apparently, Buddy's sons had played some sports for the high school,
so they knew each other. Robbie didn't tell Christine what they
talked about, but when Robbie got home he told her she could
go back the next morning.

"I wanted to *kill* that guy," she said. "I was going to grab one of
Buddy's meat cleavers."

"People are going to talk."

"My father wouldn't have done something like they were saying, would he?"

"No, he wouldn't have."

"But he didn't even know me."

"Then he wouldn't have done it to *me*," Robbie said. "No way
he would have left me holding the bag with all this shit."

"You got left holding the bag?"

"Dying doesn't free you from the bureaucracy, Honey. I got
the insurance company that doesn't want to pay off on the loss
of the boat, because your father missed the last three payments.
Some bank must be holding the note on his boat, but I can't find
any sign of it. I'm hearing that the estate of Santoro may sue
the insurance company for negligence. I got the Coast Guard
people who keep grilling me about the safety inspections on

the boat, and the safety inspector who's telling me not to talk to anybody."

"I guess you're not dead until a piece of paper says you are," Christine said.

That particular piece of paper came after ninety days, and there was more paperwork for Robbie to do related to that. She saw him on the street one afternoon so angry he couldn't speak. A court-appointed lawyer had asked him to submit a notarized statement stipulating he had no knowledge of her father's whereabouts.

"Now I'm accused," he said.

Court papers notwithstanding, Christine thought about what she wanted to do to make it official in her own mind. She had a pitiable 68 Facebook friends (everyone else seemed to have 500); of those 68 not one had wanted to come to the little memorial service they put on. Of course she realized she wasn't a very good Facebook friend, either. Gina never had any money for them to actually own a computer. Facebook was blocked on the computers at the high school. She used the public library when she could, so she was more or less a Facebook ghost, and presumed a lot other friends had friended her just to pump up their own numbers, just at she had, statistical evidence of manufactured popularity.

But one afternoon staying with Sarah, Christine went to Robbie's computer and logged in to her account.

We got the paperwork for something we already knew, she wrote. *My father, lost at sea. Officially and legally dead. RIP, Quinn Boyle.*

Within a day, below that post, right next to the thumbs-up icon, it said *28 people like this*.

Sarah was coming to see Robbie more often, because her mother worked and school was out for summer. On days when Christine worked the early shift at the restaurant she'd take Sarah for the afternoon, usually at Robbie's apartment, or on nice days to the park or the water. They walked around town, enjoying the early summer weather before the humidity rolled in. One day they were sitting on the bench in front of the ice-cream shop when Jared Kelly drove up.

"Hey," he said.

"Hey."

He was in his baseball uniform.

"Going to the game tonight?" he said.

"I can if you want."

"Nobody's making you."

"Is that an invitation, then?"

"Yeah. It is."

"Okay. We'll be there."

He drove off. Christine had always thought he liked her. And she had always hoped he liked her.

"Is that your boyfriend?" Sarah said.

"Not yet."

She was smiling, indeed, but why was she feeling kind of bad, too? She knew why; she just didn't want to admit it. To her regret, she couldn't avoid thinking, *If my father wasn't dead, none of this would be happening.* That wasn't a very fitting memorial.

13.

SO THE YEAR SINCE QUINN'S DISAPPEARANCE HAS passed, and they enter the new cycle, another spring and summer. Toward the end of August, Robbie comes to the diner as Christine finishes her shift. He sits her down at a table and says, "I got a call."

A cod boat out of Aberdeen, Scotland, has found something floating, far out there, north of the abandoned and isolated island of St. Kilda.

Robbie has brought them in a paper shopping bag, which he opens.

It's a torn-up pair of the orange lobstering pants. On the suspenders, he shows her, written in faded Sharpie, it says *Christine II*.

"The cod boat crew saw these floating in a field of seaweed. We don't know whether these were from Quinn or from Santoro," he says. "But I thought you might like to have them."

That night, she spreads the pants out on the floor next to her mattress. She arranges the tattered edges, so they're like half of a chalk body outline. She wonders if they'd been pulled off by someone trying, in the last minutes, to stay afloat. This thought will set off a whole week of bad dreams, the movie visualization in her head, of desperation and futility.

"We should bury them," she tells Robbie, finally. "It's something that was really there."

"In the long run, I think you might want to keep them."

The rubber pants glow with a power of the religious artifacts, those ancient touchstones and relics. A chip of the cross; the Shroud of Turin. If such things are real, they have meaning. The pants have floated for nearly a year, so to be found in a particular place yields no clues. If relics are fakes, they seem to prove the pointlessness of belief. She sits there looking at the pants and fights the urge to extend her hand and touch them. When she succumbs to that battle, the pants feel as if she is touching cold flesh, even though she hasn't touched her father in all the time of her memories and experience. She must have, once. She must have curled in his lap and felt his warmth, but that memory was purely hypothetical.

A pair of rubber-coated pants. When they rolled off whatever factory line they must have come from (her diner-sensitized nose can almost get that scent of hot rubber being bonded to fabric) there was no humanity in them. The only thing that gives them any kind of life is that handwriting on those salt-yellowed suspenders, the hand of her father. Her regret is nearly crippling in this moment, now that there's nothing to be done.

All evening, she feels numbed, even as Jared Kelly arrives at her empty apartment and they get into her empty bed, and fill it up, and she gives him what he is here for. Christine wishes afterward her first time wasn't so disconnected, so off is she in the fog of all the missed connections of all the years, ticking away inside her head.

"Was that your first time?" Jared says, afterward.

"Yeah, get serious," she shoots back.

When she awakens in the morning, Jared has already left for his job. He's replaced Santoro, running the yacht club's launch in the harbor.

She hasn't been completely ignoring her mother. She makes the obligatory visit once a week, and actually finds Gina at home about one out of three times. On this Saturday, Christine goes over early before Gina has headed out to party. Gina is in the kitchen in a bathrobe, with white gym socks on, black on the soles from the unswept dirt of the kitchen.

"I saw your Facebook post," Gina says. "Like, seriously? You're that broken up about it? Because he didn't really care about you."

"Maybe he did it in his own way."

"Yeah, kids in your situation tell themselves that, to feel okay."

There's the razor. The sting of it makes Christine recoil. She mumbles something and she's out the door.

"I'm the one who did all the caring," Gina calls after her.

It's all she can think about, walking back to her apartment. That perfect little statement has succeeded in destroying her, maybe because there's just a thread too much truth to it. Christine has to admit she's far more comfortable with the father she only needs to imagine. His death has freed her up. Now she doesn't walk the streets of this town worrying endlessly that she'll run into the actual person, Quinn Boyle, and how awkward that would be. Christine always guessed he walked around town the exact same way, anxious about the possibility of looking up and having her there. His movements were a tiny triangle, between the docks, the bar, and that one room he rented.

Kids in your situation tell themselves that, to feel okay. She knows exactly those kinds of girls at school. The one who goes on about how awesome Dad is, even though she hasn't seen the guy in ten years. The one who sees the gone-away Daddy only in counterpoint to asshole Stepdad, who might not even be such an asshole. Christine is part of a generation of kids who barely know what "Mom and Dad," that singular unit, really means.

The kids who have an actual Mom-and-Dad thing going on tend to be going to private schools.

But autumn is here. She's paid her tuition in full, from all those extra shifts at Buddy's. She knows the bus route to the campus. The last dregs of her money goes for books; she imagines herself being a nurse, maybe, if she can cut it in the intro courses. She thinks about Jared, who has arrived three more times at her apartment, the third time with the condoms. He's moving up to Salem State Labor Day weekend, to try out for baseball, but he's saying he'll be back all the time to see her. She knows he will, before she abruptly thinks, *That's what kids in your situation tell themselves.*

When she comes to her uncle's a couple of days later to spend time with her cousin, she instantly knows something is wrong.

"Did they find something else?" she says.

"This isn't about your father, this is about you," he says, and she nods.

"Apparently Jared Kelly has had a lot to say about you lately," his voice holding back the anger.

"Meaning?"

"Meaning he's telling all the guys about his conquests."

"Guys do that. How did you hear?"

"I cover sports, Honey. Stuff like that gets right back to me."

"Don't worry. It's not a problem."

"It is a problem!" he says in a rising voice. "You're seventeen."

"I'm eighteen now, actually. I live on my own, work, and now I'm going to school. It's okay."

"So you think you have it all figured out, do you?"

"I know what I'm doing."

Robbie is shifting his weight back and forth on his feet, and he seems to be trying to find the right way.

"I've seen all this before," he says. "I've seen exactly how one stupid mistake affects every life around it."

"Meaning my parents."

"Exactly meaning them. Too young, too naïve, then too much on their backs, too many responsibilities they weren't ready for. We all paid a price. Every one of us."

"That won't happen."

"Are you sure you're not pregnant?"

"Oh my God, did you just actually say that?"

"Are you sure you're not pregnant, is what I just asked you."

"Yes, I'm sure," she says, even though she knows no such thing.

"Are you sure you even love this boy? This boy who brags about you in ways that I, for one, find kind of disgusting?"

"Not sure."

"And does he love you?"

"I don't *know*."

"There you go, then."

"Times are different, Uncle Robbie."

He's shaking his head and walking around in a tight circle.

"Everybody has failed you, including me," he says. "You're eighteen and living out on your own. That's just not right."

"I'm fine," she says. "Really."

"Kids like you only think you are."

He can see her glaring at him now.

"Someone needs to give you some kind of grounding."

"You're grounding me? I don't even live with you."

"*Grounding*. Yes, in a different meaning of that word. Structure. Consistency. Do you not understand what I'm saying? I'm saying you need to move in here."

"I don't want to impose."

"Impose? *Impose?*"

"What?"

"It would *impose* on me if you got yourself pregnant and had to quit school and take some awful job. It would *impose* on me to have to watch you fail to be what you might have been, fail to be remotely happy, start drinking, start doing drugs, get into debt. It would impose on me to sit quietly by, worrying on your behalf. That would be imposing on me."

"What are you talking about? I haven't done anything."

"I spent most of my adult life helping your father clean up his messes," Robbie nearly shouts. "It's not happening all over again."

He's overreacting, she thinks. And as quickly, *That's what kids in your situation . . .*

And it occurs to her that for what is probably the first time in her entire life, someone is actually giving a shit.

14.

CHRISTINE MOVES INTO THE EXTRA BEDROOM (HARD-
ly a bedroom at all, no closet in it and more a closet itself). Labor Day Weekend; Robbie takes the girls to a discount furniture
store to buy bunk beds. Sarah can't seem to stop grinning up on
that top mattress, the princess on her pea. If he'd known that all
it took was a bunk bed to get his daughter begging to come to see
more of him, he'd have considered that money well-spent a long
time ago. But then there are more sheets and pillows and towels
and a cheap desk and lamp for Christine to do her homework.
That night he fans the receipts out on his desk. Robbie lives in
constant worry about money; he's drilling down into savings
that were never healthy to start with, given his meager wages.

He does the math when he's driving, or showering, or struggling to drift into sleep. Christine keeps on waitressing as she
can. They save the bit of money she was paying for that stun-
ningly depressing little apartment she shared with those girls.
Robbie takes any overtime he can. That, minus the daily expenses. Minus the school money for Christine because she'll come
up short after this term. Minus the child support he sends to
M. And minus the money he spends seeing Jean. In the night,
he looks at the clock, creeping toward two in the morning, then

three. Here he is in the binding of his own life. When he was a kid, he liked being the oldest. It was as if it gave him certain prerogatives he never chose to exercise. Perhaps he has only put this on himself, this accountability, but now he feels it chronically, like heartburn.

Christine says she wants to get an iPhone.

"I can pay for it out of my waitressing money," she says, hopeful, but he knows that game from his own teenage years.

"That only subtracts from the total," he says. "It's still total income versus total expenditures. And the monthly charges to be on a plan."

"But you have one . . ."

"I have one that the paper pays for, because I need it for my job," he says. "You've gotten along without one until now."

"That was when people were texting," she says. "But now there's Twitter and Instagram. You kind of need to use those. Otherwise I'm kind of a leper. I'm trying to make new friends."

The phone thing has put the first parental pall on their relationship. When he goes out the door to take Jean for a cheap dinner, he feels Christine's quiet and burning scrutiny. And knows she doesn't even mean it. But he gets that it's important to her, that to not tweet is to not belong to the human race as defined by teenagers, which in turn is the problem with letting teenagers set any definitions. At dinner, Jean asks him what's on his mind, and he says, "Nothing." Then he excuses himself and goes outside and calls Christine at the apartment.

"You can get the phone," he says. "I'll help with the payments."

Christine mumbles a thank you and he'd swear she was sniffling on the other end.

The relationship with Jean progresses easily, incrementally, in the deceptively simple ways his lunging efforts with Dawn failed to be. Jean seems amused by him, and them, and lacking any urgency. He maintains his stumbling sense of how these things work.

But he's a parent, too, really twice over now. When her daughter is off on sleepovers, he stays in Jean's bed until midnight before heading home. He won't be out all night with Christine in the house. He worries about her, in indistinct ways. He also knows his already-lean budget is getting leaner with the new phone.

"She's a girl who just wants to do what the other girls do," Jean says as the old clock's hands rise toward apex. She is warm against him. "Being a girl just keeps getting more complicated, and more expensive."

"Tell me about it," he says.

Okay, Quinn, I'll take on your daughter. I'll get her through the next two years, or four, or what it takes. I'll give her some foundation that you and that goddamned Gina could never give her. The foundation the old man tried to give us, but failed on at least half that account. I'll shut my mouth and do this for family. And then when she's out on her own, I'll turn around and hope I have enough left to give my own daughter what she needs.

Thanks again, Brother.

Shock has gone to anger with no real weeping in between. He fights the burn with empty platitudes: Quinn was doing his best. Quinn was working as hard as he could. Quinn didn't seem to get the breaks. But his mind goes to Botelho, that event being the beginning of the end, the first piece in the movement for Quinn toward his own death. What did happen that night? Quinn always said he never saw anything, but why? Was he doing heroin? Or was he just sloppy, too used to thinking the dangers weren't really so? Or it could have been something Robbie doesn't want to think about.

Anger turns in time to an even more disturbing feeling, one he wonders is "part of the process," as Jean keeps saying, but one he will not divulge to her.

I'm glad he's gone.

It was too much, he tells himself. His brother's mistakes, and his troubles, hung as a shroud over all their lives, all bad weather that would not clear.

15.

BACK ON A SUMMER DAY OF THEIR YOUTH. ROBBIE IS, despite his best instincts, sitting at a bar waiting for his brother to return to the adjacent stool. Quinn's beer stands warm in its glass, the foamed head collapsed like a failed soufflé. His fake ID has gotten him easy entry, and he's enjoying the pleasure of passage under an assumed identity. The ID, of course, was arranged for him by Quinn, about whose shadowy contacts Robbie does not inquire. The picture on the counterfeit Rhode Island license is actually Quinn's, but close enough. The name, laughably, is Doyle. The mask wrought of a single changed consonant.

Quinn has said he'd be back in ten minutes, and it's been nearly an hour. The afternoon sun angles in, so that this place, facing the harbor of Newport, is brilliant and clean; the air conditioning is on full rattle against the heat outside when Quinn comes through the door, grinning as bright as the glint off the sunlit water.

"You look pissed off," Quinn says, needling. "Am I that late?"

"I'm fine," Robbie says, his own mug long emptied.

"I'm buying everything from here. I have all the money we need."

"All I really need is another beer," Robbie says.

Robbie is home from his first year of college, as humbling as that has all been. School, for him, has always meant sports, and little else. He'd enrolled at Stonehill on a $3,000 student loan, intent on playing hockey. This was a Division II program, so he thought he had a chance. His career had lasted about twenty minutes. At an open tryout, he was sure he was good enough to make the team and work his way into a scholarship. The coach had all the players skate laps of the rink until they were warmed up, maybe sixty guys competing for five or six available slots. Then, in groups of ten, they lined up at the end boards. Coach blew the whistle and each group blasted down to the other end, then all the way back. In the final yards Robbie could feel himself flagging, the legs burning in those last half dozen strides. He finished at the back.

"Okay," an assistant coach said to him, "you can change up."

"You don't want to see me play?" Robbie said.

"Sorry, son, you're cut. You're just not fast enough."

In the locker room, he changed into his clothes without showering, and went back to his dorm and wept. What he had left was a student loan on his back and no actual interest in college, if "college" was defined by whatever there was besides hockey. The truest pain was in being told he wasn't good enough at something he cared so deeply about.

Now, his freshman completed, he's left Stonehill and is enrolled for the fall at the state college. That isn't so much affirmative movement as it is a seeping bewilderment about what comes next. And now he's here in a bar in the slanting sun, watching a younger brother who seems to brim with confidence, nearly cockiness.

Quinn is seventeen but waves to the bartender for a beer and gets one.

"What's the matter with you?" Quinn says.

96

"I'm just getting hungry," Robbie says.

"So get something."

"In here? Too expensive. Let's go over to the deli."

"I said I was paying."

"We've been sitting here for an hour already."

"I was taking care of some business. Let me relax for a second."

"What kind of business is that?"

"I'm making some deliveries."

"You're delivering lobsters?"

"Don't be an idiot," Quinn says. "I'm delivering powder."

Robbie looks around as if drug agents are about to swarm them.

"You're *dealing*?"

"No, I'm not *dealing*. I'm only *delivering*. It's a favor I kind of need to do."

"How much do you have?" Robbie says.

"Just these little bags. I'm just helping a guy who helps me. There's a bunch of girls from Boston in a vacation house that I need to go to next."

"How about eating first?"

"Look," Quinn says, reaching into his pocket for a smaller bag. "Here's some I kept for myself. Take it and go in the men's room and powder your beak."

"Why would I do that?"

"So you won't be hungry."

"Using what?"

"Just stick the tip of your car key in, and snort up. Then you won't worry about eating."

In the men's room, sitting in the stall, Robbie does so. Back to the barstool; indeed the hunger is gone. But thankfully he has no urge for more, and never will again. In the years that come he'll wonder if that becomes the only true difference between him

97

and Quinn: not the exercise of superior willpower or morality, just the fact the stuff doesn't take hold.

As Robbie is spending this summer of '85 working for a house painter (and trying to come up with any kind of vision of what he will be next), Quinn is still rushing into things at full speed.

Quinn's life has been arranged by parents, their own and Gina's. Quinn still seems to be trying to ignore the situation. He'd told Gina to keep quiet while he figured out how to handle it, but she'd confided in her sister, who immediately told her parents, who immediately called the Boyles. Much shame and weeping ensued. The sister, apparently distraught, then told everybody at school, and that was that. The loose talk had birthed the baby as much as the act itself had. Adoption seemed off the table in light of wide disclosure. And other things as well. In such circumstances, even when a church-going Catholic might be convinced of the necessity of thinking more liberally, for nothing to happen at the end of nine months (when so feverishly shared at the outset) would have been the darkest of sins.

And so the plan was forged at a dining-room-table summit between the pairs of embarrassed parents. Quinn would finish high school, they pledged, as would Gina. When both had reached majority age, they would marry. The baby, born in late September, was in the care of Gina and her parents until a proper home could be made. The baby, named Heather, was made available to Quinn one day a week, in plain sight of Gina's parents. He mostly declined.

Quinn seemed to have made that two-year gap into something like a nonstop party in which nothing was truly being celebrated. He did not graduate high school, somewhat purposefully; recalibrations had to be made. The old man, whose slow boil rose over time and made him grow old too fast, wrestled

Quinn down to Chuck Joyce's boat, telling him it was damn well time for a man's work, if Quinn thought himself man enough to be a father.

Now it's come to a summer Saturday, and they're at an air-conditioned, harbor-side bar with enough coke stuffed in Quinn's pocket to get them both into very serious trouble. When the next round of beer comes to them and he sees what Quinn is tipping, he understands why no one is asking them how old they are, or why they're here.

"You need another snort?" Quinn says.

"No," Robbie says.

"It's not like I'm charging you."

"I just don't want any."

"Okay, be a pussy, then."

And Robbie feels like one, for not snorting down more of the white, for not being willing to give himself over. For being scared, or for being a straight arrow, which might have been one and the same. For whatever reasons, he doesn't want to, and he feels weak because of it.

16.

ROBBIE HAS ALWAYS SUBSCRIBED TO THE THEORY THAT he and his siblings effectively killed off their parents, although what's less clear is whether this theory can be applied generally, that it's always our offspring who hasten the inevitable march to the grave.

The folks are gone in one way and the other now. Dad is measurably dead, and Ma figuratively so, in the last of the degrees, the relentless scrub of memory from her head nearly completed. He cannot bear to go up there to the nursing home to see her, sitting with that blank stare, the continuation of a years-long wake. She knows nothing of Quinn's disappearance; she checked out mentally even before he went to prison. But she breathes on and the heart beats like a piston.

Sarah had only seen Ma, at best, as the flighty old lady, bird-like in her final nervousness, the lightness of her bones making her seem nearly translucent. Then she faded away. The visits to the nursing home are of staring at a wraith, gone in all ways except corporeal. Robbie could try to tell his daughter about the formidable wills his parents had both exerted, but it would be like a fairy tale.

Dad had come into the world in a storm, and been made by another, and left in another one still. He was born during the first waves of the Great New England Hurricane, September 21 of 1938, delivered in a brass bed that shook as if it were on the deck of a ship as the winds tried to pull the house off of its pilings. His parents had only lately come from the old country, and they'd occupied a fisherman's shack, built like a pier outward over the water of the Sakonnet Passage. The hurricane had come so fast, and with so little warning, that as his mother held him in her arms, the waters had begun to rise up through the floorboards. The day was one of both the autumnal equinox and of a full moon; by darkness his parents had pushed out the door into the winds, the newborn Dad wrapped in a blanket under his mother's waxed coat, the older children clinging to its hem. Up the hill, to higher ground and stronger houses, banging doors, where finally at the third door they were admitted. They'd spent the night worrying about their house sliding into the sea, which it emphatically did. In the morning Granddad had found the house gone, the piles standing as aimlessly as the unroofed columns of Greek ruins.

How was the old man shaped by what followed, the progression of rentals and falling fortunes? The family had never been well-off; Granddad Boyle had worked as a maker of dentures, the dusty office up above the storefronts of South Main Street, the long shelves like a faceless audience of disconcerting Cheshire grins.

The War came and went, and Dad learned about heroes and martyrs, and then in a few more years, Hurricane Carol came along, in '54. Dad was a few weeks short of sixteen, but already built like a man, making his mark in sports at the high school. The devastation of the storm had been significant in town, and the need to rebuild was offset by the lack of able bodies to do said rebuilding. Dad simply skipped school and went to work. He was not a carpenter but quickly became one. After a month gone, he returned to school for

102

the sake of the football, but he never really stopped working, picking up gigs steadily and turning full to it summers. He was tireless, and a quick study, and by the age of eighteen, while he and his contemporaries marched through the diploma line out at the high school, he was already a skilled finish carpenter with a brand-new pickup truck, and on the door of that truck the stenciled name of his company. He was hiring men by the age of twenty, and by the age of thirty employed several dozen. He'd married late, when he was sure he had the money, and Ma wasn't much younger.

Had it been Dad's plan to bring Quinn into that fold, by first sending him to sea, and making him wade through the testing waters? Neither Quinn nor Robbie had ever expressed much interest in becoming nail-bangers; Robbie guessed that Dad thought a few months on a pitching deck in roiling seas was enough to make any man pine for carpentry, the quiet precisions of the plumb and level. When Robbie went off with the espoused goal of a higher education, Dad may well have assumed his return as soon as the hockey coaches had scratched that inked line through his name on the tryout roster. Dad had said he'd pay, but Robbie was the stubborn one, sure he'd end up on scholarship. He kept on with college just to forestall the embarrassment of leaving.

Dad had been shaped not only by the work that had seemed to have chosen him, but by the men he chose to work for him. Childhood visits to Dad's work sites, be it the framing of a new house or the careful re-sculpting of an old one, had the din of camaraderie that Robbie didn't much know of at home. By the time of evening that Dad came through the door and deposited that dented old lunchbox by the kitchen sink, he was far too worn for ebullience. But Robbie could remember, as a boy in shorts and rubber-toed P.F. Flyers, approaching a house-in-progress and hearing the sound of real men talking. The shouts and jibes, the curses and laughter. He thought he would grow into that easy rapport. But by the time he approached swearing age, Dad was largely withdrawn, pulled back through his frustration with Quinn and the boy's on-going wildness. Nothing seemed funny anymore, nothing worthy of an unabashed laugh. The jokes had all become bitter. The old man fell to silence, and even on the work sites, the voices went on without his. Maybe it was the inevitable hush of midlife; Robbie saw it overtake Quinn like a seeping fog, and then felt his own register falling a few years later. Maybe he had only come of age in the early stages of Dad's colloquial demise.

Robbie had clearly been the least problematic of the lot, at least by the usual measurements. But it seemed that his own sudden lack of ambition in adult life created in his parents some deep well of consternation. His and Quinn's unrelenting energies toward hockey and football and baseball must have had a ring of familiarity to Dad, who had then thrown himself so unquestioningly into the carpentry trade at the same age, and not ever really let up. Robbie had always had some kind of drive, but then when sports stopped for him, he fell back into a malaise that has continued, even now, into his gathering middle age. It had probably cost him his marriage as well. Everybody seemed to expect better things from him, only to be found wanting.

By the time Dad passed, a heart attack as he and Ma sat weathering not a hurricane but the blizzard of 2006, they lived then in a downsized house out along the breakwater; the lashing seas and the howl of high winds might have come to Dad as a voice, a beckoning home as the rocks of the seawall began to crumble just as the piles had in his delivery. Robbie could find no true measure for the old man's ledger of disappointment. Bound by two storms with many in between.

The second thing that may have killed his parents is moving away from the church. Oh, the Sunday snowstorms of his youth, those windblown drifts, them all trying to get to that ten o'clock Mass on time! His parents had the sidelong glances of people trying to sneak quietly past eternal damnation, although he saw no evidence of powerful sins nesting within them. But when Robbie announced he was through with it all, his mother had the horrified look of having learned he just went down in a commercial airline disaster.

"*What?*" she said.

He could have gone on forever, trying to explain, but he didn't. He realized they'd already consigned Quinn to the trash heap of Damnation, and probably Margaret as well, the good person who had foolishly married a Jew, lapsed as he was. With Robbie now mathematically eliminated by his obstinate refusal to *just go to Mass one hour a week*, it was as if their mother had already formed her own upside-down version of eternal suffering, of making it to Paradise but then knowing her children had not. Waiting perpetually at the Gate for arrivals that did not come. As if waiting on the observation deck as the "up" elevator arrived again and again and again, opening and always empty.

The third thing that probably killed his parents was the inability to see their grandchildren. Margaret was in North Carolina with Ken, Quinn had lost contact with Christine, and Sarah was only three when the divorce happened and Robbie was left with sixty-four hours a month with his child instead of every one of them. The resentment all around was palpable. Robbie had folded too easily on the matter of visitation, M. was apparently irritated by her former mother-in-law's early-dementia badmouthing of her; Sarah seemed to think grandparents, these wrinkled beings bending toward her with bilious breath smelling of browned-out internal organs and pan-fried onions, were mildly frightening. In the end, Dad had simply pulled the existential ripcord and dropped through the trap door of life, while Ma had taken the opposite route and begun a comprehensive memory dump. Yes, she was still alive by vital-signs definition up in the nursing home, but Robbie knew in his heart they'd killed her off long ago.

Which left only him. He has found himself the presumptive head of the now-decimated family only by the process of elimination, not by acclamation. Quinn had been numbed by his life, but that didn't mean Robbie didn't have to take on his problems. Margaret, more than a little insulted by the parents' objection to her marriage to a man named Ken Rosenberg, sends the obligatory check for Ma but otherwise remains a distant cipher.

And in reality, the family now narrows down to Christine, the only person fully depending on Robbie. While Sarah has her pleasant hours here, and she then on Sunday afternoons at five skips home to M., Christine is both in need of Robbie's help and becoming ready to break free from it. She seems smart enough, and the decision to go into nursing is a piece of wisdom he knows both he and Quinn lacked at her age. She's been going off to the classes at the community college for three weeks now, and here in waning September heat she arrives back with a soft smile, the extant signs that things are going well for her. In a few years she'll be off to her life. Robbie wonders how much he'll ever hear back.

17.

FALL SPORTS ARE IN FULL BLUSH EVEN IN THE INDIAN summer of this dry September, and Robbie happily takes his place in the hut-like press box above the bleachers at the high-school stadium. The halide floodlights buzz slowly into full illumination. His laptop is in front of him on the narrow transom, and his binoculars around his neck. Up here, the faint cool of the evening breeze is more pronounced, the slightest incantation of true autumn. There is a peace in this, a symbolic end to his conflicted grieving period. But Jeff Williams, dormant over the summer, has returned with a vengeance, and has apparently found little closure. Billy has graduated, but now a younger brother, a five-feet, four-inch sophomore named Jack, is already on the varsity football team. And a good player, too, as his brother was in basketball.

The father goes not much taller, and tends to wear those thick-soled work boots that help get him some height, possibly with gel inserts for one last skyward push. His left arm, issuing from a rolled-up sleeve of T-shirt, bears that unfortunate barbed-wire tattoo. Young Jack is playing tailback on offense but does not participate on defense; when the Hawk defense takes the field, Williams kills most of that time glaring up at Robbie. In turn,

Robbie hopes for the offense to get the ball back, and hopes as well that young Jack can honestly make a good run, so that Robbie may record and report it. He wants Williams to back off, but his son has to earn it for him.

But there's something in these Williamses that has a lilt of the contrarian. Two short sons, trying to succeed at sports custom-made for boys built bigger. He wants to say to Williams, "Get them into wresting!" but he suspects they've pondered that, the sports diced into size divisions so the little men can succeed against other little men. Flyweight boxers, diminutive weightlifters, lightweight rowers. But the Williamses, clearly, want badly to be big.

At halftime, and the score at 10–10, the teams withdraw to sit in circles in the opposite end zones. Up in the stands, the spectators stretch, and then wander down the runways to the food carts. While the scorers tally up the first-half numbers, Robbie comes down the ladder from the press box and gets himself a hot dog and a Coke. Sports food, a gustatory pleasure he's never shaken. Under the shadows of the floodlights, he eats gratefully. The clusters of parents group up in the brighter side, loudly; the cheerleaders giggle on past; the little boys throw a soft football around, readying for their eventual time under the lights. All is well. But now Williams comes toward him, and Robbie thinks to ask where Billy's gone to school, and if he'll try basketball there. Of course, Williams would probably see that as sarcasm. It hardly matters. Williams makes the first parry, calling out to him as soon as he's within fifteen feet.

"So your brother killed Santoro and himself the same way he killed Botelho," he says.

"Nobody knows what happened out there," Robbie says.

"Based on past performance, you can probably make an educated guess. Seems like he fucked up as usual."

The truth of sports means that if young Jack Williams breaks open a run, Robbie will faithfully document that, and the yardage gained. But that mention just dropped a half dozen paragraphs in this hypothetical story, just on principle.

Williams stands with a triumphant-looking grin, breathing a bit too hard.

"It's a dangerous business, they were in," Robbie says evenly. "It comes with its risks."

"So does running drugs."

"That's actually safer, unless you count the legal dangers."

Williams looks at him, trying to get the point of what he just said. Robbie isn't sure, but it's worked as a bit of a deflection.

"Your brother was a piece of shit, like you," Williams says.

"And your son is still short, and there's nothing I can do about that."

Williams isn't charging at him on this evening, but Robbie is suddenly aware of just about everybody else watching.

"I have nothing against your sons," Robbie says.

In the second half, in a tie game, Jack Williams does finally break that run, twenty-five yards down the right side of the field. Robbie feels his mood lifting in that flash of hope. But as Jack is tackled, he loses the ball, and the Chiefs recover in a frenzy of dancing and fist-pumping. Jack walks off the field with his head down; he's probably crying under the face cage. The truth of the moment, and needing to be written. But Robbie has no fight in him anymore, so he does the best he can when he types up his revised lead on his laptop.

In a sorry turn in what was a breakout game for sophomore up-and-comer Jack Williams, he fumbled the ball in a tie game that . . .

He watches and waits to finish his sentence as the Chiefs bang the ball down the field. In minutes, they have scored, and Robbie types . . . *turned the tide in what had been a tight contest*. It goes like that. The Hawks, deflated, cannot come back. The Chiefs score twice more, and at the final whistle he finishes his lead. *The Hawks went down to defeat 31–10 in a game that should have ended up much closer.*

He imagines Williams's fury tomorrow morning, down at the café, reading the Saturday morning paper. But this is the hard fact, and Robbie must stand by those hard facts.

He lingers in the press box until the parking lot has emptied and the high-school janitor begins to power down the floodlights. He's sent his story to the desk by email, and he'll swing by in an hour to check the edit. But for now, he's happy to sit alone as the last filament dies off and he can finally hear the end-zone trees rustling in the breeze, unimpeded by school bands or screaming parents.

The white lines of the field still show in the waxing moon. This was a venue of at least some of his modest glories; he and Quinn had both those moments, of turning as you come out from behind a block and "seeing the front lawn," as they said in their team slang. Open grass, unimpeded by defenders, and the hash marks ticking by in measurable progress. He'd had the ball many times, as Jack Williams had tonight. But he hadn't ever fumbled the goddamned thing in a tie game. He hadn't lost games. As much as he feels for the kid, again there is the meaningful truth for Williams and his anger. *He was weak, your son. He couldn't finish the job when he needed to.*

18.

NIGHTTIMES AT HOME ARE NOT YET PAST THEIR AWK-wardness. Robbie tends to stay in his room, reading or just drifting; Christine sits on the couch in front of the television, textbooks around her, furiously thumbing at the iPhone he has finally bought her. At times, she giggles out loud (*lol!*, he thinks).

She likes to turn the heat on as the fall evenings cool down; he likes to turn it back off. It is purely domestic, all of it, and he wonders if it turns out to be a dress rehearsal for his future with his own daughter, something he can effectively prepare for.

Robbie tends to wander to the kitchen around nine to eat. Christine follows, cued by his movement, but loathe to admit it. This has become their ritual, to silently put out the food, to heat and toast and boil, cut and chop and mix, then sit and eat. Only as the plates are left with the whorls and swaths of sauce and gristle and crumbs, of the footprints of food now departed, does the conversation begin.

"So are you in love with Jean?" she says, apropos of nothing.

"I definitely like her," he says. "Maybe that's so far, so good."

"Hmm."

"You're a teenager. You believe in destiny. I believe in main-tenance."

111

"She really likes you. She may even love you, for whatever reason."

"I'm happy if she likes me. I'd worry if she loves me. That would be too quick. If she loves me, it's not based on experience. It's based on expectations. And I'm not exceptional at meeting those."

"Sounds like an easy out."

"I'll take all the easy outs I can get."

Christine sits looking at Robbie as if examining a specimen.

"What?" he says.

"I realize I'm trying to figure out my father through you."

"Is that something you learned in your psychology class?"

"Kind of."

"So I'm your homework?"

"Not yet. I skipped ahead."

"I can tell you what you'd like about your father, you know."

"You tend to tell those stories protectively."

"Of him?"

"No, protective of me. I wish you could realize I've seen a lot already."

"I'm sure that's true."

"No, really," Christine says. "I don't think I'll even be that surprised. I think the truth might not even be as bad as I've heard. I always expect the worst anyway."

He thinks about what tale he wants to tell, and which version of it.

The world, of course, is larded with artifice. The old stories have their charm, and their indictment, and they come to him strangely, at odd hours. One late night, a few weeks before, Robbie had remembered his brother and himself, as children, being piled into that old station wagon. They were making the obligatory trip to Olde Plimoth Plantation, that historical replication of Harder But Better Times, seventeenth-century style. Summer-vacation fare,

112

to witness the lives of the Pilgrims south of Boston, where one could understand some nascent truths about the Protestant Work Ethic, which Dad pointed out was hardly limited to Protestants.

They'd arrived there on a hot late-August afternoon. The parking was that gritty aggregate where flinty Massachusetts was giving itself over to the sands of Cape Cod (the Cape, a place they never really visited, but which was dismissed by Dad as a geographical elbow comprised of soft men who made easy money and exercised the obscenity of second homes). "Plimoth Plantation" was a re-creation of the Plymouth Colony, circa 1627, and an obligatory tourist spot in those years before the giant plasticized theme parks. Here were the suggestions, at least, of straight-backed adventurers who lived life at the edge of a razor. The Boyle family, the men in their Bermuda shorts and Fruit-of-the-Loom pocket T-shirts and the women in sweat-soaked summer dresses, walked among wool-clad figures with their ponderous buckles and chimney-pot hats. The Pilgrims stayed resolutely in full character: "What be this strange box 'round thy neck?" they intoned as Ma, with her Instamatic camera on its strap, sent the three children to the photo-op public stocks and had Dad stand behind, the old man mugging a look of theatrical exasperation, with two seventeenth-century wayfarers on either side with arms crossed on their chests like early-American bouncers. The photo survived for years, three smiling children fixing on their mother's lens, the father behind them in faux fury at their presumed crimes. Then the picture was lost, gone from its place on the refrigerator door, only surviving in memory.

Robbie still remembered that rough collar of wood on his throat. But what he remembered more was wandering in search of a restroom a short time later, and coming upon a cedar-fenced pen where several of the breech-clad time travelers from *Mayflower* days were partaking of the familiar red-and-white of a pack of Marlboros, and discovering their fire at the end of a Bic plastic lighter. "My dogs are killing me in these goddamned clown shoes," one of the Pilgrims was overheard to utter, in a decidedly modern voice.

Robbie must have been ten or eleven, Quinn a year younger, and Robbie hadn't realized his brother was up behind him.

"Hey," Quinn shouted through the fence, gleaming with the moment. "Any of you fat-ass Pilgrims got a spare smoke?"

The Pilgrims turned then, hunching, looking through the slats of their confinement, with that shamed look of men pinched and buttoned into the robes of their own silly fortunes.

"I'm on break, you punk," one of them said, in a thick Boston accent. "Run back to Mommy and hold on to her skirt before I give you a beating."

The other Pilgrims laughed at that. They were probably in their twenties, and Robbie can still think back on that, wondering how they had landed such jobs.

"Well you can try, motherfucker," Quinn said in a voice that hadn't even changed yet, high and soft like a little girl's.

They were coming over the top of the cedar fence now, cigarettes clenched in their lips. Quinn and Robbie were running, but Robbie was slower, despite the surging thump of adrenalin. In an instant, the hand was on his shirt, pulling him to a halt. The Pilgrim was sweating, breathing in heaves, hot-red with anger.

"What did you call me?" he said. "Huh?"

"Nothing."

The hand bunched the shirt more tightly and the face moved in closer to Robbie's own. The pneumatic breaths pumped into Robbie's face. The Pilgrim was, even then, falling back into character.

"What pox did thou cast on me, ye mewling child?" he nearly shouted. "What doth thou sayest now?"

114

Robbie was frozen in his own amber. The Pilgrim grinned, and then looked up at Quinn, fifty yards away, in his shorts and his sneakers.

"Get back here," the Pilgrim shouted, "or, verily, I do kick the living shite out of this one."

Quinn stood there staring, as if for a moment he might have come up with a plan. But then he seemed to come to something else, and he shouted back.

"Go ahead!" he yelled. And then he turned, making his exit.

In the station-wagon ride back, Dad kept looking at Robbie in the mirror, as Robbie tried not to whimper and Quinn tried not to laugh. The Pilgrims had not beaten him, but they had applied their own timeless brand of justice. First there was the apparently indigenous practice known in schoolyards everywhere as the Indian Sunburn, and here in the car his arms smarted from the friction. Then, as well, they had hanged him, not about the neck but in nether regions, in what Robbie might have described as a Colonial Wedgie.

"I'll get you back for this," he had whispered at Quinn.

"You can try," Quinn had whispered back, grinning, as Dad kept his eyes fixed on their reflections, instead of the road ahead.

Writing yet another sports story late in the evening, it occurs to Robbie how it is, so often, that he's trying to squeeze the messy events of life between the neat lines of the arena. Sports can be that way. They at least provide a definable ending. You win or you lose. There is a measurable score. You levitate, or sink, through the grids of standings and statistics. It does seem a truth that may have come to seem not so much untruthful, just utterly beside the point.

The story at hand is along the order of, *Despite tumor, Hawks sophomore leads team in scoring.*

In these stories, one's afflictions, faults, bad luck or illness simply asserts itself as "a challenge to be overcome," in pursuit of the redemption of the big win, the championship or often in the even-more-poignant character-building exercise of a tough loss. Robbie has suddenly begun to hate it, writing these stories in which all manner of agony is made right by stuffing a ball through a hoop, or a puck into a net, or landing that vault, or hitting that pitch over that fence over by the faculty parking lot.

He understands why people like these stories. He all too frequently gets compliments when he does them. The stories are easy to write. There seems a sense of completion in these tales, which is exactly what is lacking in his current existence.

He had gone down to the school in the early afternoon to watch the Lady Hawks' field hockey practice, where young Alexa Shea, sophomore phenom, was brought to him by the girls' coach. Alexa had come at him head down, carrying her crook of a stick, pigeon-toed in her big cleats and athletic skirt. The tight rubber headband that now seemed common to all girl athletes was taut across the crown of her head, looking as if it might tear her hair from the scalp. She had the mien of a pre-adolescent boy, sort of a brooding shyness. Probably a notch under five feet tall, she shifted nervously from foot to foot. She stood with her mouth distended by the big rubber mouth guard, before the coach nodded for her to spit it out in her hand.

"Alexa, do you know why I'm here?" Robbie said, knowing various parental releases were already signed.

"Yeah," she said, with what might have been a trace of disgust.

He knew that she knew why. He'd been called not only by the coach, but by Alexa's mother, who thought Alexa could use some encouragement through a positive notice in the columns of the local sports pages. Robbie had been offered direct contact with the doctor.

"How are you feeling these days?" he said.

"I feel *fine*," Alexa said, as if he personally had already asked her this question a thousand times.

The day before, he had gotten the backstory: a benign brain tumor had been stumbled upon, after a summer-league basketball game in which she'd been knocked down and hit her head on the court. An MRI had been ordered to evaluate for concussion, and there it was, an unexpected mass, something that had been slowly growing, unbeknownst to anyone. There had been no headaches or seizures, no vomiting or nausea. Just the ghostly dark on the sliced-cabbage topography of the scan. What followed, of course, were the consequent urgent whispers, the surgery, and then the good-as-could-be-expected news. Low-grade glioma. Not malignant. No chemo or radiation indicated. Alexa, a three-sport athlete, had begun her return in the gym in late September, shooting free throws incessantly, running long miles, going to work on the weight machines, getting in the batting cage. She had turned into a fairly clichéd comeback story, and of course clichés were the hard currency of sports writing, the same base story told an infinite number of ways. She was going to beat it. She was going to triumph. And indeed, so far this season she has been tearing up the court.

"Do you think you learned anything from the experience?" Robbie said, as the coach hovered nearby, beaming.

"Like *what*?" Alexa said.

Robbie had been down this pike many times. The self-possession of a successful high-school jock was often fascinating to behold. He might have been exactly the same at that age, as might have Quinn, although the internet seemed to have amplified all eventualities. Now, the college-recruiting blogs conferred a kind of digital royalty even to kids who might only have a narrow shot at a scholarship. Everybody was a celebrity.

Robbie already knew he would get no considered perspective from young Alexa, no pearl of wisdom that would further punctuate her journey. He could just write up those sentiments himself, later, in the office.

In what had felt like the cursory call to the doctor, he had expected little. Sitting at his desk with the phone to his ear, he was unwrapping his sandwich and presumed a bridge of two or three minutes to the pleasure of that first bite. The doctor got on the phone in that gravel tone Robbie had long come to expect from such calls.

"It's my understanding you're authorized by the family to discuss the case," Robbie said, to a grunted assent.

"So it's a happy outcome?" Robbie said.

"Happy enough," the doctor said. "Patients often hear what they want to. But I think if you characterize this as a very happy outcome, you're not being inaccurate."

"Is there anything that isn't happy?"

"You actually want to know that?"

"I guess . . ."

"The diagnosis is of a low-grade glioma, a tumor that grows out of the glial cells. Now if it had been a high-grade glioma, the prognosis is a seventy-five-percent chance this young lady is dead in two years. So it being a low-grade, the prognosis is much better."

"I didn't know there was a prognosis," Robbie said.

"There always is, pretty much," the doctor said. "But it's much, much better. Recent studies have established that the survival average for low-grade gliomas is about seventeen years."

"But she's only sixteen."

"I understand that."

"So she might only live into her early thirties?"

"It's possible. The seventeen years is an average. She could live much longer. Or much less."

"That doesn't sound as good, Doctor."

"I explained this all very carefully to the patient and her family."

"I'm not doubting that."

"Now don't forget how much treatment has improved. Ten years ago, studies showed average survival of just under eleven years. By the time this young lady reaches adulthood, the average may be thirty years."

"That is good, then."

"If you're twenty-five years old with an estimated survival of thirty years, that's as good as you can expect," the doctor said. "I mean, you're then competing with car accidents, other cancers, gunshot wounds, and poor health brought on by your own bad habits. The mother has diabetes so the genetics are there. Something else may have the final say, because there's always something, as a medical certainty."

"And the family knows all this, exactly as you say it?"

"Exactly."

"If I simply write that the tumor's removed and she won't have problems for the foreseeable future, am I incorrect?"

"I'd say you're not incorrect. And besides, that's exactly how the family wants to think of it anyway. Why get into what's really going on, right?"

So now, approaching deadline, he writes his sanitized version, of a brave girl beating her illness decisively, of compiling a three-goal-per-game average, of the doctor's certainty she's as good as she could possibly be, and of his own sportswriter's voice laying in the mortar, of lessons learned and chances regained, of the unexpected turns in life. Of course he knows all this is only foggily true. He knows the complications of existence. But hearing that doctor's voice talking confidently of our own uncertain marches toward mortality, Robbie doubts his own assuring words. And he knows that Alexa will as well.

19.

DAWN CALLS ONE NIGHT AT TEN O'CLOCK, ASKING Robbie if he's asleep.

"No," he wheezes, rising from the couch.

On the other end, she's amused. "Why do you always say you're awake when you're not?"

"I don't know," he says from the ether. "It's like I'm being caught at something. But why do you always ask, if you know I'll lie?"

"Both stuck in our bad habits, I guess."

"Are you all right?"

"I'm fine. I didn't expect you to be sleeping so early. I just wanted to talk, if you have a minute. Are you alone?"

"Yes," he says, assuming she means Jean.

"I want to talk about your niece."

Christine, in fact, is in her room, but the music is playing and she won't hear him, out here.

"Go ahead," he says.

"Well, I hear she's living with you now."

"That's right."

"So you're giving her a free place to live."

"Right."

"Why?"

"She needed help."

"She has a mother, doesn't she?"

"Her mother is a train wreck."

"So was your brother."

"Which is exactly the point."

"I'm not attacking," Dawn says. "I'm just asking. You have your own life. You have your own daughter to support. After all those years sticking your neck out for your brother, now you take the niece on?"

"Just while she's in school. Then she'll be on her own."

He hears Dawn's sigh, long and soft.

"People in your family seem to have a funny way of never being able to be on their own. Are you sure you're not letting yourself in for a permanent headache?"

"Dawn, don't take offense, but what is this to you?"

He hears that sigh once again, the too-familiar disappointment.

"This isn't about me, it's about you—someone I care about, regardless of what's worked out or not worked out with us. Honey, I think you get used too easily."

He's thinking that she's got an angle on this, maybe about how the niece-in-residence may affect their own prospects.

"I know what you're probably thinking," she says, "but don't worry, I've given up on us. I'm seeing someone else."

"You are?"

He's not on the defensive now, but hit with a well of unexpected sadness. It was never going to work out with Dawn, but that doesn't mean it doesn't feel strange. He's been fending her off and now he has that familiar feeling of wanting her back, kind of.

"Couldn't wait forever," she says, more softly.

"Anyone I know?"

"Probably not."

There's silence and then she says, "Take or leave what I'm saying. But one part of being in your life is seeing you get caught up in things. Hopefully not me! I just want the best for you."

"Thanks," he says.

And he knows, hanging up, that's genuine.

He and Dawn never truly aligned. They'd met within an hour of Robbie exiting divorce court, which seemed like a good start at the time. Divorce court: that sad moment of standing next to your spouse in the waning seconds of a marriage, unable to even turn and make eye contact, while a judge sits on high and asks if this is all the way you agreed it should end. You mumble something, of course—faint assent, or restrained glee, depending upon which side of the equation you reside. And moments later, on a blustery gray day, you're heading one way toward your car, while your ex-spouse moves off in the other direction. And so commences the new life.

In Robbie's case, it was sitting in the oyster bar down by the harbor in Newport. He was feeling waves of relief, and of a depression gathering like the far gray clouds. The first of these reliefs had been the night he moved out, a month before. For all the hurt of it, he felt a rush of near-euphoria when he lay on the couch in that quiet apartment and thought, *I don't have to live with that anymore.* It wasn't completely true, but it was solace of the moment.

This was in early winter; the back deck of the bar opened onto the cold breeze off the harbor. He took his drink out into the elements, which somehow made sense. He felt pioneering, an unthinkably divorced man. Like Quinn now, a failure.

Robbie sat in his coat and wool watch cap, defeated. There were long sheets of translucent plastic hanging down to keep the weather out; they rose and fell silently, in the rhythm of lungs busy in their inspiration and expiration. He was alone among the tables and chairs. He'd taken a bottle of champagne and a glass. It was eleven in the morning, and while the bar wasn't even open he'd pled his case and been served. He'd thought he should mark the moment, as if he were trying to talk himself into something. Then a woman came toward him and said, "You look like you're celebrating something."

It was Dawn; she was a sales rep, then, for a restaurant supplier. She said later that something about the way he was looking out on the water had made him seem a man who badly needed a friend. So she told him that.

"I do," he said back.

"Is that an invitation?" she said, commencing their long succession of not-quite-on-the-mark comments, asides, remarks, and unintended slights. For someone he would grow to love, even if he didn't know if they could have ever have made it work, she was always coming across about five degrees off-kilter.

"Join me," he said.

And as with the early-December air that puffed the plastic sheets and told him the bitter winter was ahead, she sat and laughed loudly when he said he had come directly here from divorce court.

"Story of my damned life," she said.

He didn't mean to get her in bed by that weekend, but there they were.

"Let the buyer beware," he said to her as she put key to lock.

"I'm a shopaholic," she said. "To my everlasting regret."

Afterward they just lay there, and his gratitude was boundless. For the first time in months, he wasn't overthinking. For the first time in years, he felt as if he was really with a woman. But like a junkie sliding out of his high, he began to feel a kind of sexual of sexual food poisoning, too rich and too quick after the sparse offerings of the always-overwrought M. He got up in the half-light and began to dress.

"Don't take offense," he said.

"Like I said, story of my life," Dawn murmured in the dark.

20.

THE WHITE FOG, AND THE SHARP-ETCHED SUN. THE IN-
finite waves, and the hard wind. The vastness of possibilities,
and the footprints left.

Robbie is at his desk in the office, typing out a girls' lacrosse
story, when his head comes up, the snap of realization, the sift-
ing so many times through the facts that he abruptly sees that
one microscopic gap.

He's back in that recollection. He's back on the front steps of
Santoro's parents' house. Though right now it's a late afternoon,
the low sun a glare in the window, in his mind he's in the dark,
back to that night. He is remembering scuffing his foot against
the worn gray paint on those three front steps, with the old people standing in the doorway in their bathrobes, smelling of cigarette smoke. He is back there, in the cold push of wind from the
harbor and the faintest warmth escaping from their door. He is
asking where their son is.

"Freddy said he was going out on a lobster boat," the old man
says right then, seeming bewildered. Robbie thinks, right then,
I knew it.

That seems, in the dark, the confirmation of all Robbie's worries
and speculations. The old people shiver in the cold, now deathly

worried by the stranger at the door, bringing news of missing men. Robbie feels that guilt, but also the rising anger. *A bad-luck boat.*

So the work begins in earnest then, the three-headed search not only out on the far water, but on near land. The casting for signs of either man—foolish, given the absence of the *Christine IIs*, but the simple fruit of that kind of desperation. It's checking just to check. At Quinn's room, Robbie knocks and knocks and then gets the landlord to bring the key. Swinging open the door on its groaning hinges, he steps into to a room that reveals only the dirty clothes and a cheap mattress. He should not be shocked by the bareness of it, yet he is.

And now in the sun from the window, months after a few shreds of gear from the boat is found floating hundreds of miles out, and months after the whole thing is discharged as another lost boat—one of so many, over so many years—he looks up from his keyboard and realizes there's never been any proof at all that Santoro ever got on that vessel.

He stands, agitated. It's all been assumed. All set into motion by Robbie's own unfounded perceptions. All going back to a tendril of conversation on an ass-shined barstool.

But he ponders what that means, and he can't come up with anything. If Quinn had found a crew other than Santoro, he thinks, why hadn't anyone else been reported missing? He wonders if Quinn would have just gone out alone. Robbie follows the thread and moments later it's all dead-ended. It doesn't matter. Even if Santoro somehow evaded that fate, Quinn has not. Robbie knows it's just the recurring frustration of not having answers, and knowing there are likely to be none. And he knows when these thoughts come to him, it's the survivor's guilt he's feeling.

Quinn was mourned as a local legend, even as his death was reduced to a few paragraphs in the local paper and no mention at all on the Providence TV stations. What Robbie realized was that Quinn's stature was both real and tiny. He was well-known in that small circle that was the world of Atlantic coast lobstermen, as all places have their small circles, with the occasional and overlapping edges he remembered from high school as inscrutable Venn diagrams.

Quinn was always pushing it, and admired for it. He ventured farther and farther out on the ocean. His favored grounds had become Great South Channel, less traveled than Georges Bank and away from the Maine lobstermen, who seemed to feel the sea was theirs alone.

Somewhere in their middle thirties, Robbie had asked Quinn why he wasn't coming inshore, doing shorter runs and staying safer. Quinn dismissed that with a wave of his hand. The waters were too crowded, he said. Up along the coast, lobstermen were having their lines cut, in disputes over who could lay claim over certain compacted waters.

"One good long line with the traps costs me a couple of thousand dollars," Quinn said. "I'm not taking the chance of that all going to the bottom because some clown who can't look me straight in the eye thinks I'm stepping on him. Everybody's got a piece of bottom he thinks is his own."

It had been vicious for a while. One smaller boat had been sunk in the harbor, and some guns had been waved about. The inshore men had secret meetings, and secret votes, on whom they chose to allow on their waters. Quinn wanted no part.

"All that prom-queen bullshit," he said. "Better to deal with the enviros."

Out where he went, there were the right whales, and those who worked among this endangered species seemed to be seen as the worst kind of people. Right whales could get caught in the lines, although it had never happened to Quinn and he had never seen it happen to anyone else. But the rights were an increasingly rare beast and had become a genuine cause. "I guarantee you a whale will kill me before I kill a whale," Quinn said, bitter at the notion that, even with a vast ocean out there, he was still feeling squeezed.

"Come on," Robbie had said. "Just try to work with it."

"So easy for the sportswriter to say," Quinn had answered.

Robbie doesn't precisely remember when he first began to get sick of his brother, but one day the feeling was suddenly there. It was toward the end of his own marriage, what had been theretofore the solution to Quinn's dissolute ways. Robbie, at that point of the marriage, was still playing defense, still opting for the easy thing; M. was the first somewhat decent woman who came along, so he'd just gone with it. At a certain age, this made for a mindless march toward The Next Step. Eight years later the marriage was done, immediately pitching him into a sense of failure and regret; he never quite figured out what it was he'd done wrong.

He noticed, as if all of a sudden, that his one successful relationship was in being stuck at this little newspaper well past what would have made any sense. He'd become a lifer. He awakened in his late thirties, realizing how much time he had already lost. He was a man who presumed to have options now, although none came immediately to mind.

Up until then, Quinn's troubles had made for an easy counterpoint. Quinn was what Robbie was not, what he'd chosen not to be. But now Robbie found himself pitched into utter disbelief of his own falling fortunes, and spent increasing time at the bar trying to center himself.

Dawn had come along. She was kind to him. One might assume she had a motive, but if the motive was based on liking him genuinely, it seemed fair enough.

It was in a wind-howling January snow that M. was taking off to Aruba with the new boyfriend and needed Robbie to take Sarah for a week. They had been divorced all of five weeks. M. talked to Robbie on the phone as if it were she were doing him the favor, sending Sarah over on a week in which he was supposed to work long days.

He'd only known Dawn for a month, but he called her to tell her this, his voice leaden. Sarah was four, and M. was dropping her off that afternoon so she and the new boyfriend could get to the airport. They had to beat the big snowstorm that was supposed to come overnight. The exchange at the front door was as tense as he'd ever had with a human being, as the man watched from his Mustang in front of the building. Robbie supposed that this all happening while Sarah was so young was good strategy for M.; the little girl was happily oblivious. In an hour, she was tucked in and asleep, and Robbie sat the window watching the storm, feeling the true aloneness of someone just out of a marriage. His doorbell rang then.

It was Dawn, out in the blowing snow.

"I was at the mall, and began to wonder how you were doing," she said.

Her arrival felt like the nicest thing, at the right time, anyone had ever done for him. After M.'s yearlong campaign of growing coldness, a shunning that never stopped mystifying him, he had lost the ability to imagine anyone cared at all about him. Even as he and Dawn have faded, his gratitude for that gesture stays with him.

They ended up in bed that night, but still clothed. His daughter was in the other room, after all. But having a woman next to him, softly snoring, brought him out of that singular agony. But it was odd: M. was flying to Aruba with the man she'd denied to him she was even seeing. Why, with a woman sleeping next to him in her jeans and sweater, with the divorce final, with M. having systematically made him doubt everything about himself, did he still have the unremitting feeling of being a cheater?

It all felt too strange. He pushed Dawn off then, even in his gratitude. Dawn, meanwhile, laughed it off. "Why do I always get involved with guys right out of the gate?" she said. He was even grateful for that bit of presumed understanding. It was the first turn in the on-and-off they'd struggle through for the next year.

Robbie kept his thoughts at bay by working. He covered games and relied on the statistics for the parts of the game when he'd zoned out, caught up in his own ruminations. He sensed that he was bottoming out, which cheered him for the return. Around him he had mostly silence. Quinn acknowledged the troubles Robbie was going through, but seemed unable to hear much. He was wrapped up in something else; Robbie was most often happy enough not to know. Indeed, in his marriage, Robbie had too easily taken one step back from his brother, and then maybe another, to the point he rarely saw him. It seemed odd now, at such loose ends, that Robbie found himself wandering down to the docks.

That summer, he sat out on the stern of the *Christine* on sunny days and drank beer as Quinn went through his silent routines. In a beach chair carried down from his car, Robbie let the sky warm him, and drifted into half-sleep, trying not to think. Quinn would have at least tried to listen if Robbie had wanted to talk. Robbie, though, was exhausted. Too many sleepless nights worrying about things, about where his life was going to go. And, guiltily, he knew he'd never much listened to Quinn.

"I need an adjustable wrench," Quinn said, and Robbie opened his eyes. "I'll be back." Quinn jumped off onto the pier in a surprisingly graceful leap, then shuffled up the hill in his search. Robbie, full-bladdered and bored, went down into the cabin to look for the head. He needed to piss, all of a sudden, and the dirty toilet of the boat would have to do. Underneath, he saw the tight space Quinn occupied. On the small bunk he saw the paraphernalia, in a Ziploc bag: the foil, the spoons, and a dozen syringes in their sterile wrapping. And on the floorboards was an object he first registered as a long pistol. As his eyes adjusted, he realized it was a sawed-off shotgun. He'd never seen one before, and he stood at it as if it were a relic.

By the time Quinn got back, Robbie was thinking he wasn't off searching just for a tool. Quinn came wandering up, empty-handed.

"Find what you were looking for?"

"Not a loose wrench in the whole town," he said.

"So you need a shotgun for something?"

Quinn grinned at that one. They were brothers, and only a week past being Irish twins. Being born fifty-three weeks apart, and sharing a room as kids, and playing every sport together had made for very few secrets.

"Yeah, I kind of need that."

"What for?"

Quinn shook his head. "This isn't working for the sports pages, Bud. I live the life I live, with the shit that comes along with it. Everything I have is down below."

"Like the drugs and the needles?"

"That, and other stuff. I don't even have a bank account, you know. What reserve I have is down there in cash."

"So maybe you should get a bank account."

"I don't need the paperwork."

"Meaning what, that you don't pay income taxes?"

Quinn sat next to Robbie on the gunwale and motioned for a beer, which Robbie fished out of the iced bait bucket.

"Most of my life is off the books," he said. "I get paid in cash, a lot, and I declare only so much. I have a deal with the distributors

131

that I give them a low price and we settle difference on the side. The child support was based on the best year I ever had, and I don't have years like that anymore. I haven't had years like that in years. It's not as if I can wish those bugs into the traps, but Gina doesn't want to hear about it."

"Have you ever used that gun?"

"Never. Never shot it once. It's got one shell in it and if I fired it, I'd have to try to remember how to reload it."

Quinn sucked the beer out of the can in one draw and said, "The trouble I needed it for is mostly gone."

"But you keep it by your berth."

"Just in case."

"And what about the other stuff? Is that heroin?"

"Why bother asking questions like that?"

"Quinn, Jesus Christ . . ."

"Think what you want to think. It's just to smooth out the rough spots. You'd have to be in my situation to understand."

"How often are you using?"

Quinn let out a long breath. "I've had a lot of rough spots lately."

When Botelho disappeared and the *Christine* was seized, there was oddly no mention of a shotgun, and no charges for having possession of one. Nor of heroin. Quinn was up at the jail, his bond too high for anyone he knew to help him. There in the visiting room, Robbie wasn't about to ask. They recorded everything.

Quinn pleaded out quickly and went into prison. Robbie drove up to visit on his midweek off-day, but Quinn generally had little to say. Gina had called Robbie at his office to tell him Quinn would no longer be allowed to see Tina; Robbie assumed Quinn knew this, but the conversation never went there. Quinn was even quieter now, shedding himself of the years of drugs.

132

He seemed, in that, to have become reflective. But he still shared nothing.

"What are you going to do when you get out?"

"What are you talking about?" Quinn said, seeming to awaken out of something.

"You lost your boat."

"So I'll get another boat."

"Don't you ever think about making a change?" Robbie said.

"Not really," Quinn said, sitting in his khaki prison outfit. "What would be the point?"

Robbie felt a tang of frustration, but at the same time wondered if he was all that different. He'd given little consideration to what he would ever do if he wasn't writing sports. He assumed he could do a lot of other things. But he'd never tried, despite the boredom he had come to have with the work he did. He was afraid to try, and Quinn had probably been afraid in the same way.

Quinn came out of prison after five and a half months, twenty pounds off and clean-shaven. Nearly a different man. He laid over at a halfway house near Boston. Robbie picked him up on a Thursday afternoon and they drove back quietly.

"You can stay with me for a while," Robbie said.

"I already got a place to stay," Quinn said. "I rented a room."

"From prison?"

"Halfway houses have the internet, too, you know."

"That's good, that you have a place to live."

"They help you get set up, when you're finishing," he said.

"Good."

They fell back into silence and then Quinn said, "Do me a favor?"

"Sure."

"Don't ever ask me anything about what's happened before today."

"Okay."

The conversation ended there. Robbie imagined Quinn must have been, at least in small part, savoring his release. A silent hour later, Robbie dropped him at this new apartment house, a shambled Victorian diced into closet-like units. Quinn carried his small pack up the front steps and closed the door behind him.

When did he lose hope? Robbie thought as he drove home. A very long time before, it seemed.

And now, years later, Robbie drives down the hill to the harbor, a brotherless brother. It's still early, the dawn after a night when the sleep grudgingly comes and goes. Robbie looks at the water and counts what's gone for himself. The family gone, one way and another. The wife, long gone. Robbie has two years to give to Christine and then it's open water from there. Sarah, he knows, will be that occasional visitor, the father-and-daughter connection already irrevocably compromised. He's already grieved that, and made his peace with it, even as she comes blasting through the door. She's too young to know what will have been missed. How do you have a daughter who sees you twice a month? He supposes there was a time when men simply moved on, but he hadn't really asked to give up his daughter. If he goes back to those days at the end of the marriage, Sarah was the reason it was worth it. But then it was over, and he has had to learn to live largely in her absence.

They'd had their memorial service for Quinn, but Robbie, the night of the suspended search, had conducted his own one-man Irish wake, he and a bottle of Glenmorangie, at the kitchen table with *SportsCenter* on the TV with no volume. It was the only way to find sleep. He awakened in the morning reminded, forcefully, of the pain of life.

He gets out of the car and goes to the edge of the water. The rocks are smooth, and flattened, rubbed smooth by eons. He picks one up, his version of contact with some eternity, and throws it. The shoulder pulls a bit, too many years removed from the baseball days, but the stone yet has a nice backspin. It hangs in the soft air for a moment before arcing, as if meant to stud the morning sky, as if in its natural place, defying the imperatives of gravity. And then it plunges. It loses all of its loft, almost defying its own moment, and hits the water with a fierce slap. It sinks. Robbie watches the momentary ripple. Then all is again as it was. Lost.

PART THREE

21.

HE AWAKENS EARLY NOW, IN FIRST LIGHT. HIS HEAD IS clear, and his body absent the bone-deep aches that had so long plagued him. His sparse room is clean and cool, and takes the east light rising over land, the reverse of what he lived for so long. He breathes in slowly, filling himself.

His hair is buzzed down to a stubble. Seventy pounds are gone in a year, both fat and muscle, molted and shed. He hasn't touched anything in that time, not heroin or coke or weed or even beer; in his early forties he feels the odd salve of calm for the first time since he was a child. Between that, all those long nights chasing sensation, be it standing buckle-kneed over a urinal, beseeching relief, or sinking into a foam couch cushion, letting the fix whisper to him, or pressing up against the hot skin of some anonymous woman, not really wanting to know.

His life, now, is of the ascetic. Far more so than prison, which brought with his fellow inmates its own complications. He knows himself now as a man in a small, bare room, with a bed of cut foam topped with sheets and a blanket, and a sagging upholstered chair in the corner (which he'd carried on his back where it had been left on the sidewalk). He has no television, and wants none. A radio sits by the bed, and he likes to play the music low. No news, no sports, a minimum of human voices. He makes little noise, walking so softly across bare floor his neighbor below doesn't ever have to think of him. Indeed, his footprint in the world has become nearly unseen, shallow tracks in sun-melting snow. He has a bottle of water in the small refrigerator, and he drinks from it standing, as if in ritual. He'll walk today, in the rain, the hood of his sweatshirt shrouding him, his eyes down. He'll look for the small bits of traceless occupation.

The ledger's balance is even, for the first time in his adult life. Or more aptly, blank. Since the age of sixteen, he was always mud-footed in obligations he could not shed. Always under the crush of demands that lay above, out of his reach, like an ocean's sunlit surface to a drowning man. Now the ledger was wiped clean. In this new year of new existence, he needs so little to live that he needs to earn little in turn. He knows for the first time what it's like not to have the pressure exerting on him at every lucid moment. He has been born again in a public library in Salem, Oregon, where he'd sat at a computer and Googled his own name and come up with those holy words: *Search Suspended*.

He stands now at his window in his shorts and T-shirt, surveying another mostly gray Seattle sky. He was always drawn toward coastlines, although he cannot see water from this small building in the Lake City section. It's been a rain-driven winter, which he has taken to in ways that surprise him.

He's been back in for two weeks, after two months out. He's just finished a hard stretch, working below decks on a catcher-processor, the *Siberian Wanderer*, a 240-foot ship that had pushed far up into the Aleutians and come back fat with cargo. He is not a fisherman now, though. He is just another anonymous worker down on the processing line, in a windowless below-decks vault that could as well be a landlocked fish factory, if not for the roll of seas that register in the stomach but not underfoot. The pay scale of this legally grayish operation is commensurate with being an

140

employee not asked to provide any convincing proof of who, exactly, he is. This arrangement fills out an 800-ton ship that powers up across the threadless boundary of the Arctic Circle. The *Wanderer* is a churning predator in pursuit of Pacific cod. One night under the midnight sun, his shift boss let him come up to the deck and look at a black line on the horizon, so they could say they once saw Russia. Then it was back underneath, sixteen hours of work, minutes for quick meals, and the remainder for sleep in the crowded bunks. The smell of fish and human effort pervaded. Dozens of men, working endlessly for two months, and then all back to port for a cash payment he can now stretch out for a few months before he goes back, looking to sign on again. He'll fill gaps between with day labor and rest. He spent his time in the belly of a ship, a Jonah in his whale, earning money so he could fall again into anonymous, landed existence.

It all feels temporary, but he doesn't know what's next. Down in Oregon, they don't lobster, they crab, but most of it is the same and he thinks about hiring onto a boat, with the risk that goes with it. He can feign being the newbie, the quick study who picks up the skills.

Then he stops himself from such daydreams. Strange: You walk away and decide you can start your life all over again, but then you find yourself drifting toward exactly the same old life. You imagine you have every choice in the world but you find yourself swirling into the same narrow funnel.

We think we make an imprint in the world and then find out it's so small, as small as crabs' feet at the edge of the ocean, washed away by each pulsing wave. They never missed him when he was alive; they surely can't miss him now.

He goes by the name Ken now. *Quinn*, he hears, in a voice he does not know. Ken, he repeats aloud then, more clearly, saying it softly over and over, for good measure.

He is clean onshore, always. He showers twice a day, sometimes three, in those first days back, scrubbing hard as the last traces of fish stink fall from himself, shedding that self as the bugs do, molting one shell for another. On his slow way across the country, he forced himself to be a different man, an inscrutable man, speaking with the sharper, smarter tone he always could have used, but had always chosen not to. What he did, really, was just mimic Robbie, occupying the voice of the college boy he'd never had any notion to be. As he did, he saw how people reacted to him, and how easily he could make this work. On trains and buses, where nobody needed to see identification, and staying in motels where any name was fine if the payment was cash, he'd kept moving.

He'd settled here only because he had run out of land to cross. Alaska had been a thought, but that involved borders. First morning in Seattle, he'd gone to the Salvation Army store, squat and gray up on Fourth Avenue in the shadow of that big football stadium where the Seahawks played. He was there to find himself appropriate costuming. He tried on suits dead men had once worn, and bland Christmas ties that probably were never worn; when he needs to, he can be that guy. But mostly, alone, he dresses like the athlete he was so long ago. He wears track pants and gray T-shirts and blank-chested hoodies, no team or school logos to bespeak affiliation. And he has made a bit of investment in some good running shoes. One day in his first week here, he ran a half mile, at great effort, gulping breaths and fighting a searing stitch under the ribs. That night, he'd been kept nearly sleepless by his aching legs. But two weeks later, he was up to three miles. Then eight, and then ten, and then to the now-regular the habit of Sunday eighteen-milers that loop the city and allow him on those afternoons the indulgence of one good meal. He's eaten nearly nothing now for the cycle of a year.

If someone from his former life passed him, he doubts he'd even be recognized as himself.

The turnabout of opposite shores: on the *Siberian Wanderer* he has stood endlessly at a rear-lighted conveyor, in his hairnet and surgical mask and latex gloves and rubberized apron, sorting and cutting; there is no time to mark when underdecks, no affirmative light or darkness to know the true hour by. The paper he signed was explicit, nearly cautionary: shifts were doubles, standing, with five minutes breaks on the hour, and then eight hours off, then back, no days off, no weekends. They were all younger men around him, most of them illegals, some Inuit guys with that weakness for The Drink ("We're the Irish of the Arctic," one of the Inuit men, working next to him day after day, had said more than once, jolly in his forced sobriety) and some recovering from one abusive relationship or another (vodka, women, poker, oxycodone, the ponies, fortified wine, the greyhounds, and, of course, heroin). Alcohol was forbidden on board, and everything else. Everyone was searched as they boarded. He could already see how his fellow men would inevitably burst from this oppressive cloister to the first bar or dealer they could find. But now he came down a gangway with the pressure of his anonymity keeping him quiet, and the promise of rest, and the chance to run miles again, after months locked on his feet. The first night back on land, he had the burning urge to lace up his New Balance running shoes and run in the late-night mist, looking at the tall buildings lighted against the sky and hearing the bars close, ranging far from home. For two months he'd been convicted, at his own signature, to a place where there was no ranging at all.

Yes, that signature. He came to conclude the best name to be rechristened by was the simplest derivation from his given, despite the risks. *Ken Doyle.* Close enough, but far enough. Anyone who knew him would laugh, but nobody knows him now and he expects it to stay that way. He's exited the grid, fully: no credit cards, no cell phone, no bank accounts, no utility bill. He lives in an apartment with everything included. He pays in cash or money orders and keeps his mouth shut, an action and non-action largely synonymous.

There is, however, an exception to his vow of solitude. The weekly Alcoholics Anonymous meeting is in a church basement, a half-mile walk from his place. The meeting, and its specific vows regarding alcohol, serves to stand in as a disavowal of all the diverse and damaging excesses of a previous incarnation. The irony is that alcohol was never really the problem. He just figures it as the one place he can be among other people and not be pressed as to who he is.

Long miles run in the rain, in extended penance. He has learned to calibrate; when the thoughts begin to intrude, he can push his pace and wipe them clean. He has never been a retrospective man, but he works to cut the mental sinews that attach himself to the past. He is learning the exacting skill of forgetting. His brain is at repose, freed from the currents of worry and frustration.

His body morphs, part of the process. The heavy knots of muscle that had yoked his shoulders and neck and chest are now lean. The legs are more vascular, the veins cording the skin. He has his sets of pushups and sit-ups, many times through the day.

His second exception to calm silence also threatens to compromise it. In his newfound health, in his calm, and in his fitness come the physical urges that had been so long dormant. This is the surprise, although it shouldn't be; he's just turned forty-three, in the kind of shape he hasn't been in for twenty years.

He'd done his share of whoring in those drugged days, but he sees it now as sad efforts to uphold a faded reputation. He'd knocked up a girl at fifteen, to the awe of those acne-pocked contemporaries around him; could he really have been done with sex by age thirty-five? He'd decided not. He'd paid for what he needed, one way or another, if not by clear transaction then by the shifting of assets, the consideration in exchange for another. Women had come and gone but with no stake in any of it.

Back when he was with Gina, though, there had been that one girl. She was working the office for the seafood broker, and seemed to be trying to catch his eye. She was nice; she was the good daughter of a lobsterman, which served as dubious endorsement. He presumed she then knew the vagaries, and risks. She did seem taken with him. He was twenty-eight then; there was still a shred of hopefulness in him as well. She was probably twenty, and prone to heavy mascara and frequent shows of small, pearly teeth. She wore lipstick even in that dank warehouse. She was always saying he should take her for a drink, which she delivered as a half-joke he couldn't quite read. And it was always within earshot of people who ought not have been hearing, making him wonder if she were serious. Gina was at home with the two girls; he and his wife had effected a soundless kind of peace, their resentments and provocations temporarily put away. That was the closest they ever did get to a happy marriage.

He would have been, with that girl behind the counter, the one to upset the calm. A few months later the girl was seeing another lobsterman, one of the straight arrows. He felt a pang of regret upon hearing this. The girl and her lobsterman married six months after that, and were still married these years later. Quinn could not stop seeing it as that one missed chance. Once he had gotten into the drugs, such aspirations faded. Women were around, but not a woman he wanted among them. It would have been trading in one Gina for another. Sometimes he saw the girl with her straight-arrow husband and their kids, walking up State. He thought, at times, she might have looked his way. It was, however, hard to say you lost something if you'd never had it to begin with.

Now, for the first real time since back then, he feels infused with sexual energy. The solution is mostly that he remains in isolation, but walking in the city he finds himself noticing women to whom he cannot aspire, even now. In the AA meetings there are no real temptations, until a night when a woman walks in who defies the expectations he's come to have of the proceedings.

She wears a thin wedding band. She's probably thirty-five and she's small, and very slender, with narrow shoulders and a flat chest. She's nervous, he notices, which in turn makes him notice how closely he observes her. She's dressed crisply, pressed jeans and a blazer, really put together among all the falling-apart others. The reality of this group is the numbers who do so rapidly fall off; the first night he was paired with a sponsor, an older man he hasn't seen since. There's so much turnover he'd not ever been asked to give his testimony and doesn't intend to do so; no one seems to realize he is now sponsorless.

He watches the woman, trying to piece her story together by extant details: the steel men's wristwatch dangling loose on her arm, the cut of the clothing, the careful curls of the hair, planned and set. But she, looking at him in his khakis and button-down blue shirt and brown shoes, his stubbled scalp and clean chin, might never guess. An office man, she'd venture; a family man.

Tonight, an older gent speaks first, detailing the usual descent, the booze and pills, variations by a quarter-tone on an endlessly familiar theme. The man seems close to tears, welling up genuinely and unprepared, then coughs hard and pulls back. It is a convincing performance, the reason Quinn comes, all the witnessing he needs. They all break for coffee then, and at the pot, the woman is there, edging up behind him for her cup.

"So what was your drink of choice?" she says, cheerily.

"Beer," he says. "I drank a bit more than I wanted."

"That sounds kind of tame."

"Things can have a way of spinning out. You?"

"Vodka, when I was college. I thought it was cute that it came in fruit flavors. Then it got to where it wasn't so cute anymore. I was good for a long time, then I wasn't. So wine, mostly, but the same as you, just too much, and then *way* too much eventually."

"Your husband a drinker, too?"

"Oh, the ring. I should really throw it away. He's long gone. I'm just wearing it until the final divorce decree. To make a point about living up to the vows."

"Did he leave you because you drank?"

"No. I drank because he was with me. Then he cheated and I was shocked at how hurt I felt. I'd always probably liked my drinks a little too much, but I've gotten very bad the last year and I really kind of need to stop."

"That was the reason to drink?"

She smiles. "I can't think of a better reason than that, can you? You sound like someone who never got cheated on."

"Maybe, maybe not. They were like ghosts I never saw but knew had been there."

"Your wife managed that, did she?"

"I went out of town on business a lot," he says, already feeling as if he's saying too much. "Long trips. God knows what went on."

"And you? Alone in all those hotels? Those extended absences? Handsome guy like you?"

"It wasn't exactly like that."

"Are you military? Were you in Iraq or something?"

"No," he says, looking at her more directly.

"I thought because of the haircut, or actually the lack of one."

"It's just a style."

"Well, it looks damn good," she finally says.

147

There's the moment, right there, but he keeps on.

"You don't seem like someone from around here," he says.

"I'm not. Lots of people are from somewhere else."

"I understand that completely," he says.

Someone rings the little bell, and so he and the woman part, back to their far-flung chairs. When the meeting ends, he moves to the exit and slides out. He walks quickly, head down, and cars pass and he doesn't look back for her.

But he keeps thinking of her, in a way that ripples the calm of his out-of-the-way life. Who does she think he is? Not some worker in the deep belly of a ship, slopping cod entrails for sixteen hours. That's for sure. But he doesn't have to be that, he thinks. Why couldn't he be something different? But now he is a man determined to hide his whereabouts, and that has its liabilities. Why did he end up the way he did?

It was Dad who pushed him into the hard life before he'd had a chance to think about it. Punishment disguised as a lesson, so clear now. Maybe just the old man's pure frustration, the buildup of steam that had to be bled off. Shit, he thinks, at fifteen I was always nosing after trouble, always pushing for something. At seventeen I was even worse. Not anymore, he tells himself. When he gets back to his room, he does a hundred pushups, just to short-circuit his teeming head. Later, he does a hundred more, to short-circuit the lower regions. Then, finally, sated, he slumps onto his bed, sweating into fitful sleep.

22.

HARD RAINS FOR THREE DAYS KEEP HIM PINNED, MOST-
ly. He makes brief and stabbing runs in which his pace feels like
a sprint and the turn home is always into the lash of the winds.
His is not a sunny disposition, but rueful by nature, and the rain
seems to frame it well at the moment, as sunny summers can
frame a different mood. This will be his second summer without
a boat loaded with lobster pots, heading eastward.

Away from it, he better understands what made him love it.
There's a straight gratification to the work, despite the problems.
You push your boat into hard ocean and drop your traps deep.
The bugs crawl in, entrapped and destined for the boiling pot.
You pull in your lines and count up. Fair trade in that; you can't
outsource that to China and you can't concoct a computer pro-
gram to replicate the job. Every time Quinn made some phone
call and heard a computerized voice on the other end, the exchange between a human being and a binary code masquerad-
ing as a human, he felt a small but meaningful gratification, the
proof he still lived resolutely in the physical world.

He stands at his window watching the rain veining the rattling panes, and he considers something that he has not before:
a future. He'd already sworn, as he put his foot back on land and

began the journey, that he should do no such thing ever again. Life was right here, finally, without the ballast of all the years and obligations. Life was going to be longer, with each ticking minute, than it could ever have been before this. Back there, with his debts and his sins, he was already in negative time.

In the evening, he runs again. Six miles, pushing the pace into redline, running against headlights with the watch cap low on his eyes, spitting out rain as he goes. He monitors his cravings, and how the urges that come with a woman are not just sexual. He wants a drink now, too, suddenly and surprisingly. So he runs more, not back into the apartment until near midnight, its refrigerator shelves mercifully bare. He puts the shower as close to scalding as he can bear it and falls into a still-restless sleep, going back to long-gone days.

The old man was a tough one, but being tough was how he'd made it through life. Quinn sees more of him now, striding through his dreams, his appearances in Quinn's night stories delayed by so many years of dreamless, substance-aided sleep. The Dad he sees is the version of the man at the height of it all, still well-muscled, still tan and lined and straight-backed. The declining version of the father, gone softer in voice and affect, gone white-haired and pale, was simply denouement. The man, in his intensity, was a force in all their lives. Quinn thinks he knows the man far better now. He thinks that the essential, and previously missing, ingredient to his heightened insight has turned out to be his own compounded slog through life.

Back then, though, Dad's steel will was the point, to which Quinn became the endless counterpoint. The old man had a way of looking at the world that was all straight lines and clean corners, level floors and low ceilings of expectation. He never once told his children they could do great things, but he always warned them not to do the wrong things. That list was precise on matters of behavior, conscience, and obligation. It tracked closely with the Bible, Quinn supposed, which had been fed to him by the nuns as the most bloodless tome. There was no fun in the Bible, ever; no passage spoke of Jesus and the Apostles doubled over in good belly laughs or simply grinning madly at some high moment. Even when The Big Man appeared live that Easter morning, could He not have had a bit of a Told-You-So smirk?

The old man taught them all the dirty words, and then he taught them never to utter them. For Quinn, the most dangerous two words that could come out of his mouth were not the vile swears forbade in good households, but rather these:

Watch This.

Whatever followed those childhood words were generally calamitous. Headlong plunges from rooftops and high limbs, fingertip matches on combustible substances, water balloons, riptides, sharp sticks, long knives, and wanton trespasses onto all manner of forbidden property.

And then later, emboldened, these three other words:

Hold My Beer.

Fist fights, headlong plunges from even higher rooftops and limbs, long swims in rough waters, ill-considered remarks to large and dangerous people, old cars pushed too fast, old cars driven with no credentials, cars driven long before the designated age without the sleeping parents realizing the keys were off the hook by the back door. And then, girls. Squeezed flesh, torn buttons, the hum of a zipper, the whoosh of silky garments, the hot touch of flesh uncovered. It was a life of going out to the edges of things, then returning from it to celebrate, too long and too hard.

The thrill of it was only compounded by the old man's voice, echoing in the back caves of Quinn's dark conscience. Life for

Quinn was less straight lines than shortcuts, less clean corners than pried-open seams. On and on. Tirelessly. Then the first crashing entry into sex, with the first girl who would let him there. Gina.

Dad went to work in the mornings exactly on time, and returned again with like punctuality. No amount of chaos stirred him from his own codes. But they could all tell he was at a loss. In Dad's powerlessness to tamp down the mayhem coming from his own blood, he began to die in little bits, but not without a fight. He hit his disfavored child, sometimes sweaty-palmed slaps and sometimes with the closed fist. He shouted, barking until he roared and went hoarse. He threatened, and thunderously promised dire consequences. Quinn laughed, enjoying his indignation. And in time, all the promises came true.

In so many ways, his father was the love of Quinn's life, the passion unduplicated by any human being. Passion of a loving kind was not the old man's provenance, so enraging him was the only way to draw out the true measure of his marrow, the only way to see his heart pump. Quinn was the impossible son, and in that he got the attention he'd failed to garner through all the acceptable means. Robbie got pushed aside as the brother who caused no problems. But Quinn eventually lost all of it.

The night Dad got the phone call from Gina's father, he sat waiting for Quinn to come home from practice. As Quinn and Robbie came through the back door, dropping their hockey bags and sticks in the mudroom, they found the old man with a cigarette vised in his lips like a heat-seeking missile set to launch. Dad nodded to Robbie, severely, in that way that sent him sliding up the back stairs and out of harm's way.

"I got a phone call from some people I don't even know," the old man said, just to make it a puzzle. Quinn, ready for the game, began to smile.

"You think this is funny?" Dad said.

"I don't even know what it is. How can I think it's funny?"

The old man was breathing so hard his nostrils flared in steady pulses.

"Your mother is upstairs, just dead ashamed of you."

"That doesn't narrow anything down," Quinn said, unable to help himself.

"Who is this girl Gina?"

"Just a girl." Now Quinn knew.

"Just a girl, huh?" the old man said, the voice becoming strained and guttural, in a way Quinn knew was the prelude. "*Just a girl . . .*"

"Yeah, I know a lot of girls," Quinn said.

"Mr. Grownup here," the old man said. "Mr. Know-it-all. Mr. Can't-Tell-You-Anything. You know what your new name is going to be?"

Quinn said nothing.

"Daddy. Pop. Papa. Congratulations, because this is what you earned yourself."

"What are you talking about?" he said, knowing exactly what.

"What am I talking about? You got 'just a girl' pregnant."

So she'd told someone. The act had happened outside the high-school dance, on her coat, in the grass, as the music thumped through the cinder-block wall of the school gym. Their breaths tanged with cheap beer. The smell of first sex, so unexpected. Now, Dad sat there staring at him.

She had promised not to tell anybody until he figured out how to solve it. Being the one who caused all the hell was a way of never feeling that shock, but now. He felt the shake of wanting to cry but he pulled back and toughened.

"So how much does the abortion cost?" Quinn said. "I'll pay you back, don't worry."

The old man spat at him in a way that made the cigarette skitter across the floor and to his feet.

"There will never, ever, be any of that kind of thing," Dad said, unable to mouth the word. "Do you think we're like that?"

When Ma came down to the kitchen to warm up supper, Quinn saw she had gone silent, and he might have even suspected it would be permanent, which it largely was. She blinked furiously, not one to let the tears flow freely. The late supper after hockey practice was usually something that allowed Ma to sit with Quinn and Robbie and listen to them tell about their day. This night, traditions had abruptly ceased. It wasn't the silent treatment, specifically; it would be impossible have anything resembling small talk with such ponderous matters looming just offstage. In those ensuing months, she would leave the room whenever it came time to discuss the pregnancy and what would happen next. In time, Ma left the room almost whenever Quinn would enter, unwilling to even bear him. It took a long time to make sense of that. He assumed it was the shame of having such a sinful son, who'd gone so bad so young. In time, he'd come to a more direct truth. She simply never forgave him for making her a grandmother at the age of forty-four.

Dad got right to it, though, as if the conversations themselves were part of the punishment.

"Let's talk about what having children costs," he said that first night, smoothing a sheet of loose-leaf paper out on the dining-room table, and taking that stubbed pencil from his shirt pocket, as if he were doing a building estimate. Food, clothes, doctor's appointments and medicine, second-hand cribs and carriages, toys. The list Dad penciled in was a long column, and Quinn was already tuning out. He was a sophomore in high school. What did he care?

Dad grabbed his arm and shook him back.

"The last part of this is what you pay me back," he said. "My obligation was to support a wife and children. That will be your obligation now. I simply have to front you the money until you get out of high school."

"What about her father? Is he paying for anything?"

"Yeah, he'll put the roof over your child's head. And you'll owe him plenty, too."

Quinn felt again as if he would cry, but he knew such things were for children, and that had all just passed for him.

"You might as well enjoy high school," Dad said. "I'll give you that much, to see through my obligations. But the minute you graduate, you'll have a hefty balance against your name, and you had better be ready."

Dad pushed the piece of paper across the table at him. "You might want to keep this, for the future." Quinn knew the old man was being sarcastic. What future was there now?

23.

HE SEES HER AT THE NEXT AA MEETING AND CAN'T fool himself into believing he didn't hope she'd come. All the wrong buttons are there, and ready to be pushed. He's a man living a dark-gray existence who'd do best to avoid. But she comes right over to him and seats herself.

"How many meetings do you do a week?" she says.

"Just the one."

"I'm feeling good, doing this. I feel like I've turned a corner."

"I'm happy for you."

"Am I fooling myself?" she says.

"I don't know. How much were you drinking before your husband started cheating on you?"

"A fair amount. But not nearly as much as I did after."

"Then you'll probably be fine. It was situational."

"Isn't all drinking situational?"

"I meant, as opposed to constitutional. As opposed to genetic. Those people don't have to have a reason."

She's looking at him more intently.

"Which one are you?"

"My genetics would suggest it was situational. My family is otherwise a bunch of lightweights, at least as the Irish go."

"So you're Irish, then!"

"Isn't everybody at this meeting Irish?"

"Can I ask your full name?" she says.

"No. Rules are rules. Just Ken."

"If I take you for coffee afterwards, can I ask?"

"Yes, you can take me for coffee. Yes, you can ask. But no, I won't tell you."

They end up in a coffee shop she's chosen, and that's uncomfortably close to his apartment, although he doesn't tell her that. Having a conversation proves a new challenge. He wants to give her nothing, even as it's obvious she's trying to piece things together. He's worked to suppress the accent, but here and there it comes out.

"Boston," she finally says. "That's where you're from."

Rhode Island is not quite Boston, but close enough to the untrained ear. He declines to tell her where he's from, what he does for a living, if he has a family. She's newly divorced and seems to be looking for a new man in her life, but it can't be him. She asks him about his alcoholism, and he freelances a story that leaves out the heroin and coke part, but adds in liquid dependencies he's never had. The hard stuff never was his thing, for whatever mysterious reasons.

"You've spend a lot of time in the sun," she says, looking at the keratoses across his cheeks and nose.

"I used to golf a lot," he says.

"I love golf! Let's play sometime."

"I gave it up," he says.

She grins now.

"Those aren't golfer's hands," she said. His hands are bulb-knuckled and scarred, healed over of many splits and gouges, sunburnt into a permanent hide, as if salt had been rubbed in by a worry stone until the skin held a permanent patina.

He's in negative space. He is simply disavowing who he was, without a clue as to who he'll become. He suspects he'll sign on once or twice more with the *Wanderer*, if he can't find any no-questions-asked work on land, but that's not truly what's ahead. It's just a way of putting some money up. And he still has some of the cash from when he stepped back on shore from that last run out from home, when he walked up a street he didn't know and began to find a way of continuing west.

She, on the other hand, is uncomfortably more than forth-coming. Her name is Alix, she says, noting the spelling, but he stops her before she can get her last name out. She flows into the particulars. The husband had some money, so she's been working light duty, the part-time manager of a boutique in "U-Village." She grew up down in Tacoma, but went to school at "U-Dub." She married when she was thirty and now she's di-vorced at thirty-five. They never got it together enough to have children. She's worried she won't be able to control her drinking "now that it got out of the bag."

She reaches into her purse and takes a thick pen out, and hands it to him. "Write your phone number down," she says.

He smiles, and declines, and returns her pen.

She's good-looking, and as before, well-dressed. Why him? He forgets, at times, that he looks pretty good these days, all that weight shed, the set of his "good" clothes telling a story he's not sure even he believes in, the speech and affect no different in most ways than his brother, the writer. He neither fractures the language nor struggles for words. He realizes he can keep up with her, easily.

"I was already drinking too much wine when I was married," she says. "Not falling down, not missing work, just wondering why I had to have something every night. But when I tried not to drink, I'd think about all the shit in my life and that was that.

The husband starting leaving me home alone at night. The more I thought about not drinking, the more I drank. Then the husband not coming home at all, so now throwing some vodka into the mix, and some gin, and then becoming the puking college girl I thought I was rid of."

Quinn listens.

"You?" she says, as if he owes her now.

"I've made a lot of mistakes in my life," he says. "I'm just trying to have a fresh start."

"That bad, huh?"

"Yeah, that bad," he says.

Being in prison was the only respite he had really known. He'd had an odd sense of relief the day he had gone in. The guards worked him through the processing and saw what he was. The wayward hockey player. The lobsterman with a load of bad luck. They were mostly guys who could have reversed roles with him and it would all have been pretty much the same. "I have a license to bust balls," one of them said, laughing. "And yours got suspended for a while."

And so it was. For the first time in what seemed like his entire life, there was nothing to plan, nothing to chase, nothing to worry over. His boat was gone, and many of his possessions, save for a waterproof bag he'd filled with the things he needed months before, answering some odd intuition. He'd hidden the bag in the soft ground under the front porch of what had once been the family house. He knew its crannies and had crawled under in the dark, flashlight in hand, beneath its sleeping owners. He had begun to take so seriously the thought that his decrepit boat might fail, he didn't want to lose his worth with it. There was, among those personal effects and hardware, two bricks of triple-Saran-wrapped cash. Nearly twenty thousand, his entire life's worth, scooped quietly, and incrementally, over so many years, decades, with a likewise sense of hope. In some way, he saw that squirreled cash as the promise of some kind of alternate life. After he'd met his obligations to his boat, his crew, the child support and his habits, he'd lived such a Spartan life he could still put something away, in tiny increments, over years. But he didn't dare tell anyone. He'd imagined a thousand outcomes for his hidden money, the life it could buy. But when the moment was there, he fell back to what he knew. He fell back to what, he had to admit, he really was. He was neither educated nor skilled at much else, even if he thought he could be in another circumstance. He felt, at that moment, as trapped as a bug in its bedroom, waiting to snap and rip at the world.

The money went in a block, and was just enough to start him anew when he was released from prison. Enough to pay off the books, so the seller could skip the hated capital-gains tax. For a bill of sale of one dollar, another unpromising boat that was a bit too small for comfort on far seas, blessed with a failing engine, gutted of its electronics and equipment, and bought stealthily from another failed fisherman. He was right back to zero.

He was pushing forty. He was utterly without illusion now. He was thinking about when you begin to shift in some fundamental way. You begin to suspect that life is winding down when you don't dream about who you want to be, but instead dream about who you used to be.

So he was on the water with that new vessel, to the consternation of some observers. Nearly immediately, Robbie had asked him once where he'd scared up the money.

"I got a loan," Quinn said.

"From who?"

"The bank."

"What bank gave you money?"

"Out of state."

"Unbelievable," Robbie had said, but had ventured no further with his inquiry. But it soon became common knowledge, however incorrect that knowledge was, that Quinn must have been backed by someone with money and a reason to help him have a boat. Many theories ensued, at bars and in diner booths, about what that situation might have been.

But that was all afterward.

At Ray Brook, after the processing and the temporary cell and the issuing of clothing and toiletries, they ushered him to his "permanent" cell in General Population. It looked fine to him. Small, square, white and silent, with a bunk bed, the top already occupied. Really just a new berth in the chain of his life, and nothing more. The rest of the prisoners were at their various jobs and pastimes, but he was allowed that first day, after "orientation," to just sit. He was right out of the van and it had been a long ride.

Jacob, his new cellmate, came in an hour later, grinning, shaking his hand as if Quinn were a new pledge at the frat house.

"They keep the white guys together," he said. "I'm not in a gang in here, and I'm guessing you don't want to be."

And it was a relief, that. And clearly more of a relief for Jacob. Quinn sat on the end of the bunk and thought for a moment about praying, but that seemed forced and at this point disingenuous. He'd never really believed anyone above had ever been looking out for him. But this place was something else. Lots of guys in there for real crimes. Guys over their lunches talked about their release dates, far-off years that spoke to their malfeasance.

The first night of serving his sentence was much like the night the call from Gina's parents came, and the long harangue from Dad. Quinn had sequestered himself in the bedroom then, lying on the mattress staring at the ceiling and feeling sorry for himself. He was too young to conceive of his problem as being that of a new human life; he was thinking about Gina, who as he made his tumescent approach, atop her on that high-school lawn, had just kept saying, "It's okay, sweetie, it's okay." He had taken that as some assurance along the lines of birth control, but apparently had been nothing more than an exhortation, which he had hardly needed.

Robbie came into the room near bedtime that night, and was clearly avoiding all of it. In his brother's brooding, Quinn also sensed a secondary complication: Robbie, never having had sex, was resentful that Quinn ever had. The older brother, and his assumption of prerogatives. The first true thing that had made them different.

Robbie, already in his sweats, had crawled under his blankets. Quinn was fully clothed and on top of the covers, still in his boots. His head was tight with the worries of finally having gone too far. Robbie settled himself in his blankets, the older brother now woefully a boy on the night Quinn was forced to become something resembling a man. In the dark, Robbie spoke, hardly above a whisper.

"You're making the right decision."

"What?"

"What you decided. It's the right thing."

"I didn't get to decide anything."

"This is going to change a lot. And Ma and Dad are definitely in the situation."

"Oh, they'll enjoy watching me have my comeuppance."

Robbie lay in the dark, seeming to think about that.

"There may be some truth to that," Robbie said as his voice trailed off toward sleep. "But I'll help you out."

Quinn lay awake for many hours, knowing he wasn't going to get much help from anybody.

Prison made for an unexpected shift. On his boat the work was always up against a ticking clock, and nautical miles refigured as a function of their waning fuel, and where at least there was, at the end of a fallow day, the hope of a better day. Prison became the slow killing of days, the choking of days, and the hatred of their breadth, and the impatient wait to sleep. The next day would be exactly like the one just passed. When he finally lay down on his prison mattress and the lights cut out, all things were equal: sleep allowed him all the freedoms and escapes of the dreamscape. And in the hardest hours, he thought that this blank march toward the blank hours was no different than simply checking out: he understood why the lure of the handmade noose or other terminally clever ways of beating the system became seductive, even in this lightweight prison. He was surprised at his own thoughts, not suicidal but thinking about the act, and not frightened by them. But the odd thing was morning. Even prison mornings had their redemption. The cool hand of the air just at dawn, when the small slot of window allowed a shaft of sun to crawl across his wall, and the stomach ready to take whatever came on that plastic tray, and the simple pleasure of that coffee. Mornings made him want to live, with those gold sunrises whispering to him to him to just hang on.

His months in prison passed with relative peace. He was left alone, except for Jacob's anxious nattering. Jake, a kid who'd popped a loudmouth in a bar and been sent up on a hate crime because of various oaths and provocations uttered in the drunken moments just before.

"Luckiest punch I ever threw," he said. "One-in-a-million shot. The guy went right down, totally out cold."

He seemed excited to have now been government-certified as a badass. That he was now a convicted felon seemed not to have sunken in, nor a notion of how it would affect him. He treated

Quinn with an apparent deference, but wouldn't stop asking him questions.

"How much did you dump before they got you?" he wanted to know.

"Not that much," Quinn said. "I really wasn't trafficking. They got it all wrong."

"They did with me, too!" said Jacob.

"It was a business necessity," Quinn said, to Jacob's continuing laughter.

It had been, though. He had in those years of his early thirties fallen into his own ebb and flow, the tides of work, rest, anxiety, calm, hopelessness, and scant optimism. He was through with his twenties, and had come to the realization that the work he was doing, despite Dad's notion it would straighten him up and allow him to get back to important things, had never released him from its demands.

It had all made sense early on. At eighteen, he was making more money on the boats than he could have in the usual jobs he might have had, bagging at the supermarket or working for a landscaper, or even working on a construction site for Dad, who seemed not to be able to stand the sight of him. On a boat with a really good catch, he could bring home nearly a thousand dollars for a few days' work; he was young enough and strong enough to be almost constantly out on the ocean, splitting his time at times between several crews. Dad was getting paid back in install-ments, and Quinn was able to rent an apartment for Gina and the baby and himself, and to buy a well-used Ford pickup truck, and to begin to put a small bit of cash away that Gina didn't know anything about. He wasn't precise in his own mind as to why he was doing that, other than that it gave him some small presumption of eventual escape. Someday, somehow; the math was easy enough to realize. If he could hang on until thirty-four, he'd have an emancipated child and no more responsibilities to Gina, presuming they continued as they had, which was very, very badly.

He'd never even liked Gina that much, although early on he hadn't disliked her, either. Had he ever been in love with her? He'd come to the eventual conclusion that he'd been way too young to have any meaningful handle on that. The last two years of high school had been as if in a limbo; on some Saturdays he would go to Gina's house, and as her parents glared hotly at him, he'd play with his child for a few hours. Gina seemed bored: had she ever once loved him?

Ironically, fathering a child seemed to raise his stock around school, as much as the sports. The girls seemed now to really understand how dangerous he was, and it seemed to make them a little wild. As his football teammate Brice would say, as they passed by some smitten girl stealing glances, or past another one backed up against the lockers with her books across her breasts like armor, "Steaming . . . hot . . . panties." So as Quinn and Gina waited for their forced pairing, their roles as a cohabiting couple with their baby, she began to become resentful. They had a cheap wedding in July after senior year, peopled mostly by gray faces and little cheer. The honeymoon was a rainy overnight in a Cape Cod hotel room, in which they didn't touch each other; Monday he was gratefully on a boat, pushing out to Georges Bank.

He didn't want to feel sorry for himself. Thirty-four is a long way off when you're eighteen, but it was there, a neon marquee. He stayed mindless in the work, and somewhere along there, on an especially brutal late-autumn run on rough seas, somebody let him have a snort of coke. Its use was purely results-driven, converting spiked energy into hard dollars. Coke was cheap enough, and Quinn knew that working hard through two nights fueled by blow was giving them all a measurable profit margin.

But when they came back to shoreline, he needed something else altogether. He needed to land easy instead of crash, and alcohol was of no help in softening that first touchdown. The boats did not run on hard schedules, and sometimes, coming in late, he'd not go back to that small apartment. As the straight arrows started up their pickup trucks and rolled home to their wives, he'd follow those dissolute stern men to places where they all found what they held as their reward. Heroin was remarkably present; he was living in a world where he'd not understood what secrets lay behind each closed door. For small withdrawals from the cash he'd squirreled away, he could find a peace from his aches and worries that felt no less than magical. Those first few years, the needle in his arm was the soft welcoming kiss at the end of hard travels. It was a reentry into glaring fact. The drugs were in some ways a frontier for him to cross. When he did come through the door, soothed, Gina was raw from days alone with a baby. Or so it seemed. They were hardly having sex at all by then, even still so young. He'd spend most of his time home sleeping, awakening at odd hours to see his thumb-sucking daughter standing by the bed, considering him with puzzlement. He never did get to know her. He was counting time now, thinking of reasonable exit. At twenty-three, he had five years of relentless work behind him and a nearly nonspeaking existence with Gina. She'd gone bitter, but still looked pretty good in her better moments. He thought it was time to split. Divorce was fair enough because he'd done the right things. Five fucking years! It was time for Robbie's "things will get better for you" prediction to happen. She'd still get most of what he brought in. He didn't care about the money, only about some life he had only dared to think about.

It was somewhere in the end of that year that Gina announced she was pregnant again.

24.

HER NAME IS NO MORE LIKELY ALIX THAN HIS IS KEN Doyle, and he prefers it that way. He's not foolish enough to think he's fully clean, or so easily shed of the problems he walked away from. To relax fully is not a possibility, and never will be. Staying so deeply hidden in his anonymity is a blanket, and gives him great comfort. Only if he were dead would he be having less of an effect on the world. Yet he goes to his AA meeting again, denying to himself that he hopes she's there. The running, the pushups, the lack of drugs and alcohol, they all contribute to a deep imperative that's as bad as the rest in the way it can pull you off course.

And there she is, as clearly looking for him. She smiles and turns away, a more subtle approach now that they've sat together outside of the meeting. He looks away. *In due time*, he thinks.

On the way out of the coffee shop that previous week, she'd lunged at him, kissing him, and for the first ten seconds of it he was imagining himself in her warm bed. He felt the sexual energy, without doubt; attraction was a funny business but he wanted her. As they kissed by her car, though, he was coming out of it, his head aswim. By fifteen seconds, he was disengaging. She stood with her hot mouth still open, her eyes wide with surprise.

"What is it?" she said. "What's wrong?"

"I just want to go slow," he said.

"Oh, my, a gentleman . . ."

"Exactly," he said.

He couldn't sleep at all that night. He was thinking of that pen she'd handed him. The time in the legal system had left behind the indelible record of fingerprints, on databases across many jurisdictions. He had, in his time anew, avoided touching things. On the ship, they wore latex gloves as they processed the catch, and those felt like unexpected security. He had left his prints all over the city, on every door handle and coffee cup and light switch. He was feeling something approaching phobia. He'd stopped going to bars as much as to stop drinking as to leave no traces on emptied beer bottles, that army of dead soldiers that could whisper of his existence. He thought of that pen in her handbag, glowing like radioactivity.

He just wants things to be simple. Maybe people have a capacity for excitement that turns out to be a finite quantity, which runs out and can't be replenished. He's on empty, and has no urge for a refill.

New faces here at tonight's meeting, stricken faces. First-timers, eager to tell their stories, eager to begin the journey. He's been coming long enough he can now choose to defer, and to listen. But when the call comes, it's Alix who leaps up, and as she prepares to speak, he cannot help think he is the audience, and no one else.

"My name is Meg, and I'm an alcoholic," she says, and he cannot help but smile. When they all call out *Hello, Meg!* he does not voice it with them. Such is the luxury of contrived personas. He cannot logically fault her.

But the story she tells does not match the one he heard in the coffee shop. It's as if she's circled certain words and made her substitutions. The husband is now a boyfriend, the substance of choice now Cuervo Gold, the profession not retail but something toward finance. And she says it all staring right at him, knowing he knows.

And he's withdrawing, and does so realizing it's because she's a liar, just like himself. If he's going to move forward, that's a bad scene. But at the end of things, she's coming at him, smiling.

"Coffee again?" she says.

"Can't tonight."

Her frown pinches at the edges of her mouth.

"I thought we had a date."

"I didn't realize that. Rain check, then?"

She instantly looks suspicious.

"Well, it is raining out," she says.

"Okay, then."

"Sure, but why not tonight?"

"I just have things I need to do."

"Are you seeing someone at another meeting?" she says, smiling in a way that doesn't seem amused.

"I just can't," he says. "Not tonight."

She nods, thinking on it.

"Can I ask your real name?" she says.

"Ken. Doyle."

"And can I ask what you do? Where you live?"

"No, you can't. That's the 'anonymous' part."

"That doesn't seem promising for a second date."

"I'm really sorry."

"You know," she says, "I'm really not that much of an alcoholic. I was just going with it tonight. I felt like white wine was wimpy for this crowd. I felt like I didn't want them to make the connection if they were to walk into my shop."

"That's all very understandable."

"So let's have coffee. I won't keep you long."

"Like I said, something else has come up."

"So you really do have a busy schedule, do you?"

"Busy enough."

And that's it. Walking home, he realizes the tightness with which he is enveloped in his small existence. A car passes, and he wonders if it's her, seeing where he's going. The rain begins again, steadily heavier, and by the time he keys the lock of his place, he can only peel the wet clothes off and turn the shower to the hottest he can bear.

He goes to bed early and awakens at two in the morning, wishing he had gone running. He still waits, on his worse days, for the inevitable knock on the door, or tomorrow's tap on the shoulder, or the hand firm on his arm. By three he has calmed himself. No one knows to look for him. They think they know where he is, fathoms deep at the crest of Georges Bank, forever lost. His problem won't be so much that he will be found, but that the person he has become is very much a suspicious one, unable to fully explain himself. It is only in the gray before dawn he can finally fall asleep, and only because he's decided, his past experiences notwithstanding, that a boat is the safest place to be.

He's at the shipping office early in the morning, sidling up to the boss, Bernard, who says, "You're back sooner than I thought. Did you already run through all that pay?"

"No, just bored. Ready to work again."

"Bored enough for this shit? What happened?"

"Nothing. Seriously."

Bernard goes to his computer and pulls up his file, and looks a little irritated.

"We really need better paperwork for you," Bernard says.

"Like I said, it's on the way."

"I mean, I know you're not from Mexico or Guatemala, but we need the documentation so we don't get trouble. It doesn't even have to be real. Just enough that we said we covered our end."

"Send me out. By the time I'm back, it's waiting in my mailbox. I sent away for a duplicate license."

"Well, Jerry says you work fast. That helps."

"I work my ass off. I make you guys money."

"A white guy who works harder than Guatemalans is a hard worker."

"How do the Guatemalans get on, then? Where's their paperwork?"

"They have their system."

"I'm asking. Wherever they get it, I can get it, if you tell me."

"Why not just wait for the documentation you say is coming any day?" Bernard says, amused.

Quinn has the urge to turn and bolt, but he says, "Bernard, help me out."

"Who are you trying to avoid?"

"An ex-wife, if you know what I mean."

Bernard laughs. "I guess I do."

"Until the paper comes, which it's supposed to, where can I get some temporary coverage? Just to bide me over."

Bernard puts his hands up. "That's not my business. I just need to comply with the law, at least enough to keep myself from getting a headache. You remember Nello? He worked with you on the last run?"

"Vaguely."

Bernard writes down an address. "Go to him, and maybe he'll help. And then when you have something, come right back. Make sure you have a Social, too."

171

Quinn stands looking at the address.

"It's easy," Bernard says. "Every illegal in town, and every under-aged student at U-Dub, has a fake ID. It's really not going to be that hard."

The night of the next AA meeting, he's hesitant. He's hoping she won't be there. And if she is, he's hoping she'll let it all go. He should not have come. But in fighting his dependencies, the meeting has now become the dependence. He was surprised how shaky he felt even contemplating not going. Out on the *Siberian Wanderer*, you don't need AA meetings, three hundred miles off Alaska without a drop of alcohol on the ship. Out there, the work mutes all urges other than for sleep.

But here, in the city, it's the only place he knows to go, the only place to sit easily among people, to be in the flush of body heat and noise and the smell of humans. To cycle through a week without, and then another, leaves nothing. *Why did I talk to her?* he thinks. *What was that even about?*

He goes. She's there. He has come in purposely late, taking a folding chair at the end of the back row, knowing she'll look, which she does. She flips her hair, casting a sidelong glance at him, then she doesn't look again.

He'll wait until the break, and head out then. He's gotten enough of what he needs. Up at the front, a new guy tells a story of too much damned gin and tonic. Amazing, in Quinn's mind: each to his own downfall, all the different booze, all the various brands, the many tastes, the infinite paths to the same singular ruin. He does find himself fascinated, the way people sneak it all past themselves, the way they make it palatable. There's a woman here, older, who talked about how she only drank champagne, as if merrily muting the downfall. The new guy is a bearish man with a pursed mouth and short fingers, somehow both delicate and expansive, fascinating in his shame. *It was just gin and tonic,* he seems to say. *Who in hell knew?*

The break comes when the big man cuts his story off and retreats to his chair, stifling some rising sobs. Everyone stands up. Quinn turns and is off for the back door.

"Ken!" he hears her calling. "Wait up!"

The clack of her heels sounds off the meeting-room linoleum. He turns and she is up at him, eyes maybe trending toward crazy.

"Why such a hurry?"

"Things to do," he says.

"Always so busy. Always so rushed."

"It happens."

"So what's going on, *Ken*?"

"Going out of town soon."

"Oh, really . . ."

"It's the work."

"Which is?"

"Remember the 'anonymous' part, Meg."

She smiles at that.

"After the meeting last week," she says, "I went to the coffee shop where we'd gotten together, just to see if you might come in on your own. I thought it might be nice, to chat, away from all this AA stuff. So I sat for a while, and just when I thought I'd been wrong, here you came, up the street. I thought, 'Maybe this was meant to happen.'"

"Relax on that," he says. "All we did was have a cup of coffee and a kiss."

"But then you walked right on by. I realized you weren't coming from your car, you apparently didn't have a car—you were on foot. It was *pouring*. I watched you go down the block. You'd walked by the window of the shop and hadn't even noticed me, didn't know I saw you."

"So be it."

"I saw you go into your building. I saw where you live. Like, what's the story? You live in that dump? That's a place for crooks and junkies."

"I can live wherever I want."

"People don't live in places like that because they *want to*, just because they *have* to. So who you are, and what you do, has become incredibly fascinating to me."

"Why is it your business?"

"It's not," she says, and she's smiling now. "I just really am curious."

Two days later, Quinn is coming up the gangway at four in the morning as the *Arctic Star* finishes loading. It's smaller than the *Wanderer* by twenty feet, and also the first ship out. He's heaved his foam mattress into the trash bin behind his building, stuffed the clothes he has into the bag he carries, and terminated his week-to-week lease.

"Back out to sea?" his old landlord said the night before, surprised perhaps by a departure in the middle of a paid week. Quinn regretted having told him anything when he filled out the application. He'd felt the need to justify, then realized afterward this building did not have exacting membership standards. In his pocket, he's got the new driver's license Nello procured for him, Kenneth G. Doyle deadpanning into the camera, a Minnesota document with a matching Social. Quinn's never come close to Minnesota, which is apparently the point.

Puget Sound is dark water ahead, more foreboding than in the East, where he'd watch the dawn light creep up in invisible increments out of the flat sea horizon. Here, they sail into darkness with the light only slowly catching them from behind. But he will be, in a few hours, back into the belly of the ship, first to prep, then to squirrel all the bunk time he can get before the true work begins. And then they all file like inmates to the conveyor line as the *Star* begins to ingest fish, a ravenous factory lumbering over high seas, where they likewise become machines in the bottom levels. Working and sleeping and working. The hours will seem to take forever to pass; the months will slide by quickly. He will feel the ache of his running legs as, after the weeks of building up, they again go fallow. He'll feel it as his wind decreases and his shoulders sag from hour upon hour on the belts, sorting. But he can look forward to land not for the old pleasures of heroin and sleep, but for those new miles, swiftly afoot.

He realized that night at the meeting that the reason he went was simple: so as not to be a man so utterly alone. Now he will clear his mind and think anew. By the time the ship turns back, east southeast, he'll be of clearer mind, or better plans. He will leave Seattle, he will think. By the last night, when he finishes his last shift and falls into his berth with only the payout left and the attenuated thrill of the big ship sliding silent into its slip, he'll be ready to be a new man, again. He'll go to the deck, cleaned and shaved and packed, to take in the cool morning air and watch the shore loom up slowly. Coming to port is a silent journey, down the Strait and then into the Sound, and finally narrowing down more into Salmon Bay, with the rows of docks and moorings. He'll watch those last minutes of the journey, as the pilot takes the laden *Arctic Star* in, anticipating the soft kiss of the piles. Then, just before the bump, he'll notice someone down there, waiting, oddly familiar from the distance and out of place. He'll see what seems like the look on the face, even from a hundred yards. And when he's sure who it is, he'll know his life as he's imagined it is already over.

PART FOUR

25.

ROBBIE ISN'T MUCH OF A FLIER. THE FACT IS THAT HE'S never had many chances to go farther than a gas tank's drive away from home. His honeymoon was his first time flying, rough air all the way to Aruba, and it made its imprint. He suspects M. may have first begun to doubt him as she watched him white-knuckle his way to their presumed paradise. Since then, he hasn't avoided flying, but has also never come up with a good reason to do it much more.

So now, as the plane releases its brakes and the jet engines roar and it lurches forward on the runway, he's feeling fully hurled into more turbulence. It's been more than two years since Quinn disappeared, and yet Robbie's remained haunted by his doubts. He's been stuck, and he knows that.

The plane picks up speed on the rumbling tarmac, and now it noses upwards and the ground falls off beneath the wheels. Robbie feels the familiar fear in his stomach and he begins his deep breathing. Houses, far below his window, the grids of streets and neighborhoods. And everything he knows is behind him now.

In a strange way, his mourning has restarted, this much later.

On the one-year anniversary of the *Christine II* leaving port for that last time, Robbie had allowed himself the notion that everything had found its proper place. That year had been a slog, but maybe they'd arrived somewhere. Christine had settled into a comfortable routine, and Sarah was feeling more at home around him because of Christine. And then Jean: a thoroughly happy presence when she came by, often with her own daughter in tow. Robbie was feeling as if he had gained some renewed worth. Jean liked to cook for them all. On Saturdays, when Sarah came to stay, it was a family meal, all of them at the table, the food and the laughter so unlike his own childhood.

At *The Record*, he worked any extra shifts he could. Christine did likewise at the diner. At night she'd sit at the kitchen table and do her homework. She was finding it a challenge. The two of them would sit on Sunday afternoons and work through their expenses, keeping just ahead of things. Yes, they'd eked out the money for her precious iPhone, and for Robbie to keep his old car running, maybe another year or two. This was how life was. Jean offered to help, but he was adamant that he couldn't accept it. Her support and closeness, yes; her cooking, yes. But no money.

In these last few years, through different tragedies, his life had become quieter. First the divorce, M. and all the ensuing nonsense. Then Quinn coming out of prison, and all that went with that. Then the *Christine II*'s vanishing. Robbie was left responsible for all manner of things. He dreaded the chance encounters with Botelho's wife, still aflame with rage. If he'd thought the idea that Quinn's death could have allowed her some peace, he was wrong. She still turned up, coming up and spitting at him one night when she was drunk down the bar. It seemed ceremonial. He was the proxy. But Robbie had largely abdicated the complicated pleasures of the barstool, with thanks to Jean, and owing as well to his brother's absence.

Likewise, he'd softened it up at work. He'd had enough of the pissed-off sports parents. He didn't feel compelled to dole the honesty anymore. Now he wrote his pieces trying only to praise, stories in which the only slight was to not mention a player, rather than mention his or her bad play. Sports, ever an arena of truth, but he no longer felt the obligation to report the more disturbing of those verities.

On a Monday morning in November he was at his desk in the Sports Department, looking out on the sun-shimmering water, waiting to head for an afternoon soccer game. The receptionist called him to say someone was there at the front desk for him. He had no guesses. Down the back stairs, he came into the small foyer to see Dawn, looking very nervous.

"Can we talk?" she said.

"Haven't we done all the talking we can?"

"I have something I have to say, and I need to say it privately."

"I'm kind of in the middle of something."

Dawn looked as if she was about to burst into tears.

"It took a lot for me to come here."

The receptionist had her head down, but was listening to everything. Robbie shrugged then, lame assent.

Out the door they went. In the back booth of the restaurant, empty at mid-morning, Dawn lowered her voice into raspy exhalation.

"I believe I mentioned I've been dating," she said.

"I'm glad," he said. "Is he a nice guy?"

"You know him. Bob Clarkson."

"The cop?"

"Yeah, the cop. Is there something wrong with dating a cop?"

"I didn't mean it that way."

She looked around, as if afraid of being seen.

"Is he being okay to you?"

She glared at him now. "Yeah, he treats me very well. He's great."

"So, you just wanted to let me know."

She shook her head. "You're really being an asshole right now. I'm trying to tell you something."

"Then say it."

"I need for this not to have come from me. Or from Bob. You need to promise me."

"I guess I don't have a choice, do I?"

"That's not much of a promise."

"I promise, I promise."

"Okay. Look . . ."

"Just say it, for Christ's sake."

Dawn looked around, making sure no one had come up on them from behind.

"It looks like Santoro is still alive."

Now, reflexively, Robbie found himself scanning across the restaurant.

"Bob told you that?"

"I'm not going to get into that," she said. "Leave Bob out of it."

"How do they know this?"

"It has to do with a prepaid debit card from the Walmart. The cashier remembers Santoro buying it. She used to buy drugs from him outside the high school, but he didn't remember her. The card was bought for four hundred in cash, so it stuck in her mind. She let the police know. Apparently the card was used for two days, starting the day after your brother's boat went out. The transactions went as far west as Pendleton, Oregon. Bus tickets to Portland, and food. No motels or anything, just a straight shot across. Then it just stopped."

"They just found this out?"

"No, they knew months ago."

"So where is he now?"

"Nobody knows. It's been a year."

"Are they looking?"

"No."

"The guy's a bail jumper and a drug dealer."

"Apparently no one wants to hassle. There's no real proof it was Santoro, except the girl saying it. They put out a bulletin and left it at that. I guess if Santoro crosses anybody, he might turn up."

"What about Quinn?"

Dawn reached across the table and took his hand. "They checked what they could. Nothing. They think he's dead."

"And they're not going to go after Santoro."

"They don't even know *where* to go after him. The DEA is supposed to be keeping their eyes out."

Robbie slumped, pondering.

"Was there a name attached to the card, or anything like that?"

"They didn't tell me."

"Can you find out?"

"Probably not. Bob knows about us, obviously. About our history. He doesn't even know I'm speaking to you. This is all I can offer you."

"Okay."

Back at the office, he sat looking at the same water as an hour before, but now he beseeched it to share its secrets. *What happened?* Whatever hard-won peace he'd gathered in the past year had just fallen through the bottom. He wanted briefly to believe Dawn was lying, but she wasn't that cruel. But still he wished she hadn't told him. Now he had to think about all that.

Santoro: always trouble, always pushing. That was a sports story, too. The tale of the angry kid who couldn't play well enough to get into the lineup. The kid who was no good at school, had no real social skills, wasn't especially good-looking. Yet one who burned to be something, even if he doesn't know what. The resentment came from that. On the football field, Santoro would start fights with guys he wasn't fast enough to chase down. Sometimes Quinn, sometimes Robbie. You'd come out of a pileup with the coaches shouting and the whistle going, and there was a hand on your facemask, yanking. Santoro, torqued about the stiff-arm you'd just got on his throat, twenty yards back.

Freddy Santoro was always the guy who felt he was never getting a fair shake. In hard fact, he was the guy who didn't see the truth of his own limitations. He was forever raging, and at times the Boyle brothers got their share if his venom. Into adulthood, as Quinn worked the boats and Robbie eased into his small-town sportswriting life, Santoro still had a tendency to go off. One night, mouthing about past slights, Santoro started in about how he was always a faster runner. Quinn had looked up from the silence of his drink and said, "I could beat you in any footrace then, and can beat you in any footrace now." And it had come to that. A nocturnal dash down Water Street in the 1 a.m. pall, some stop sign the finish line, Santoro pulling up when he saw he was beat, claiming a pulled hamstring, pledging that this matter would be settled definitively at some future date. What Robbie always marveled at was watching Quinn still able to run at all, even with the bulk, the foot speed something that couldn't be taught, nor apparently unlearned. But down past the stop sign, bent over in a pool of streetlight, Quinn choked and spat and walked it off with that growing tightness in his lobsterman's back, and they all looked at each other, the definitive result of the race only being that they were all getting older, and still acting like fools.

It hadn't surprised Robbie when Santoro got pinched. While Robbie had no idea to what extent his tight-lipped brother had invested himself in the drug scene, Santoro had been blowing air about it for years. It must have made him feel like a kingpin.

Santoro had apparently made connections, because in his several years of vigorous, low-level dealing, he'd become very well-known. Even before the arrest that would bring Santoro his conviction, Robbie had heard a couple of reporters on the news side talking about him one night in the break room at the paper.

"How does he not get caught?" one had said to the other. "I hear he's selling like crazy at the high school."

"What's he selling?" Robbie said, and the two of them looked up at him, the nosy sportswriter.

"You know the guy, right?" the one named Jane said.

"I knew the guy in high school," Robbie said. "That means I'm kind of stuck with him for life."

Jane had glanced at the young guy, Trev, and said, "He sells tons of weed to the kids, but now we're hearing about other stuff. A lot of prescription-grade stuff. Oxy, Ritalin, Xanax, Adderall. We also hear he's got a bit of a heroin pipeline, although maybe not so much in the school. Do you know anything about that?"

Robbie honestly did not. But neither had he ever known the source of Quinn's mysterious heroin habit. He had to have gotten it somewhere; on the other hand, Quinn seemed unlikely to accept anything from Santoro, even for the right price.

Robbie had shrugged it off. "So if everybody knows, why aren't the police on him?"

"These guys?" Trev had said. "I mean, I know they're small potatoes, but there's got to be something more they're after."

In the time since, Robbie has heard more about Santoro from Christine, about Santoro sitting in his truck outside the high school with a toolbox filled with Ziplocs of pills, quarter-ounces and disparate powders and presumed bromides, taking cash from the high-schoolers.

But within a month of the newsroom conversation with Jane and Trev, Santoro was more surprisingly busted by the DEA, getting off that boat in Newport loaded with product far beyond what Santoro had previously been associated with. It didn't look to be a solo venture. Everything from there was speculative, and as he awaited trial, bonded out at the price of his parents' and sister's houses as surety, he began to blow hard once more. Now that he was exposed, Santoro took on the role with a certain unexpected aplomb, both denying the obvious as well as playing the stand-up guy.

"The Feds want me to tell them where I got it," Santoro said, drunk and infused with that odd kind of honor. "No way I do that!"

But the stuff on that boat, and in Santoro's pickup, had to have come from somewhere, and somebody. Given that volume, whoever had supplied Santoro had to have held very much indeed. And holding that much must have made somebody nervous about loose lips.

26.

AS CHRISTINE CAME AND WENT, ROBBIE BATTLED THAT urge to tell her what he'd heard from Dawn. But what would it prove? The original story, of two lobstermen going down in a failing boat, had always been too easy, because it was such an obvious outcome. But the complications of what had really happened now had a multitude of disturbing dimensions, none of them favoring Quinn or his survival. Robbie felt the ache of mourning welling up once again: it was one thing to imagine an accident far at sea, and different to imagine something not accidental at all.

Deep in his nights, after filing a night-game story, he came into the dark apartment with Christine gone to bed and the dishwasher humming. He sat with a drink and catalogued the many ways his brother had fooled him before. Such is the nature of drunks and druggies, to maintain for a time that convincing front. Such is the nature of prison conversations through heavy glass, hearing a voice on the telephone receiver that matches the mouth moving on the other side. *It was just stuff I got for myself. There really wasn't that much. They thought I'd thrown over a lot more than I did.*

His brother's mysteries. And always the ghost of Botelho. *What happened out there?* A question now endlessly repeated, a many-spined urchin. A bristle of scenarios that had come to plague many a sleepless sunrise. *What happened out there?* And of all the scenarios that were painful to absorb, the most painful was the one that had Quinn possibly being alive.

Did my brother play me?

He met Dawn again for lunch, after several insistent messages at her office. The odd flip, of her now keeping him at bay. But she knew what he wanted, and only the final voice mail got her to respond: *Don't open up those kind of possibilities then refuse to follow through on it!*

So there she was, nervous as usual, but nervous for different reasons now. He came to her now, seated himself, and said, "How's Bob doing?"

"Bob is fine, but what you mean is whether Bob is telling me anything."

"Yes," he said, already irritated. "I'm assuming my brother is probably dead, but I'm just wondering if he was murdered. If he was, why isn't anyone doing anything about it?"

"If there's one thing I knew from our time dating, it's that your brother has been what's held you back. You've always taken on too much responsibility."

"I'm supporting his daughter," Robbie said. "At least some. She's family."

"She might actually benefit from your help," Dawn said. "But how did you ever benefit?"

"Don't worry about all that," Robbie said. "I just want to know what happened. Santoro was supposed be going to prison for some really heavy trafficking, and now he's home free?"

"Cops and prosecutors don't chase leads that probably won't ever pan out," Dawn said. "Not with the budget the police have these days. Bob said if they hear anything more, they'll check it out. But all they have right now is Oregon, a year ago. And Bob says it's really the DEA's case, and that the DEA thinks Santoro was just small-time."

"Does Bob know you're telling me this?"

"He tells me definitely not to tell you, then he tells me more," she said.

The New England office of the DEA was in a looming concrete hulk, twin structures called the John F. Kennedy Federal Building in Boston, which Robbie had never before noticed in all his years coming up for Bruins and Red Sox games. He'd called ahead, and now he was brought to a conference room that looked like an office-furniture-store display. The table was veneer, and a couple of the swivel chairs still had tags zip-tied on their undercarriages. After a while, a man with a gray suit and a silver badge on his belt entered, and shook his hand. He said his name was Powers. The agent had a folder that he put on the table in front of him but didn't open.

"So, the case of Federico Santoro," the agent said.

"Right."

"What's your interest in the case?"

"Freddy went out on my brother's boat."

"Okay. Your brother was also a convicted drug trafficker, correct?"

"Incorrect. My brother was initially—and mistakenly—charged with trafficking. He pleaded to straight possession."

The agent could not hide the heard-it-a-million-times smirk.

"You called Santoro 'Freddy.' You two were friends?"

"No. We were on the same high-school football team."

The agent turned his wrist, already stealing a look at his watch.

"So what can I do for you today?"

"I want to urge you to look for Santoro."

"I thought he and your brother went down in a lobster boat."

"That's what I thought. Now I'm hearing Santoro might be in Oregon."

"Who told you that?"

"I'm a journalist."

"Really?" the agent said. "Aren't you a sportswriter?"

"Yeah, high-school sports."

"But you have a big scoop about Santoro."

"I heard the police down my way heard this."

"Local cops can never keep their yaps shut," the agent said. "I can. Even if what you're telling me was true, I could neither confirm nor deny it. But if he was in Oregon a year ago, I seriously doubt he's in Oregon now."

Robbie pushed back in his chair. He didn't like getting jacked around. But the agent just kept looking at him, the brother of a once-accused drug dealer.

"I just want to know what happened to my brother."

"He went down with his ship, is what everybody tells me."

"And you're not going to chase down Santoro?"

The agent sat as if he'd also had this conversation a million times before.

"We investigate, and we compile evidence, and maybe if things work out, we make an arrest. We go to a federal grand jury when we have enough, and we present. We indict and we bring the suspect in front of a federal judge. The minute that judge grants bail, and that suspect walks out the courthouse door, we can assume we've lost him. When a suspect actually does come back to court of his own accord, it's always kind of surprising."

"So you're mad at the judge."

"The judge makes the decisions he wants to make."

"So you just let Santoro go . . ."

"A guy with drugs loaded up on his fishing boat is not the Mexican drug cartel. We can do better going further up the chain of command. Sometimes these small-timers help get us there. Sometimes they take off and that's that."

"At least I'd try."

"We don't have unlimited resources."

Robbie nodded, and the agent pushed to his feet, ready to go.

"I'm sorry to say this, but either way, I'd guess your brother's dead," the agent said. "There may be a possibility they were in on it together, but in my experience, bail jumpers facing most of their life in prison usually work alone."

Christine came in late from school, and Robbie was already on the couch watching the end of the hockey game. She dropped her backpack and looked at him.

"What's wrong?"

"Do I look like something's wrong?"

"Yeah, actually."

"Well nothing's wrong. But I have something to tell you."

Christine came around and dropped herself into the chair.

"I've decided to take a vacation."

"Okay."

"I'll be gone a week, maybe ten days. You'll have the place to yourself."

"That's fine. Are you going with Jean?"

He hadn't thought of that, and Christine could tell.

"Just alone. I just need to get away. Just clear my head."

"Of what?"

"I haven't had an actual vacation in about five years now. I just thought I'd relax for a little bit."

"Are you taking Sarah?"

"No."

She mulls this. "Okay . . . where are you going?"

"I thought I'd go see Oregon. I hear it's really nice."

She was staring at him now.

"Is this something about my Dad?"

"Absolutely not," Robbie said.

27.

CHRISTINE KNEW RIGHT THEN SOMETHING WAS GOING on, even though Robbie wouldn't admit it. He couldn't really hide a thing from her. A vacation, alone, to Oregon? *Please.*

And she was angry he wouldn't trust her with this. So she went through his things when he wasn't home, without any idea what she was looking for. But she kept hunting, for days. She went through his dresser drawer one morning after he'd left, with her backpack on her shoulders and ten minutes to catch the bus. She went through expecting nothing. Then, there it was.

He must have printed these things out at the office the night before, and put them in the file folder she now opened. There was a boarding pass, Boston to Portland, and a hotel reservation to a Hampton Inn by the Portland airport, and a car reservation for a subcompact, all bought off the web. But nothing else. Nothing that explained anything, other than about the travel and lodging itself. She wanted to imagine any explanation besides the one that came immediately to her: that Robbie was not planning on coming back. And that it had something to do with her father. And that he might be out there somewhere.

The community college was like a mass relocation of much of her high school, but worse. The kids in her high-school class with families that had money, or with some sort of ability sports-wise or brain-wise, had gone off to what Christine thought of as "real college." Those who were nothing special ended up at the community college, a little purgatory where they were surrounded by the same bottom slice of kids from all the other high schools around them. Nobody seemed especially happy to be there. But being there was at least a little bit of having the sense you hadn't given up yet.

In her Comp class there was a guy named Nick, who couldn't stop looking her way. She knew part of it was the boredom of school itself, but when she sat in the atrium eating her lunch from the bag, there he was. He wasn't exactly good-looking, but wasn't exactly not. Dark hair, a scraggly beard, and a bit of a shy hunch. When he sat next to her and said hello, she went ahead and said hello back. She'd had no boyfriends, other than those few encounters with Jared. But now Jared was off to college, and all the boys like him were, too, and all the girls like them. Boys like Nick were pretty much what was left over. So were the girls like her.

So without planning it, they sat and ate lunch together most days. He had a job at night at a convenience store, and she told him about hers at the diner. Their hours didn't mesh, and he didn't ask her out. She wasn't sure if she would have said yes. Maybe she just didn't want to assume that her choices were already more limited, and that the path she was taking was already telling her what she was being allowed to be. She wanted to be a nurse because she'd heard the money was good, and there were jobs. It wasn't really about aspirations.

Nick had a bit of nervousness under his quiet, just that little twitchiness. He said he wanted to be a car mechanic, because the money was good and there were jobs. But she knew he was just saying that. He was clearly, and quietly, obsessed. He told her about how he'd fix up the old cars nobody much wanted, the ones with the severe mileage or bad transmissions. He spoke like an evangelist who was saving souls. The community college had an automotive technology major, so he said he was going with that. And, he said, they turned out to have very little to teach him.

"I like to figure out how things work," he said in a bland voice that sounded uninterested in his own thoughts. "I can do most of it already. I just need the piece of paper and I can go work at one of the dealerships out on Route One. They have electronics and tools I could never afford."

In one way, it seemed good to have a solid plan. On the other hand, it was a plan that would take him to retirement. Day in and day out, flat on his back underneath cars. A lifetime of greasy hands and of breathing the smell of gasoline. But she was making a judgment that was probably unfair. Just because she hoped her life would have some surprises, it didn't mean everyone else had to.

Beyond cars, Nick liked to talk about music, so that was their topic. This band and that; this singer and that. It was the only thing that seemed to really get him out of his sluggishness. As he talked about it more, he talked about listening to certain bands at certain times he was driving. She realized in time that for him, the music was just an extension of his love affair with cars. Music was a tool for demonstrating his sound system, or for connecting to a driving performance.

"I was listening to 'The Oracle' driving back from my friend's house and you know how at the beginning it kind of speeds up? And then it keeps speeding up? I looked at the speedometer and I was doing a buck-ten."

"Is Oracle a band?"

"No, it's a *song*," he said, with a sharpness, as if Christine was stupid. "The *band* is Godsmack."

"Well," she said, "That's why it's great to have a friend who's a guy who knows about that stuff."

"Did you just friend-zone me?" he said.

Of course, she had.

"Not really," she said. "I just didn't think we were doing anything other than that."

He looked pissed, but didn't say much more. She presumed the social skills of would-be auto mechanics were not always at the top end of the scale. She didn't know exactly what he was trying for. She figured then that she wouldn't see much more of him. But the next day at lunch, there he was again, going on about cars and music.

So on this day, she surprised him by sharing what was going on in her life. He didn't know anything about her missing father—she'd said her father was out of the picture, but she'd let Nick assume he was gone in the usual way. The story about the missing boat seemed to perk him up, to her surprise.

"So you think your uncle helped sneak him off?" he said.

"I don't know what to think."

"What reason would he have?"

"He owed a lot of money he couldn't pay," Christine said.

"On what? A boat? A truck?"

"On me."

Robbie packed on a Thursday night for an early Friday flight out of Logan. Christine was in her room, awake, and shaking with anger. She felt as if she were shivering. She'd lain awake most of the night and when she heard the front door shut in the early light, and then his car start up, she decided she wasn't going to school that day.

Up, she sat at the kitchen table for about two hours, waiting for it to be nine o'clock. As soon as it was, she looked up Jean's office number and called her there.

Jean sounded as if she was exhausted.

"Do you know what this Oregon thing is about?" Christine said. "Why is he going there?"

"Is it Oregon he's going to? He only told me he had to go out of town. It's the first time he's really kept something from me."

Christine wasn't used to Jean being so forthcoming, of her voice absent her usual cheer, bemused and in control.

Jean said, "Did you know your Uncle Robbie has been seeing his old girlfriend?"

"You mean Dawn?"

"They've met for lunch, more than once, from what I've been told. And now he's taking off on a mysterious trip, apparently to Oregon."

Christine had never heard that bite in Jean's voice before. "I don't think that's what it's about."

"Really? You don't?"

"I think it's about my father."

"What about him?"

Christine paused then, because she knew if she said it, she was putting the nail into Jean's relationship with her uncle, by adding on one more presumed subterfuge. But as quickly, Christine thought, *screw him*!

"I don't know why I keep thinking it's about my father. Crazy, right?"

Jean paused then, for a while.

"Honey, I know you want to hold that hope. But this looks to me like it's just a case of good old-fashioned two-timing."

"That's ridiculous," Christine said. "Why would he do that?"

"I've sat up all night wondering the same thing."

"What makes you so sure Dawn is with him?"

"I called her office and they told me she's out, and won't be back for a while."

"Oh," Christine said, her own hopes fading with that revelation.

"Your father is not alive. What Robbie is doing has nothing to do with that. This is really about something I've done, or haven't done, or don't understand."

"I thought you two were doing so well. You cared about each other so much."

"You always think that," she said, even more tiredly.

"Christine, what's the matter with you today?" Buddy said when she brought another redo back to the grill.

"Please don't fire me," she said. "I can't afford to lose this job."

"Calm down, calm down," he said. "Why do you think I'm always going to fire you? I only did it once."

That little bit of confidence helped her get through the shift. But on the way home, she could feel her anger rising up. She was mad at Robbie, but then she thought of her father, out there, alive somewhere. Having turned his back on her once again. Halfway home, she decided that whatever Robbie was doing in Portland, it was total shit. And that maybe after years with Gina she'd learned to fight back when she needed to.

She Googled until she had the website for the Portland police, and when she got through to a woman on the other end, she said, "I have a tip."

"Okay," she said, "Let's have it."

"Are you a detective?"

"No."

"Can I speak to a detective?"

"Talk to me first."

So she felt like she needed to make it good. She wasn't going to lie; she was merely going to speculate.

"Hampton Hotel by the airport. A guest named Robert Boyle. He's possibly going to be meeting with a drug trafficker, and I think it's going to be a big shipment. He may be traveling with a woman who's in on it."

Christine could hear the woman's keyboard going at the other end of the phone. She typed fast.

"And who is this alleged drug dealer?"

Christine didn't want to say it was the brother, because she knew she needed something juicier for them to go on.

"Freddy Santoro," she said. "He got busted in Rhode Island by the DEA, but he's on the run. He skipped bail while awaiting trial. I think there's going to be a lot of drugs and a lot of money."

"And who are you?" the woman said.

"I'd rather not say." And then Christine hung up. And at that moment she felt instantly remorseful, maybe more than she ever had, maybe more than her own father ever had, even at his worst.

28.

FINALLY IN HIS HOTEL ROOM IN PORTLAND, ROBBIE WAS now seized by the realization he had absolutely no clue of where to start. He'd been so far fueled by pure indignation. He'd landed in the late afternoon after changing flights in Chicago, had rented a car at the airport, and now, on the hotel bed, he was exhausted. Back East, it was getting late. He'd stayed awake on nothing but emotion. In the last hour of the flight he'd only begun assessing what an impossible task he'd set up for himself. He had seen the downtown from the window of the plane and should not have been surprised by its size. It had an NBA team; he measured the size of cities that way. Somehow, he'd still been imagining something smaller. As if he'd stand on a street corner and Freddy would come walking by.

Now he had a gas-station map spread out on the bed. He was using his laptop to try to narrow things down. The advantage he had was to know Freddy Santoro. And he guessed Freddy was as bad at hiding as he'd been at everything else. From the more-intimate perspectives of having been on teams with him, of having sat in classrooms and lunchrooms and lockers rooms and the back rows of away-game buses grinding their way to far-off fields, Robbie knew Freddy Santoro was not very smart, and that Freddy thought himself much smarter than he was.

Freddy had always been a drinker and a drugger, but Freddy craved an audience even more. Just as Freddy thought he was a football player, he also thought he was a fisherman, and that notion seemed the best direction. Robbie had written out, on the hotel notepad, a set of directions to the water, where the fishing boats might come in. His first confusion as the plane banked toward the airport in the Western dusk was why a city called Portland wasn't right on the ocean. Portland, Maine, of course, made sense in that way, as this Oregon one did not. Robbie had looked out the windows on both sides of the aircraft, scanning for the long plain of water, and had found none. But what he knew was that Freddy's supposed trail dead-ended here, so this was the only logical place to start.

He had a photo of Santoro cut from *The Record*. In the paper, the headshot of Santoro had run side-by-side with one of Quinn, under the headline *Lobstermen missing at sea*. What had irked Robbie was that someone had placed a subhead beneath it: *Both had been convicted in drug felonies.* Robbie would have thought that could go farther down the columns, especially because these convictions were completely different matters. But, indeed, both photos had been booking shots, and both faces had the same expression, a kind of stunned resignation. At his newsroom desk, Robbie had scissored the Santoro photo from the rest, tossing his brother's picture aside. He laminated Santoro's face with clear tape, an identifier which he now placed on the bed, like the first face card to come up in a difficult hand of poker.

When the phone by his bed rang, it felt like a jailbreak. He nearly lost his balance, so startled. He picked up and the voice of the desk girl said, "Your visitors are on their way to your room."

"I don't have visitors," he said, but he could already hear the knuckles on his door.

"Who is it?" he said at the edge of the doorframe.

201

"Portland Police Department. We need a word."

When they came in, they stayed standing, but he could see them looking, the eyes scanning in some trained way. Two young men, looking like they should be manning the register at a local coffee bar. Plainclothes: plaid shirts and windbreakers and jeans. They showed him their badges and handed him their business cards. The taller one, whose card read as Detective Horton, seemed to be in charge.

"Sir, we do not have a warrant but we'd like to ask a few questions as to why you're here in Portland."

"Tourism," Robbie said.

"You're traveling alone?"

"Yes."

"And staying at a hotel by the airport. When is your flight out?"

"In a week."

"Are you here for any business purpose?"

"I'm a sportswriter. So, no."

"Have you been convicted of any crime?"

"Never."

"Do you mind if we look around?"

"Yeah, I do, kind of."

"Sir, I could make the call and get the warrant done, but it would be easier for us to clear this if we can just look around."

Robbie shrugged.

The two of them went up facing sides of the bed, and Horton looked closely at the photo, trimmed of any information.

"Is this Santoro?" Horton said.

"How in hell did you know that?" Robbie said, and they seemed suddenly intrigued.

"Are you in Portland for the purpose of meeting with Mr. Santoro?"

"Not exactly."

"What does that mean, sir?"

"I'm looking *for* him. I got a tip that he might be living out here. Everyone seems to think he's dead. He was last seen on my brother's boat. The boat went missing east of Nantucket. And my brother is now presumed dead."

Horton nodded. "Can we check the room, with your permission, for cash and narcotics?"

"Sure, have at it," Robbie said. "But I did bring some cash, you know."

"I don't mean cash," Horton said. "I mean *cash*."

"Well, I definitely don't have any of that," Robbie said.

Robbie's hands were shaking as he punched the number in his cell phone. The detectives had left, quietly and politely, seeming to have bought the story. But the call to the DEA in Boston only went to voice mail. *Are you kidding me?* It was Friday, and past closing time on the East Coast.

For two days he did not move from the room, afraid to try anything. He found himself looking out the window, staring at the parking lot below. On Monday morning, the wake-up call was at six, and he immediately dialed. Back in Boston, they were just getting their coffee.

The woman who answered put his call straight through, to Robbie's relief.

"This is Powers."

"This is Robbie Boyle. You remember who I am?"

"I sure do."

"So what the fuck are you trying to do to me, you asshole?"

"Whoa, slow down now, buddy. What are you talking about?"

"You know what. Less than two hours after getting out here to Oregon, I have the Portland police searching my room."

A pause.

"Really?" Powers sounded nearly amused.

"Thanks a lot, pal. I try to get your help and you bust my balls."

"Boyle, listen. I had nothing to do with that. How do you know it had to do with Santoro?"

"They recognized his picture I had. They said it like they knew what I was looking for."

"Fucking local cops. Look, this is our case. I don't know anything about that. Do you know how they knew?"

"You were the only person who knew why I was coming out here."

Powers was quiet, thinking.

"Do you have a car?"

"I rented one."

"I'm going to suggest something. I'm going to send you to a guy at our Seattle office. Portland is part of the Seattle Division. I'm sending you to some guys up there—I don't think it's a long drive, like a couple of hours. By the time you get there, I'll have called them. Maybe they'll have something for you."

"Okay," Robbie said. "You're not fucking with me, are you?"

"No, I'm not. I'm helping you out."

"Well, I appreciate your help."

"See what they can tell you," Powers said. "See what they might have. But don't get all fired up. I have no reason to believe Santoro didn't go down with that boat. Or your brother. You could waste a lot of energy and money chasing shadows. Trust me on that."

And then in the middle of that night, waiting in a Seattle hotel room for his morning appointment with Henning of the DEA, he's instantly and fully awake. He gets his phone and dials.

"Hello?" Christine says sleepily.

"So are you happy with yourself now?" he shouts into his phone.

"Uncle Robbie?"

"What the hell was the purpose of that, exactly?"

"Calm down. Let me talk."

"Absolutely unbelievable. Goddamned ungrateful kid. I gave you a goddamned home."

"You've got to let me talk."

"They searched my hotel room, Christine. They were watching me when I checked out of the hotel. What am I, a criminal now? Are you enjoying that?"

Now her voice swung.

"You lied to me!" she said. "You and your vacation. Not to mention who went out there with you. I know he's out there. I know you're going to meet him."

"I was here with who?"

"You know who."

"I'm here alone. So there's your first mistake. And who am I meeting with?"

"Is my father with you?"

Robbie's heart drops. "You got to get off that shit. I can't believe he'd be alive. If he were alive, we'd know it. Or at least I would."

"And you're in Oregon . . ." she says with a tone of accusation.

"I'm looking for Santoro. I'm trying to find out if he's even alive. And if he is, then find out what happened to your father."

"I don't know what to believe anymore."

"You ungrateful shit," Robbie said.

"Ungrateful? Ungrateful? I have a goddamned father who didn't ever do a thing for me, and you helped him. I got left out on a long limb, and you could give a shit. He's my goddamned father and you should have told me what you were doing."

"Assuming he was your goddamned father!"

Silence, at both ends. The faint sound of someone knocking on a door behind her, asking what was wrong.

"Christine . . ." he said. Silence. The line gone dead. He thumbed the numbers again, and voice mail came up, and her cheery voice: "This is Christine Boyle!" He dialed again, then again. Each time a voice that reminded him of what he thought he had known of her.

"Goddamn," he said.

Then, a half-hour later, waiting for morning to make his Seattle appointment, he said, aloud in the dark, "Who did I supposedly come out here with?"

29.

CHRISTINE WASN'T OLD ENOUGH TO BE IN A BAR, BUT nobody cared. Not at a place called Topsides, her mother's venue of choice. She came through the door at about eight o'clock, hoping Gina hadn't drunk herself too far down the pipes. And there Gina was, at the end of the bar, cigarette hung from her mouth and some scrub of a guy sitting next to her. Gina turned and saw Christine and the smirk seemed pure reflex. The filter of the cigarette was stuck on her thick lipstick. The tip of it moved a bit. Christine knew she would have been way better off to catch her mother sober, or maybe even in that subdued reverie of one of her epic hangovers. But that was a small window of opportunity, and Christine wasn't in any mood to sit around waiting for answers.

"Oh, look, it's the princess herself," Gina said, the throw of the first punch.

"I have one question for you, and I want an answer," Christine said.

"Oh, does that mean we're *speaking*?"

"For the next thirty seconds at least, and no promises after that. What I want to know is, who is my real father?"

Somehow no one in this bar reacted. Christine had a sense this kind of scene wasn't all that unusual. Gina tilted her head in a way that made her realize how drunk Gina was, how sloppy. The smirk only got wider.

"I thought Robbie Boyle was your new daddy," she said.

"Give me a straight answer."

"Robbie's your daddy now, isn't he?" she said.

"Shut up and tell me the truth."

"Do you want me to shut up, or do you want me to tell the truth?"

The man next to her was laughing now, clearly amused by the two crazies, going at it.

"So you're telling me Robbie is my real father."

"I'm saying what I'm saying, so go figure it out."

"You're telling me Quinn Boyle is not my real father."

Gina, who was revealing herself as more drunk than Christine expected at such a tame hour, who in fact was nearly glowing vodka, said, "Well, I don't see him looking after you. I see that Robbie is doing it."

Christine walked out of that place trying to stop herself from crying, but she could feel the tears at the rims of her eyes like boiling water. *Assholes!*

I have such a fucked-up family.

She felt as if she hadn't slept in days, but she went to work anyway. She couldn't afford for Buddy to cut her loose, not now. Jean had tried calling her multiple times, and had left a note on the door at the apartment: *Need to talk to you.* But Christine wasn't biting.

But now, late Thursday morning, here was Dawn coming into the diner. She was with a guy Christine recognized as a cop who usually ate here in the morning. He had her by the elbow. Dawn didn't look well, and he was obviously hovering. Christine had never really known Dawn. She wasn't sure Dawn had any idea who she was. Her involvement with Robbie had been when Christine didn't see much of him; she remembered a time when she'd come across the two of them walking on Water Street, and he'd introduced them. Christine must have been fourteen. A completely different person.

Christine could sense what was going on with those two, a heaviness about the way they carried themselves. On a lot of other days she would have just left them alone. She took their order (club sandwich, scrambled eggs, hash browns, Diet Cokes) and didn't have a sense Dawn recognized her at all. Christine watched them from a distance. They ate, they talked; they were heads-down in some whispery conversation. And then the man got up and headed to the restroom.

Christine approached, as if to clear the dishes. She knew what she was about to do could get her fired. Christine said to her, "Do you remember me?"

Surprisingly, she did.

"You're Tina."

"Christine." Dawn smiled at her correction.

"How are you these days?"

She knew the man would be back soon, so she lowered down and said, "Have you been seeing my Uncle Robbie?"

Dawn's back straightened.

"What are you talking about?"

"His girlfriend thinks he's been seeing you behind her back. You were out of your office, and my uncle has been away almost a week."

Dawn went flush, and then breathed in as if just remembering she needed to, and Christine immediately knew she was getting ready to unload.

"I'm here, as you can see."

"I'm just asking. About you and him."

"Actually, I just got out of the hospital," she said, her voice low and quaky. "I was getting a procedure. If that's any of your business. My friend Bob—my boyfriend, Bob—was there with me the whole time."

"I'm sorry," Christine said, in an involuntary small-child voice.

"Why do I ever try to help any of you out?"

"I don't know what you're talking about."

She appeared to gather herself then.

"I spent a fair amount of time with your uncle, hoping for certain things," she said. "And that didn't work out. Now Bob wants to give me those things, and what happens?"

Bob was coming back to the table now, and Christine could see Dawn had fought off the urge to cry. Bob was looking at Christine warily. He apparently knew something was up.

"What's going on?" he said.

"My eggs are dry," Dawn said. "I want new ones."

"I'm really sorry," Christine said, picking up her plate. "I'll bring some more."

"But I hope you're doing well for yourself," Dawn said, recovering. "I'm told you want to be a nurse. I'm sure someday you'll make a very fine one."

30.

SEATTLE, TO ROBBIE'S SURPRISE, WAS SUNNY. HE'D ONLY ever heard of the rain, but here he was, looking at blue sky. He'd booked a room on a website, at a hotel called Silver Cloud across the street from Safeco, the ballpark. From his ninth-floor window he could see the emerald field, and the press box hung above the backstop. It evoked in him a sudden regret for things he had not ventured in his career. What might it have been like, to break free of the illusion of comfort in a small town? *What if I had actually tried?*

He'd been walking a lot. Up through Pioneer Square and northward along First Avenue, then crossing Alaskan Way to see the water, not the Pacific but at least a body of water touching it. He sat and watched the ferries coming in and out, their squat hindsides churning foam, heading for the nearer islands. And at every moment he was watching faces, looking for Santoro, in what now felt like a futile errand.

He'd had the meeting with Henning. The man looked like every other DEA agent, tall and dark-haired and with the carriage of a guy who might have played some football himself at one time. The faint recognition of such intangibles. They sat in Henning's office, and for a few minutes Henning read over the

211

file he had. Then he said, "So you came all the way out here on a hunch."

"I guess. But I know that Santoro probably got to Oregon."

"And you think he's fishing?"

"He doesn't know much else."

"There are towns up and down the coast that have commercial fishing. Newport, Oregon, Ventura in California, Grays Harbor down south of here. You going to look in all those places?"

"I guess not. But I'm from a small town, and I know it's a lot harder to go unnoticed in small towns like that. I'd guess he's in a city."

"Which would make him much harder for you to find."

"I came out here mostly based on emotion," Robbie said. "The minute the plane touched down, I knew it was kind of a stupid idea. Portland wasn't what I expected. I wandered around the downtown trying to spot his face in the crowd."

Robbie paused, then came to his summary.

"I guess I just need to feel like someone tried. Maybe I needed to see for myself how people can disappear. I'm no detective, but it was a thought. I was going to go to the docks in Portland and show Freddy's photo around. Probably pointless."

Henning seemed to understand that. He relaxed back into his chair.

"So what's your theory? You must have some idea of what you're looking for."

"My theory is that Santoro got off my brother's boat and took off."

"What happened to your brother?"

"Dead, I'd guess. The pants were floating almost to Scotland. They never found the boat."

"That seems proof enough."

"I know. Really, I'm not even sure Santoro ever got on that boat. But to get away . . . for that boat not to come back . . ."

"Would your brother and Santoro have made a deal?"

"What does that mean?"

"I don't know. Santoro conveniently disappeared. I'm just saying anything's possible. Your brother might have had a deal with the guy."

"That's not possible," Robbie said. "If he had, I'd never forgive him. It would be too much of a betrayal."

"If he was ready to disappear, do you think he'd have worried about you forgiving him?" Henning said.

So the trip had become his vacation, purely by default. Again, Robbie was at loose ends, wandering a city he'd instantly come to love, because it harbored the notion he might have been able to led a different life. What would it have felt like, to be a person no one knew? To sit and have a drink and not cross paths with everyone from high school, or church, or the parents' world, so much so that it felt too tightly bound? Or to not be held accountable for your brother's indiscretions?

He thought his town had given him comfort, but right now the comfort was in the anonymity of a city he'd never seen before. He walked until his feet chafed. Back in the hotel, he lay on the bed with the sun through the south-facing window warming him, and room service on the way.

He felt the release of having no connection.

In the morning, his last day here, he walked by the flying-saucer-like football stadium, imagining what it might be like seeing a game in there. He went past Lake Union, and past the big *Seattle Times* building, feeling all unexpected regret, but bittersweetly so. Maybe he could, still. He was forty-four. Maybe it could happen.

The trip had become a requiem for all kinds of misplaced hopes. The year since Quinn disappeared had only raised the

213

scrutiny on Robbie. Here, he was feeling his pressure dropping, a continent separating him from all of them. Back to work Monday, but this small hiatus would inform him.

He still had the picture of Santoro in his pocket. But the hopelessness of such a venture weighted him. It was as if he was simply trying to justify having spent the money. So he went along the shoreline at Lake Union looking for ships, but what he found was mostly houseboats, oddly majestic things. Rocking on light waters, cellarless, unrooted. What an odd way to live. So foreign, though it should have felt familiar. He didn't even know where to find the real docks.

He found a cab that took him to the canal where the fishing companies were. It was a familiar scene, as out his office window. Men sailing outward, and bringing back fish. The same the world over. Nothing special. In the buildings past the docks he showed Santoro's photo to secretaries, security guards, drivers and whatever crew seemed to be around. No, No, three dozen times No.

At one big company, Northwest Processing, he'd walked along the docks looking at a ship called the *Siberian Wanderer*, and he'd found the boss sitting at his desk overlooking the docks, and had noted the man's seeming amusement as he walked up.

"I'm looking for who's in charge," Robbie said.

"That's me, I'm Bernard. What do you need?"

Robbie had taken the photo of Santoro out and held in front of him. "I'm looking for this guy."

"Why, what did he do?" Bernard said, still looking more steadily at Robbie, nearly quizzical.

"Bail jumper," Robbie said.

"And who are you?"

He nearly thought to say he was a cop. Then Robbie said, "I'm just the guy looking for him."

Bernard looked at Robbie closely, then back at the picture.

"So let me be sure I know what you want. You're looking for *this* guy."

"Right."

"Never seen him in my life," Bernard said.

Now Robbie was done with all that. So stupid, thinking he'd get anywhere. He had set out on the theory that even in a big city, when you begin to narrow things down, you can find those small pockets of people who find each other. If you took the entirety of Seattle, and eliminated people with money, people who didn't fish commercially, and people who didn't drink, that made for a much smaller cohort. He was also working on the theory that he was only person who cared anymore. Santoro could as easily have been in Seattle as in Portland, but Robbie was quickly figuring out that he was never going to find him. For hours he had asked, and was given no purchase.

In the soft-blue sky of late afternoon, this was finished. And to finalize the transaction, he took the Scotch-taped photo of Santoro and threw it in a trashcan. Done. Really. Done. It was time to go home and to stop with the nonsense.

He wanted a drink, badly. Along the rows of seafood warehouses, he found a bar where he could stretch out his dollars, a ratty place with a slice of a view of the water and setting sun. Way down the line, he could see more ships, not the little fishing boats like back home, but imposing vessels.

He supposed he liked Seattle because it wasn't raining. He was seeing it at its best. He supposed that the daily nature of existence meant you didn't truly shed the facts of your life no matter where you carried them. It was only an illusion to think you'd outrace what you chose to make yourself into.

But here he was in a bar that had all the dull familiarities. Another fish-town dive. The cheap beer and pool tables, the bottle-blond women of middling age and the drape of cigarette smoke in the air, however the law might have spoken to that on paper. He sat at the corner of the bar and hung his head, a stranger in a strange land.

The place had probably been around forever, tending to generations of people who fished. They were a fraternity, in their work, be it with lines, nets, traps, rakes or bare hands. This could have been Bugtown back home, the same rhythms of too-rough laughter, too-low asides and the swirl of people often in one another's company. He was the odd man here, and dressed like it. He was beginning to understand he was suspect, in here. The comfort he always felt in Jack's Bar, among the lobstermen, was a social construct, he realized. He was, back home, initiated into something not quite his true element. While he would think no one in Jack's would ever feel unwelcome, he was getting a palpable sense of being watched closely now in this place, and he wasn't much liking it.

A glance his way, maybe a question just beyond earshot, maybe a sidebar discussion among the éminences grises down the bar in their beards and plaid work shirts. The bartender, a stout and careful man with fat hands, served him without welcome or hostility. Robbie was already thinking that the bar back at the hotel would have made a wiser choice. Now, diagonally across the well, another hangdog face, aimed his way. A guy with the look of a drinking veteran, nearly leering at him. Robbie wasn't needing trouble. He put his head down again. Then back up, seeing the same guy in full grin, locked in.

Here we go.

And the guy getting up now, and coming at him. A man of indeterminate age (probably young and made old by his habits).

He had a broad face, the color not quite brown, the features not quite Asian, something Robbie deduced as possibly Inuit. And the man was big, expanding like a nova as he came at him.

"And how you doing today?" the big man said. "Doing good?"

"I'm fine," Robbie said flatly.

"Nice to see you."

"Sure, and you, too."

"So I wonder if you can spot me a few bucks."

Robbie, resigned, shrugged. "How much?"

"Like, I don't know, twenty?"

Robbie went for his wallet, carefully, took out a bill and handed it over. He now had very little money left in the wallet.

"I got to go," Robbie said. Another bad idea. Robbie was upwards, and onwards, heading for the door, but now the man was following him out.

"Well, don't get all like that, pal," the big man said from behind.

"No, I'm not," Robbie said, thinking how long it had been since he'd needed to defend himself, physically. Bad idea, this.

"Hey, I didn't mean to upset you."

"You didn't upset me," Robbie said. "I was just heading out anyway."

"I'll pay you back."

"It's okay. You don't even know me."

"I don't know you?" the stranger said, with a rasp that spoke of salt air and many packs of Marlboros.

"Not possible. I'm just visiting for a couple of days."

The stranger came around him, blocking him. Then he bent over, dropping down low, crouched like an umpire following the curveball into the mitt, to look upwards at Robbie's hung-down face.

"Hmph," he said.

"What?"

"You're right," he said. "I don't know you after all. I apologize."

He held the twenty-dollar bill back for Robbie to take.

"Just keep it," Robbie said. "It's really not a problem."

"Don't get upset, man."

"Not upset," Robbie said.

"But the voice, or something."

"What?"

"The way you are."

"What about it?"

"No, sorry, I don't know you after all," the big man said. "About six months ago, worked on a processer ship with a guy. I thought you were that guy. I mean, you could almost be his damned brother . . ."

PART FIVE

31.

ROBBIE SEES THE SHIP FIRST AS A BLACK SHARD ON THE hard glint of far waters. He follows its approach against the low afternoon sun. *There it is. Finally.* He's aware of his stomach tightening, the queasy sensation that someone knows he's here, and why he's here. The ship sounds from great distance; the horn's lowing cry carries and then feels as if it's vaulting far over his head. A mournful call homeward. The slowness of the dance, of a ship gliding toward its moorings, is excruciating; even now he feels the urge to walk back to his rental car and just forget all that's happened.

He'd found Quinn out. From the big Inuit in that bar, he learned that the man for whom he had mistaken Robbie had been working on the *Siberian Wanderer* months before that. Robbie then found his way back to the skeptical man at the desk, Bernard, who seemed far from surprised at his return.

"I'm his brother," Robbie had said, to no argument. "This is a family matter."

Bernard had relented only grudgingly, acknowledging little but finally telling him that he'd be interested in the return of the *Arctic Star*. It was going to be at sea another month, Bernard said. He'd given Robbie what he needed from long angles.

"Do you know a guy named Ken Doyle?" Bernard asked.

"Ken Doyle? Seriously? He's never been very imaginative," Robbie had said.

Robbie has now traced his way back, his second trip across the country, to see this through. Back home, things were not good. For the first time in all these years, he was feeling the pressure of the workplace. Two vacations in a month now, during the fall sports season no less. All the football games to cover left to part-timers. Robbie pointed out to his managing editor, Chip, that he hadn't had a true vacation in years. But given the slack of summer he always had, when he's stayed on the payroll with little to keep him busy, Chip has been telling him he's playing it both ways.

"Is it a woman?" Chip said. "Because that's not a good enough reason."

Robbie denied nothing, but this time he didn't say where he was headed. When he told Christine he'd be away for a few days, and maybe as long as a week, she had soured even more resolutely.

"I'm not your father," he had said once again, pointing his finger at her the way a father would.

What a situation! With a few drunken words from Gina, Robbie's act of avuncular charity now looked like cold guilt. Of course he'd never laid a hand on Gina. Never had an inkling to. But Christine was not being assuaged. With the news he was taking a second "vacation" within a month's time, she flared again.

"Tell me what's going on."

"You really don't need to know."

"Where are you going?"

"A place where cops won't be at my hotel room two hours after I get there, is where the hell I'm going."

"Is he alive?"

"No."

"Are you lying to me?"

"No."

So, there it was, the lie. Maybe. Robbie had no idea what he was going to do when the *Arctic Star* put in, or whether Ken Doyle would really be Quinn, or just Ken Doyle. He'd left Seattle only with the notion that his brother might possibly be alive, and might possibly be at sea on that processing ship. The Inuit had told him a little, and in a way that obliquely reinforced his theory. Even in a large city, when you drilled down to a particular kind of life, the numbers got small enough for chance encounters. The momentary charge he'd gotten when his search proved out had been short-lived. He only wanted to see if his brother had survived. Whether he wanted to see him ever again after that was something he'd figure out as they went along.

As his flight had descended toward the runway at Sea-Tac with the western sky fading red, he looked northward at the city, shimmering in its light, roads like capillaries feeding a vast and pulsating body; down below him, a lone car on a dark road crept along, the person within probably lost in his own thoughts.

Now, here on the dock, on the last of his savings and vacation time, this is it. The ship moves toward him now, its hull the affectless black-and-white of a working vessel. The Olympic Mountains backdrop the horizon, no snowcaps yet. Robbie is feeling the chill air of a different life, but this time not his. He wonders which version of Quinn he's looking for.

When he spots his brother, up at the rail, the Inuit's confusion is now understood. Quinn is considerably thinner, the beard is gone, the haircut high and tight. Robbie holds his hand up, the first test, and Quinn's hand rises, grudgingly, to signal back. They really could be twins now, with Quinn so changed.

On the highway an hour later, the day edging toward dark, Quinn sleeps in his seat, slumped against the window. Robbie knows he's worked hard on that ship, but this nearly seems a final act of avoidance. Almost as soon as they'd gotten into the rental car, Quinn had closed his eyes, evasive once again. Robbie had started telling him about what he had forged with Christine; Quinn had registered what looked like muted surprise, but as Robbie told him about it he'd escaped into sleep.

That first moment at the bottom of the gangway they had shaken hands, awkwardly as pure strangers. Quinn's feet touched land, with no hugs or tears. Robbie waited as Quinn went up to the office for his pay, watching the edges of the building for some sneak-out route. Quinn came out an hour later, as Robbie meanwhile obsessed about being caught. Caught exactly for what, he didn't know. He needed to hear what happened, and he wasn't going to do so until they were checked into a motel with some beer in front of them, and some time.

Quinn grudgingly nodded when Robbie said this. Robbie supposes that more so than the desire for fraternal connection, Quinn's acquiescence may rest only upon Robbie's ability to turn him in. Quinn rides shotgun in the rental car like a captive. Even as their elbows nearly touch in that tiny Hyundai Accent, they remain a continent apart. Quinn's awakened only at the stop they've made coming out of the city, at a highway shopping center down off Interstate 5. Robbie has no destination other than an isolated motel from which Quinn can't fashion an easy escape.

"We need to get some beer," Robbie says as he takes the exit ramp.

"I don't really drink," Quinn says.

"Well, then I hope you don't mind if I do."

He pulls into a Walmart, because in Washington they sold booze like that, another indisputable sign of better things in better places. Inside, he grabs two six-packs and two bottles of Washington State wine, perhaps anticipating the collapse of Quinn's will, and of his will not to speak, or maybe the collapse of his own. He goes up the aisles grabbing packaged underwear and T-shirts and socks and a couple of sweat shirts, guessing that Quinn's size is basically his own. Tooth brush, toothpaste, deodorant, shampoo. Quinn has come off the boat with a bag of dirty clothes. In the car, he frankly stank.

When he comes back out to the parking lot, he's half-surprised Quinn is still in the car, and half-wishing he weren't.

As they pull out onto a road called Federal Way, Robbie thinks only of prisons, maybe now for both of them. He doesn't know exactly what he's done now, and what statutes apply. The rain has begun. Now, Quinn sleeps to the metronome of the wipers. He looks remarkably younger with the weight off, and with a faintly healthy flush of the skin. He's nearly that long-ago kid brother again, freckled, waiting to run onto a field or skate onto a sheet of ice. Something has happened in this year.

Robbie thinks, *Is this a rescue or an apprehension?*

Out of the shower with the steam haloing behind him, Quinn is wrapped in a white towel. He's nearly as pale, from the months under decks. He's spent the first sixteen hours in this cloverleaf motel sleeping, as Robbie has drank and fought the urge to keep looking at his watch, worried about his flight back out of Seattle. But now they both know what's going on.

Quinn sits on the end of the bed, rubbing his hair with a facecloth.

"You want to eat in a bit?" Robbie says.

"That's fine."

"You need anything to drink?"

"I'm good."

The television is on, some early-season basketball game on a Saturday afternoon, with the sound down. Washington and Cal. Neither of them really ever liked basketball, but it's what's on.

"You need to tell me what happened," Robbie says.

Quinn watches intently as Cal moves the basketball around the perimeter.

"I need to know," Robbie says.

Quinn sits silent for a bit, and on the television the ball goes out of bounds.

"I don't have any idea," he finally says.

Robbie leans forward.

"What is that supposed to mean?"

"It means I don't remember."

"You have got to be shitting me."

Quinn says nothing.

"Come on, it's me. Just tell me what happened."

Quinn rises and goes back to the bathroom. He tears open a package of clean underwear, pulls out a pair of white boxers, and slips them on.

"The cops aren't going to want to hear 'I don't remember,'" Robbie says.

"Did you call the cops?"

"No."

"Then why did you say that?"

"To make a point."

Quinn pulls on a clean T-shirt from a package. He pulls on his jeans then comes back and sits on the bed.

"So why are you here?" Quinn says.

"To make sure you're okay."

"You can see I am. I'm fine."

"They declared you dead. I spent months on your *paperwork*. If you don't remember, why did you change your name?"

"I don't know."

"Jesus Christ, Quinn, enough with the nonsense."

"Why are you here?" Quinn says, his voice even.

"Do you have any idea how much bullshit you left behind?"

Quinn keeps watching as a Washington player drives for the basket, then sees his layup spin off the rim.

"Do you have any idea," Robbie said, his voice rising, "how I've taken on your daughter and tried to help her out?"

Quinn doesn't turn his head.

"My daughter," he says.

"She is your daughter."

"How do you know that? You weren't there, were you?"

"She is legally your daughter," Robbie says. "Your name is on the birth certificate."

"My name was already on the birth certificate when I got back from out there. It was a four-day run, and then I got back and I'd been marked down as the father."

"You named your boat after her."

"I was trying to lay claim, despite all evidence. Which was just kind of stupid, wasn't it?"

Quinn is palpably exhausted, even after all the sleep.

"I've given everything I can to her," he says.

"You just got paid."

"I need that just to keep living. That's why I just spent two months working sixteen-hour shifts, sportswriter."

"You need to tell me what happened," Robbie says.

"I don't remember," Quinn says again, bloodlessly.

"You're so full of shit, Quinn. I don't believe that for a second."

Robbie can feel his face heating up while Quinn remains maddeningly stoic. There's too much in the space between then and now, an entire continent's worth of unanswered questions.

32.

Christine is back to avoiding Gina now, completely. Gina has messed her head up for the last time. But Christine also can't stay where she has been. Every time she's come into Robbie's apartment, dark and quiet, she thinks of him off on his secretive travels again. Some scheme. Some pack of lies. Something she is again excluded from. So she just has to go, somewhere.

And with nearly no choices. The girls she shared the apartment with before are still there, but they haven't spoken since Christine moved out. Not enemies, but no longer friends, and they've already gotten someone to take her closet-scale space. Getting her own place isn't something she can afford, not while she's paying for school. And without school, she's back to waitressing the rest of her life.

Then there's Jean. Christine has felt a connection with her, and she needs a place to think things through. When Christine calls her, it's a cold voice at the other end.

"How are you?" Jean says, that voice so flat it sounds like someone she barely knows. She has broken off contact with Robbie, who has seemed mystified. Christine hasn't mentioned their conversation. She's instead waited for Robbie to reach out to Jean to mend things, but Robbie never has. He seemed to go silent after his return from Oregon, and then one day he was packing to leave again.

"Robbie's gone off on another vacation," Christine says.

"With *her*?" Jean says.

"I don't think so, about that. I think he's alone."

"She went with him the last time, didn't she?"

"I think I need to talk to you about that."

"But it's really none of my business, though, is it? Where he goes and with whom?"

"I need a place to stay."

"What about your mother?"

"Are you serious?"

"Christine, what exactly are you suggesting? That you stay here?"

"I was hoping. Maybe just for a little bit. I mean, we're friends, right?"

"You are the niece of a man I thought was a friend," Jean says.

"Oh." Christine shouldn't be surprised, but she is. "So that's it?"

"Sorry, Christine. I have my daughter to take care of. I can't be trying to take on your family, too. Maybe you should stay with Robbie and just try to straighten things out."

"Gina was saying something about how he was my real father. Has he ever talked to you about that?"

"No," Jean says, so low Christine can barely hear her.

Christine is waiting for something else, but it isn't there.

"I have to go now," Jeans says.

So that's it. All exits sealed.

Where is Robbie? It's making her crazy that something is going on and she has no idea how she fits into it.

So she calls Nick.

"I need a ride," she says.

Nick meets her down by the water, his old Camry coughing smoke and his hat pulled down low over his eyebrows. She gets in and he says, "I got this car for two hundred. I'll be able to sell it for a thousand, once I fix it up."

She stares at him.

"Okay, where to?" he says.

"That's the problem."

"I thought you lived with your uncle."

"I don't want to anymore."

"Then go back with your mother, maybe?"

"I don't want to do that, either."

Nick seems slow taking the hint.

"Oh. Yeah, you can stay with me," he says. "My mother doesn't care."

"Do you have a room?"

"I have my room."

"Okay, then, just for a while," she says.

"Yeah, whatever," Nick says.

The next morning, her phone begins buzzing on the nightstand, at exactly eight o'clock. She groggily picks up. It's Jean. She's had time to think about things, she says. She definitely does want Christine to think of her as a friend.

"If you need to stay here a while, I want you to," Jean says. "I made the mistake of taking some frustrations out on you that I need to address with someone else."

Of course she's in the bed, and Nick is asleep next to her. His mother is in the kitchen, making breakfast with her boyfriend, who she's apparently just recently met.

"Where are you now?" Jean says.

"At my friend Nick's."

"I'll come and get you."

"I have a shift at the restaurant. I finish at four."

"I'll come get you then."

Nick is waking up and he rolls over. His hand slides under the blanket and onto her thigh.

"I have to go to work," she says.

Buddy has that look today, the cross between anger and sorrow that signals that her career as a waitress continued to be in danger. She can admit she is, and has been, mightily distracted. She can admit as well that she has been *emotional.* Buddy doesn't much go for emotional. He just wants food-serving robots. The place is busy, Sunday morning after church, and Christine has been constantly delivering the orders to the wrong tables. And after her night with Nick, her lack of sleep is catching up with her. She wishes Jean had called her back sooner. Having sex with Nick really wasn't such a great idea, although in the moment she felt something, at least the appreciation of being taken in. Now it's all going to be complicated, especially when she goes there to get her stuff.

Jean is being a friend, genuinely. Christine wants to be hers. Her urge to get back at Robbie was like something on fire. She'd look to the ocean, east, and think of her dead father. She'd look at land, to the west, and wonder if he'd simply fooled everyone.

Dawn and the boyfriend come in for late breakfast. Christine can see Dawn glancing her way, but probably more hoping to avoid her. Christine can tell. But she's seated at one of Christine's tables, and there's nothing either of them can do. Dawn smiles weakly, her face still pale, and asks Christine how she is. The cop is keeping a wary eye on the whole situation from behind his laminated menu.

Christine takes their orders, moves on, and keeps thinking about saying something. She knows, in fact, she isn't going to be able to stop herself. She's already talked half the night, and she guesses Nick is still asleep at this very moment, recovering from Christine's epic info dump. She knows she sounded unforgivably harsh about her family. She might have said she hated them all. Nick, floating in the aftermath of sex, possibly his first time, just lay there gaping. They'd fumbled through every phase of it. He might have had skills as a mechanic, but . . . And Christine finds herself wondering then about her own abilities to be a nurse, to be sufficiently clinical about these physical things.

"I'd teach those two a lesson, if I could," Nick said in the dark, her presumed white knight. "I should kick both their asses," he said, although if he meant it she would have warned him off it lest he catch the lesser end of things.

Dawn and her cop boyfriend keep eyeing Christine the whole time. It isn't until Christine brings the check to them that Dawn says, "And how's Uncle Robbie?"

It's clearly an attempt at quickly-dispensed-with small talk, but.

"Robbie is out aiding and abetting his criminal brother," Christine says. Their faces are not of people trading small talk now, more a pair of gut-punched people unsure of how to proceed.

"You actually think your father is alive?" Dawn says.

"Why is my uncle off on another vacation? It's, like, two in five weeks."

"So isn't your uncle just trying to get some time to himself?" Dawn says. "Without having to explain it?"

"They were always pulling stuff, those two."

"Doesn't he have a right to grieve in his own way?"

Christine can see Buddy looking at her from the grill.

"After what he did to you," she says, "I'm surprised you'd say that."

Her boyfriend straightens.

232

"Why, what did he do to you?" he says to Dawn.

"Nothing."

"Was he abusive or something?"

"No, never," Dawn said. "She means things just didn't work out."

The cop is breathing hard through his nose, his eyebrows subtly twitching as his brain fires up.

"So why do you think your father's alive?" he says to Christine.

But Christine is frozen. Just staring. Then she hears Buddy, bellowing.

"Tina!" he shouts. "Pick up!"

33.

THE DRIVE BACK TOWARD SEATTLE IS EVEN QUIETER than the drive out. His flight goes in two hours. A fine rain has begun, a hanging mist that speaks only of gloom. Robbie is thinking now that he was wrong, he'd hate living out here. The hiss of the tires underneath has again rocked Quinn into a slumping doze against the car door. This seems a terminal journey. Robbie has a plane to catch.

Through it all, Quinn has remained intractable, claiming again and again to remember nothing. Robbie has reminded him of his daughter, and of Robbie's efforts to help her. The guilt seems not to have taken. In the motel room, with the sound of the traffic close from the interstate, Quinn had ruminated on this, and finally said. "I sent her money. She shouldn't need your help."

"You sent her money?" Robbie said. "When?"

"A while back. Four or five months ago."

"So how come she never said anything about that?"

"I sent it, is all I know."

"And she knew it was from you?"

"Probably not."

"Why didn't she tell me, then?"

"Maybe she didn't need to tell anybody, including you."

"You're so full of shit."

"Whatever," Quinn says, quietly.

"She would have figured out you were alive."

"Maybe not. I don't know."

It has become clear that his brother will stay as he is, a man gone underground. In Robbie's existence, one of income taxes and a 401(k) and child support and medical co-pays, it seems utterly implausible Quinn can last long this way.

"Shouldn't I take you somewhere?" Robbie says. "The fact I found you means they can find you."

"I'm fine. I'll figure it out. I have enough money to last for a while."

So, they make their way back. They'll go straight to the airport, where Robbie can drop the car at the rental place, where he and Quinn can ride the shuttle to the main terminal, to part, Robbie to his flight and Quinn for a bus back into the city. Nothing, for all Robbie's travel and expense, has truly been solved.

And now Robbie has to carry the secret, one that bears no benefit to him. He was better off not knowing, even as he was burning to know. But every time from here on out that he's asked and denies it, he's crossed over. He's aiding and abetting something, though he's not sure what. He came to find Santoro, who is out there somewhere as well, but now he's an accomplice in his brother's prevarications.

Robbie tries to imagine that there is some explainable truth to all this. He desperately wants to buy the possibility Quinn really doesn't remember. Indeed, his brother is a different man altogether. He seems done with his own blood, and it feels too calculated. That hardly is sitting well with Robbie. He must assume Quinn made those decisions when he and Santoro played out their scheme. There was Santoro's pathetic-seeming approach that night at the bar, begging for work, the setting up of the ruse. What an act those two put on! They must have choreographed that long before; Robbie was just set up as the gullible audience, left behind to relate to the skeptics what he had witnessed. In retrospect, they brought it in a bit thick. Now, his anger waxing, Robbie listens to Quinn's soft snoring and tries to find his way back to where they had begun their parting, in all those nearly invisible fractions.

It had been after Robbie's college graduation, which Quinn declined to attend, that the connection as brothers became more random. Robbie was new on *The Record*, not yet covering the main sports. He was relegated that summer to softball leagues and ladies'-club tennis. He had the entry-level ignominy of running down Little League summaries. Robbie had been told that a good start for a first-year sportswriter was to find a way of making accounts of such prosaic games latently dramatic. So he did. They put him on a noon-to-nine shift that suited him perfectly, and rarely ended at nine. Around eleven, the paper put finally to bed, the older men from the copy desk usually wandered down to Water Street after work, for their nightcaps. Robbie went along with them.

Likewise, Quinn was now of a different tribe. The door of Jack's Bar would swing open and in they'd come, shabby and unshaven, the lobstermen. They seemed not so much to enter a place as to effect an occupation; the copy editors would groan and hasten to finish their drinks. Robbie would see Quinn among them, and could usually guess which drugs were in play. Quinn was always grinning then, despite his difficult straits. Quinn, across the bar, seemed wired, unable to stop moving.

When Quinn saw him, in the corner with the older men from *The Record*, it was with a grin and the sorry shake of a head. Robbie supposed the tribal imperatives of lobstermen included a deep disregard for sedentary occupations, jobs in which risk was only in the airiest abstract. He supposed the boatmen had to see all those around them as fools, as those around them saw them as fools, men taking headlong risks for big payoffs that maybe never quite materialized.

The lobstermen would sit along the bar, the pitchers of beer and accompanying shots cycling through, sheaves of greasy dollar bills thrown too easily down. Robbie was never sure if Quinn would wander his way. On a particular night, he did so, leering, and high. The copy-desk men, in button-down shirts and loosened neckties, blinked behind their glasses and looked away. They knew who he was. They'd moved the stories of his now-past glories on football fields and hockey rinks and baseball diamonds; they knew, too, his ongoing manifest, the teenaged father who overstepped and made a sad life for himself.

"How's life in the cubicle?" Quinn said that night, on the borderline of hostile. Dad had put him out of the house by then, and Gina awaited his return in another. He was here with his beer mug in hand, as they all were, in this small twilight between responsibilities.

"We just have desks," Robbie said. "No cubicles."

"You look like you're already softening up. You got any muscle left at all?"

It was true that Quinn had not abandoned the physical life. Working on the boats was a continuation of his bodily skills, the deft handwork and the gross shows of strength, whereas Robbie had entered an extended malaise after he had failed to make the college hockey team. Robbie had kept on with sports this way, the sharpened observer, yet fallow of strength. This was just writing, eternally on the sidelines. Who, in the end, had been truer to the sporting life?

"I can't believe you couldn't make that college team," Quinn said, once again.

"Can you let it go on that? It had nothing to do with you."

"It's just embarrassing to be your brother."

"Why aren't you home with your family?" Robbie said.

"Home? Go back and listen to Gina, with all the goddamned yapping?"

"Yeah, okay, I get it."

"But I made my own bed, right? Isn't that what you're thinking?"

"You said it, brother, not me."

Quinn, standing above him, put his hands on Robbie's shoulders and shoved him. Robbie was instantly on the floor, sprawled in his chinos and collared shirt and cheap tie, as the copy editors pushed off from the table, in full retreat.

"Is this how you live now?" Robbie said from the floor. "I'm not going to fight you. I didn't do anything to you."

Quinn may have been drunker than Robbie thought.

"No, you didn't do a thing."

"So don't come after me, then. Get your own shit straightened out."

"It is straightened out. I work, and I support a wife and baby, and I don't ask anybody for anything."

"Well, congratulations on that," Robbie said.

"He couldn't even make the *Stonehill* hockey team," Quinn said, loudly and generally.

Quinn looked as if he might really swing at Robbie, but then didn't. He turned, and walked back toward his crowd, as Robbie stayed with his. It would be a long time before he saw him again. At first, Robbie wanted to hope Quinn was drinking less; that was obliquely true in that the drinking had given way to the real goods. That was the start of a long silence between them.

Maybe a year later, coming out of a convenience store with a bottle of soda, Robbie would see Quinn across the parking lot, getting into a rust-bottomed pickup truck. He'd be huge by then, the work on the ocean having given him bulk, where the work of the keyboard had taken all of Robbie's away.

Robbie thinks of all that now, as he follows the signs to Sea-Tac Airport. Quinn is awake, groggy, staring ahead, and summoning no words.

"Time to part, I guess," Robbie says.

"Yeah."

"Can I ask you one question?"

"You can try."

"Why were you always so pissed at me for not making the hockey team in college?"

Quinn is looking off at the horizon.

"Because I was just as good as you were," he says. "So if you'd made it, I know I could have. I was never going to get the chance for real."

"Putting your expectations on other people seems a little unfair."

"I know that now," Quinn says.

The car-rental place at the airport is quiet. Robbie drops the keys, but it takes the woman at the counter what seems an inordinate time to process it. She steps into the back office, as they wait, Robbie thinks only of settling into the seat on the plane and having a drink. This delay is squeezing the rest down into a rush; he's hoped to take one more stab at getting Quinn to talk, and it won't be standing at a car-rental counter. The nature of modern life, he thinks; the expectation of delay and frustration. He should be used to it by now. Robbie breathes evenly, trying to stay relaxed.

The woman returns, apologetic. Flush, she hands him his papers. Outside, he and Quinn board the shuttle, both carrying their gear. They're the only passengers. Two travelers, as always on vastly different trajectories. Quinn rose early today and did all his sea laundry in the hotel basement coin-ops, flattening and folding and organizing; Robbie has not a clue if he'll really stay in Seattle for any more than today.

"So what do you do for an ID?" Robbie had asked back at the hotel, and Quinn had grunted.

"You go to any college bar and ask any kid where to find the guy who makes the fakes. Or you work on a ship with a bunch of illegals who all have more-convincing licenses than you do, and Social Security numbers and three credit cards. Turns out it's really not that hard."

They come around a bend on the service road and he can see the tail fins of the jets, lined down the tarmac like a school of sharks. Robbie will be in his own bed by one in the morning, and at work by noon tomorrow. Back, finally, to the familiar routines. Back to the life he's more or less lived since he was twenty-two. Sarah is coming this weekend to stay. Jean and Christine, far less likely. He'll tell his daughter that family is the most important thing, even as he only sees her alternate weekends, even as she'll ask what happened to her cousin.

The shuttle comes to the curb and the door opens. They step out and onto the sidewalk, not much time left. Robbie turns to face his brother, who has in this missing year come to look so much more like him.

"Am I going to hear anything from you again?" Robbie says.

"I don't know," Quinn says. "Probably not."

"Then I wish you luck."

Quinn shrugs.

"I hope you get to where you want to be," Robbie says.

"Me, too," Quinn says, so clipped it's obvious this is not, for him, a talking moment.

Robbie extends his hand, and Quinn shakes it. That's it. He turns and rolls his suitcase through the sliding doors, moving into the high-vaulted terminal that rises in glass and steel like a greenhouse.

He can't not look back, he thinks, but his brother is already moving away from him. Quinn's already gone; close up he has seen that. Robbie turns around and looks anyway, as if answering an unbearable itch. And he can see out on the sidewalk that Quinn is stopped, and that he's being gently surrounded. Men in dark suits, quietly talking to him as they close the circle, their hands out to calm him, gentling him. Quinn submits as quickly, no scene to be made, as Robbie pivots back toward it all. A hand is at Quinn's forearm, swinging it around his back as the hand-cuffs come out. Plucked and banded, a day's catch now. A black car, two men, and then the uniformed police step forward. The scene is forming, and it is one of flat apprehension. It's so subtle in its choreography that it's as if only Robbie can see it, as people on their way to places move past.

Robbie is turned and moving back that way now, upstream against the flow of travelers coming at him. He can see they have Quinn in hand, an arm across his shoulders in nearly brotherly regard. Robbie bangs into one text-messaging woman, then is blocked by a man sliding by to his right. He looks up again and he's lost the scene. Out through the doors and past the waves of people, the sidewalk is clear, the black car now gone, his brother and his brother's captors melted that fast into the gray day.

PART SIX

34.

HE'S REFUSING TO SEE ANYONE. WORD FILTERS OUT from the Adult Correctional Institute that Quinn Boyle has declined all visitors.

He has waived the extradition hearing in Washington State and has arrived back quickly, as if on a tailwind behind Robbie's own flight. He's done his preliminary court appearance here so quickly, Robbie first heard about after it was over. Quinn was bunking in yet another jail cell by dusk.

At the airport, Robbie had first hesitated about getting on his flight. He'd had just long enough to change his mind three times over. But he had no real money left. He couldn't afford another night in a hotel or a new flight. So he decided he'd just have to find out from home what had happened. He got on the plane, ordered his drink when they got to cruising altitude, and immediately began to steep himself in his own guilt and second-guessing for the next six hours. How had they known Quinn was there, and who exactly were they? In Chicago, switching flights, he'd called the Seattle police. They said they didn't know anything about it. When he got off his plane in Providence, he turned his phone back on and had a voice mail from the same Seattle cop, saying the pinch had been by federal marshals.

The charge is failure to pay child support, now turned over to a local warrant. Of all things. Quinn has been assigned a public defender, a young woman named Alyssa who seems endlessly nervous. When Robbie called her, she told him there was only so much she could say, given attorney-client privilege. She said that while child support was a serious matter, Quinn also has had visitors from the DEA, the state attorney general's office, the state police, and the Coast Guard, indicating matters that stretch beyond simple nonpayment of maintenance.

"And what did he tell them?" Robbie says over the phone.

"That he doesn't remember anything," Alyssa says.

"He actually said that?"

"What does that mean? Do you think he's faking?"

"I really have no idea."

Alyssa is audibly souring on other end of the line. "You know, it's actually not uncommon when people are in a traumatic event to not remember. I have an uncle who had a bad car accident years ago. He couldn't remember anything after he left the house that morning."

"My brother got all the way to Seattle."

"I understand that. My uncle remembered everything before the accident, and everything from the second day after."

"I'd like to believe my brother the way you do," Robbie says. "It's just that I know him better."

"Lucky he's got me defending him, then."

"So what's next?" Robbie says.

"Your brother probably has to spend some time in jail, and then once he's out, he needs to get up to date on his back child support. The court will set a monthly payment to be garnished from his future wages."

"That's it?"

"That's it, at least until any other indictments start coming down."

"He doesn't think it was me who turned him in, does he?"

"There's one of the things I'm not allowed to talk about."

"That doesn't sound reassuring."

Alyssa pauses, and then says, "How did you know to go to Seattle?"

"I didn't, exactly. I went to Oregon first."

"Based on what?"

"Based on a tip."

"From . . . ?"

"A former girlfriend."

"Is she a cop?"

"Her boyfriend is."

"Hmm, that sounds complicated."

"It does," Robbie says. "Maybe more than I thought."

Back in the office, Robbie can feel the new scrutiny. The story of Quinn's extradition has already been in *The Record*. The obvious question in all of it is where Freddy Santoro is. People who don't normally concern themselves with low-rent drug dealers now can't help but be outraged by the notion that Freddy has gotten away. In the Comments section below the website story on Quinn's arrest, Robbie also finds himself up for public consumption.

—*Where does the Robbie Boyle fit into all this? He was obviously helping his brother, so he must have helped Santoro.*

—*The brother is obviously in on it!*

—*Arrest the brother and waterboard him a little. Maybe he'll tell you where that POS Santoro went.*

—*The brother is a rat! He led the cops right out there. Glad I don't have a family like that!*

And under that last one, sixteen "likes."

The Comments section is a cesspool of cheap shots, ill-formed theories, and off-the-meds rants. He's always known that. But it is nonetheless a fascination and a horror to see himself held out for judgment, to read about himself as if he's on display, to wonder which of these notions is becoming embedded in the collective view. He also knows that all this kind of bile has always been said—over coffee at diners, at kitchen tables, in the office break room. But seeing it published, and by his own colleagues, is nauseating. He keeps waiting for someone at work to delete the comments. No one does.

On this Friday morning, he can feel the circling. He's been covering some volleyball the last few nights, and dutifully written his game accounts, trying to find his way back to the routines he's lived by. Now, his desk phone rings, and he answers.

"Robbie." It's unmistakably Chip, his managing editor. He looks toward Chip's fishbowl office, no more than thirty feet away. Chip is on the phone, looking at him.

"Chip."

"I need to talk to you about something. Can you come in?"

Robbie hangs up and walks over. Chip looks ashen, and that's not good.

"Is everything okay?"

"Robbie, this thing. This fucking thing with your brother."

"Yes. It's my brother."

"But you were involved."

"I wasn't involved at all. What are you talking about?"

"You took two trips out there, and then they caught him. With you right there, they caught him."

"My brother is getting prosecuted for back child support. What does that have to do with me? I've been supporting his daughter for the last year, out of my own pocket."

"You know what we're talking about here. I mean, come on."

Robbie can see he's heading somewhere with all this, so he goes silent.

"I'm putting you on a leave of absence," Chip says.

"What? For how long?"

"Until this shit gets squared away."

"With pay, you mean."

"Robbie, this paper is too small to give out paid leaves."

"I'll get a lawyer."

"Go ahead," Chip says, tiredly. "We can make the case it's on the citizenship requirement in your contract."

"Chip, why are you screwing me over?"

"I'm doing no such thing. You did it to yourself. You have no credibility now. People don't want you around their kids. They don't want you at the schools. They see the connection with Santoro."

"Unbelievable . . ."

"Look, you have a few vacation days and some sick time left. Take it. But you know what I'd suggest?"

"What?"

"Start looking for a new job as fast as you can. Somewhere away from here, where none of this stuff is blowing in the wind. I can write you a good recommendation. You've done a good job here."

"A job at a newspaper? These days? Everybody's laying off, not hiring."

"Well, a job," Chip says. "I don't have any idea what kind."

"Then how am I supposed to know?" Robbie says.

At his apartment, the quiet is unsettling in a way he'd not noticed before Christine's arrival. He's supposed to pick up Sarah at nine in the morning. Saturday already. Robbie's not remotely ready for that. Jean is AWOL, and Christine is gone, although neither is of any surprise. He expects he'd find Christine at Gina's, but he's not about to go looking. He could go to Jean and try to explain, but she's already read about his Seattle "vacation" in *The Record*.

So he goes to the living room and lies on the couch and stares at the popcorn-plaster ceiling of his sad existence. He'd feel truly sorry for himself if not for his brother sitting in a prison once again. And the person Robbie truly seethes about is Santoro, gotten away as they all are left to clean up the mess.

He takes his cell phone out of his pocket and calls Jean's number. He lets it ring on and when he's sure she won't answer, he hears her voice.

"We should talk about what's going on," Robbie says.

"I'm not sure that's a great idea. All this with you and your brother is pretty upsetting."

"Do you mean to you or to me?"

Silence.

"I had no idea I'd find him. I thought I was looking for Santoro."

"Why were you even looking for Santoro? And how did you know where to look?"

"I got a tip."

"Who gave it to you?"

"I really can't say."

"And there's the problem right there. You're telling a story that is very hard to believe."

"So what do you believe?"

"I don't know what to think."

"You sound as if you don't trust me."

Silence.

"I have no idea where Christine is," Robbie says. "Have you seen her?"

"No."

"If you see her, will you let me know?"

"Yes."

"That's it, then?"

"Yeah, I guess that's about it," Jean says.

35.

THIS TIME CHRISTINE IS ACTUALLY WORRIED. HER father is in prison miles from here, but suddenly that's become the second-most-upsetting situation in her life. She's three days into missing her period, in the anxious negative time where the clock counts upwards instead of down. Plus a day, plus two, plus three . . . She imagines all kinds of things, and had all kinds of odd sensations. Is it morning sickness, or her own overactive imagination? She even thinks she feels a kick, down there. Physically impossible, but somehow very real. Maybe just the usual unnoticed rumblings in her gut, suddenly under close watch. She finds she keeps talking to herself. *Why are you so stupid? Why did you do that?* The hookup with Jared should have been enough to make her more careful. And she avoids Jean as if she has a scent on herself, some pregnancy-related hormonal air. But avoiding Jean's detection is a distancing that's hard to make happen while living in her home for free. Christine first swore to herself she'd keep it a secret, even when she knew she couldn't. When she calls Nick, his voice sounds as if it is he who feels snagged in a trap, when in clear fact it is she caught in his.

"So what are you going to do?" he says, the voice now distant and guarded and flat, like a bystander's. There is no *we* to be found.

"I don't know. What do you think I should do?"

They are circling around whatever philosophies they might have thought they held, this moment when the lifelong drone they've heard at church, or in school, or on ABC Family, are put to an actual test in three dimensions. The Right Thing. You can say you know what you'll do, until you have to do it. She thinks now of choices her parents could have made, and of her sister and then Christine herself fading from existence.

"Do you have any money?" she says.

"Like how much?" Nick says, far more suspicious now.

"How would I know how much? Like, hundreds of dollars."

"Where would I get money like that?"

"I'm just asking. Maybe sell your car?"

"Then I'd have no life, without a car. You have a job. You don't have any money put away?"

"You're acting like this has nothing to do with you."

"It doesn't. You walked out on me, remember? What do I have to do with you anymore?"

"I'm staying with a friend. A woman friend, who had no part in getting me pregnant. I stayed with you, but we weren't *living together.*"

"I thought that's what we were doing."

"You just wanted the sex."

"I wanted more than that. I stuck up for you! I did things for you!"

"What did you ever do to stick up for me?"

"Like getting your father back here, and paying for what he did to you."

"You? How did you do that?"

"I called the State Police. My cousin Doug is a Statie. I told him about your uncle going out to have his secret meeting with your father. You could have thanked me for that."

"How could I thank you if I didn't even know until now?"

"How could I tell you if I woke up and you were gone?"

Silence.

"Nick?" she says.

"I'm listening."

"Don't tell anyone about this."

"About what part?"

"About any of it."

"I won't," he says, unconvincingly.

Christine hasn't thought about her father much at all, a mighty accomplishment. She struggles to hold it off, as if a weight that could crush her if she lets it. The anger and sorrow would flatten her, surely. But it is a time of reckoning, nonetheless; she knows she's in transition, somewhere, and somehow.

In the afternoon she walks to her mother's apartment building and sits on the front steps waiting for Gina, hoping she might come home before she heads out drinking. She needs to know things. Somehow, she needs some kind of connection that she cannot readily explain. She still has her key, but it isn't her home anymore. Sitting, Christine has time to wonder, about her parents, when they were younger than she is now, having that conversation she's just had with Nick. Why did they choose the way they did? She doesn't sense any morality or responsibility in either of them. Were they forced, in all that, by the circumstances and conventions? She wonders as well if that was their one try at being good people, and that's what actually ruined them.

Gina comes shuffling up the sidewalk from the bus stop, carrying a brown bag. In her early forties but like a worn-out old lady, heavy and gray. Gina's never taken care of herself at all. The thick neck, thinning lips, and ratty hair all make her look on the edge of oldness.

"Oh hell, and look who's back," Gina barks loudly from up the block, and Christine instantly knows she isn't sober, just reloading. "You here to beg?"

Christine stands, even as the urge is to go in the other direction.

"I just want to talk to you."

"At your convenience, I guess," Gina says. She moves aside, letting Gina go inside first.

"Door's open, hello!" Gina says.

Inside, she puts the bag down, but doesn't take out the bottle that's so obviously inside it. She drops heavily onto a chair at the kitchen table, takes out a cigarette, and lights up.

"Okay, so?" she says.

Christine is metering her own breaths, trying to be measured. "You said something crazy in the bar the other night and I want to get it straight."

"What's that?"

"You sounded like you were saying my uncle is my real father. Which would make my father my uncle."

Gina looks at her through the veil of that first smoky exhalation.

"What the frick are you talking about?" she says.

"You said that Robbie was my real father."

"When did I say that?"

"At the bar."

"I don't think so."

"You said it."

"Are you shitting me? Robbie? That loser?" She laughs, as if Christine is an idiot.

Christine seems to have her answer and maybe with that relief she feels herself getting indignant.

"You're calling someone a loser? You're calling *anyone* a loser?"

"You have no clue what I've been through," Gina says. "Me and Robbie? Don't make me sick!"

"You're the one who said it."

"I never said any such thing."

"Whatever," Christine says. "I'm leaving now."

"I thought you already left," Gina says, going cold. "Go for good this time. You can get the rest of your stuff out of your room. This isn't a damned storage unit."

In the corner of the bedroom is a black contractor bag filled with Christine's things in an otherwise bare room. She unties the bag to check its contents, and what she sees startles her, like unearthing a time capsule from a long-past life. Issues of her main indulgence, *Seventeen* magazine. College brochures. Facial-product samples. "That shit's all getting in my way," Gina calls from the kitchen. "Clear it the hell out!"

Christine reties the bag and lifts it. It must weigh thirty pounds. As she swings it around to hang it over her shoulder, she feels that twinge in her abdomen. That weird little feeling. The arrival of that desperately-hoped-for cramp.

She puts the bag down and goes to the bathroom. Locked inside, she lets out a breath and checks herself. And there it is. She's fine. There will be no babies. She begins to sob, and runs the water in the sink full blast to cover her own sound. She washes her face and when she comes up from the water and looks in the mirror, she sees someone with new life, one to spend right.

She comes out of the bathroom and looks at Gina, somehow more charitably.

"You should try harder, to be better," she says to Gina. "Your health."

"How I am is none of your business," Gina says, more softly. "So see you around."

Christine wrestles the bag out the door, and up to the bus stop. She needs a tampon and it's a long bus ride. She sits on the bench with her trash bag, and opens it again, thinking to cast off some ballast. She takes out a *Seventeen* and looks at the cover. *Get your dream hair!* it shouts at her. She feels empty, neutral, like a scientist looking at a specimen. She doesn't need this stuff anymore. She's about to find a trash bin when she hears the bus, hissing up to the stop. She drags her plastic bag onboard and shows her bus pass and sits at the rear, pressing her legs tightly all the way to Jean's. When she comes inside the house, she runs to the bathroom, to attend to herself. When she emerges, she realizes Jean and Becky are already home. Becky is sitting on Christine's bed, making one pile of magazines and one pile of mail.

"Do you want those magazines?" Christine says.

"Since you're eighteen, I figured you wouldn't need them. And since they're in the trash."

"You can have them."

"Do you want me to throw the mail away?"

"I can do it." Christine takes the pile, pretty much junk, and goes to the wastebasket, and drops it all in. It's after she's turned that something registers, and she turns back. It's a manila envelope, chunky. The handwriting is plain and square, covered with more than enough stamps and with no return address. It feels heavy. She tears it open. On top is the letter.

I'm someone who knew your father and he loaned me money before he passed on. I'm sending this money back to you as repayment of that loan. I hope you can use it as support for yourself. Sorry your father had to go the way he did.

K.D.

And there, inside, is all the money. Cash. She counts out fifty hundred-dollar bills. Christine looks again at the handwriting. It seems as if written slowly, and willfully plain. But she can still see what's there. The slant of the words, and the loops of the lower zones. The arcades and garlands she'd studied so hard, so many years ago. It seems like it was trying not to be, but has failed. This is Quinn Boyle's handwriting, with a mask on.

36.

QUINN HAS BEEN SITTING IN JAIL FOR TWO WEEKS
when Robbie finds the public defender coming out of a dank
courtroom, looking winded. Alyssa is young but has a long menu
of thieves, druggies, layabouts, and robbers to usher through
these halls of justice. But he can tell she's intrigued by Quinn's
case, of a man who insists on his inability to remember, even as
everyone thoroughly doubts him.

"Let's go outside," she says. "I need a smoke."

The courthouse fronts South Main, and when they've gotten
outside, she stands in the wind of the sidewalk and leans over to
light up.

"Where's this all going?" he says.

"The DEA would love to figure out what happened to Santoro," she says. "And your brother just keeps on saying he has no
idea. Nobody can completely refute him. They had a psychologist talk with him, and his report is back as inconclusive."

"Really . . ."

"The psychologist doesn't seem to completely believe it."

"So where are we at on this?"

"There's basically no evidence. The Feds aren't all that interested in losing a case, when there's so little to go on and there's

not much in it for them. The case is against Santoro, and Santoro was a small fry. So it's really only about the child support now, and the child has come in now with the cash, saying the handwriting proves it's Quinn Boyle who sent it—and God knows where that cash came from."

"So he just keeps playing it like this?"

"Nobody's got anything right now," she says. "No boat, no Santoro, no nothing. You have a man who turns up saying he has no recollection, living three thousand miles away from here, on subsistence level, with no assets except the pay he just got. The boat had no bank note, so only he takes that loss. He didn't file an insurance claim, although the fact you did on behalf of his estate could get sticky."

"They turned down the claim anyway. He'd missed his premium payments."

"Lucky you."

"And so what if he helped Santoro?"

"Then he'd better hope Santoro stays under the radar, because that could really change things up the road. If he helped Santoro evade prison, then your brother will likely go to prison himself."

"And so he just keeps saying he doesn't remember."

"Yup. He says he doesn't remember anything from the day the boat went out. He says he doesn't even know if Santoro was on the boat. He says he doesn't even remember getting on the boat. He says he only remembers later, being in Seattle."

"The Coast Guard spent two days searching for him."

"Because you reported him missing. Your brother never told anybody he needed any help."

Robbie shakes his head, incredulous.

"I can hardly believe it might work."

"They have very little to hold him on, right now, other than the support issue, which the daughter is claiming to be settled,"

Alyssa says. "I'm sure they'll all go after him the minute they have something substantive. If that happens."

Robbie is just looking at her.

"People used to take the Fifth," Alyssa says. "Now they just say they can't remember. Post-traumatic stress and so on."

"And so now he could just get out?" Robbie says.

"Wow, you actually sound disappointed," Alyssa says, flicking her cigarette butt to the pavement.

In Quinn comes to the courtroom, in the orange of the inmate, the wrists bound, even for the lesser crime of which he is technically accused. Department of Corrections procedure, apparently. Seated then by the bailiff, who removes the cuffs, Quinn nods to his defender, already there.

Robbie is in the back of a nearly empty room, in the pew-like bench, observing what seems the drudge of another day of dispensing cases. The judge slumps in his high-backed chair, reading whatever filing he has in hand; the lawyers at the tables seem to be working it out between themselves. Robbie recognizes one of the younger reporters from his own paper, Trev, up at the front, trying to eavesdrop. Next to him is a young woman, a television reporter from the local station, and her cameraman set up in the far corner. Quinn sits staring straight ahead, not turning to see who might have come to see this thing through. Robbie is the only one.

There's no drama here at all, only the slog through dispensation. The judge closes the folder and says, generally, "Do we have any charges?"

The prosecutor, a white-haired gent with a ponderous gut, stands and says, "As to the child support, we're willing to vacate charges given the payment sent to the dependent child, and her statement finding this satisfactory outcome."

The judge sits with his eyes nearly closed, then his head comes up.

"And do we expect any federal charges?"

"I don't know of any, Your Honor," Alyssa says, and she and the judge look to the prosecutor.

"I'm aware of none, Your Honor," the prosecutor says, with scant emotion.

"Are there any representatives of the U.S. Attorney's office here?" the judge says generally.

Everyone waits, but no one answers. The judge closes the folder. This is a place where all manner of human folly is reduced to the drone of procedure. In this deadened air, the judge coughs into his hand.

"Then that's it for us. The cash has been transferred to the mother to satisfy the previous balance. The daughter, who is of majority age, says she is satisfied with that. We will set up with Family Services to get Mr. Boyle on a payment plan until such time that his daughter completes her college studies."

The judge then looks directly at Quinn, and not so charitably.

"The defendant says he's suffered a loss of recollection, as to this incident. These charges do not speak to that situation, and whatever skepticism this court may have is not based on hard facts at this time. Unless this man is charged with a crime, by *somebody*, I have no reason to hold him."

The judge looks up at them all. Quinn sits as if no part of any of it.

"Okay, then?"

No arguments.

"Let's get him back up to the ACI and all checked out. Mr. Boyle, you should be ready to be released by this afternoon. Do you need to arrange for a ride?"

"No, sir," Quinn says.

"In some circumstances, I'd tell you not to leave the state, Mr. Boyle," the judge says. "But our friends on the federal side don't seem concerned about that at this time."

"I understand," Quinn says.

The judge motions with his hand, weak and dismissive, and Quinn stands for the bailiff. The wrists are cuffed and he's led out the back, without ever looking up.

Trev, the reporter, comes over. "Hey, Robbie, what do you think of that?"

"I have no idea," Robbie says. "Really."

"So when are you finishing your vacation?"

"I'd say I'll be back in tomorrow morning," Robbie says.

Back up the stairs to the newsroom, and across to the fishbowl where Chip sits, head down.

"No charges on my brother. I just came from there. The child support is all settled. They're letting him out this afternoon."

"I'd need to know that officially," Chip says.

"Trev covered it. Ask him. My brother will be out this afternoon. Maybe I can cover a game tomorrow tonight."

"Not so quick," Chip says, and Robbie can see he's still processing.

"I could really use the money," Robbie says. "I've been kind of tapped, looking after my niece. Tomorrow, then?"

Chip is shaking his head, slowly, working up to it.

"Not that easy, Rob. Charges or no charges, people still think something's up. And they think you were in the middle of it."

"There are no charges on *me*, Chip. There was never a discussion of any charges on me."

"People wonder about your mystery trips. A journalist needs to maintain credibility."

"Journalist? I cover high-school sports."

"Even more important. High-school kids, you know? Must set a good example."

"All families have to deal with some shit once in a while, Chip."

"This is twice with your brother in jail. Then on the lam."

"They didn't ever characterize it that way. He can't remember anything about what happened. He may have hit his head."

Chip laughs at that one. "Come on, Rob, give me a break. Just be glad the judge bought it."

"So how long will this suspension be?"

"Rob, you didn't really seem to understand what was supposed to be a helpful gesture. The suspension's permanent. You won't be back."

"On what grounds?"

"Weren't you just listening to me?"

"If I get a lawyer, you could never make that stick."

"Robbie, Jesus. Trust me that Corporate will make sure you go broke in the process. What's the fascination with this paper, anyway? You should have moved on years ago. This place is for young ones who take what we pay until they have a chance to do better. You just never left."

"I've been here twenty years."

Chip looks at him directly. "But that's exactly the problem, isn't it?"

He wasn't asked to come, but Robbie is at the ACI's main gate anyway, waiting. He's called Alyssa repeatedly, but it keeps going to voice mail; he presumes her to be in a late-afternoon stretch in one courtroom and then the next. But he's got something to say to Quinn, and he'll sit here in his car until midnight if he needs to, and he will get it said.

After an hour of listening to sports radio, he sees the gate open, and then Quinn. Hooded gray sweatshirt, jeans, and

263

boots, a man who looks like he's getting off a day of work. The hood is up, as a monk's, head bowed, penitent. A guard is with him, pointing, seeming to give him directions. Robbie gets out of his car, and at the slam of his door, Quinn looks over.

"I don't need a ride," Quinn says, as the guard recedes.

"That's not why I'm here."

"Then why are you here?"

"Look, you're out. No charges. Tell me the truth of all this."

"I told you what I can."

"I've gotten fired because of this."

"No one asked you to try to find me."

"I've looked after your daughter."

"I sent her money."

"Yeah, Gina's probably out spending it now. Christine will never see that."

"I'll be sending her more money soon."

Right now, Robbie feels the urge to attack his brother, physically or otherwise. He's up close, but Quinn is completely passive.

"Where are you going?"

"Don't know yet."

"Will you let me know where you end up?"

"Christine will know."

Robbie won't let it go like this.

"I'm going to pay for a test."

"What test is that?"

"The DNA. Not that I have any money, but I told her I'd pay so she knows she's your daughter."

"I don't know that she's my daughter."

"We'll find out. You can let them put a swab in your mouth, or they can do it with me. The outcome will be the same."

"I wouldn't do that to her, bud. I have a pretty good feeling it won't be me."

"Who do you think it could be?"

"I'd guess it could be Freddy Santoro."

"That's your imagination. I remember you said that years ago, and nothing ever came of it. She looks more like you."

Quinn shrugs. "I guess people can make themselves see what they want to see. I really wasn't around to be that girl's father. I think Santoro always enjoyed that. Trying to get the better of me. And you know Gina did."

"Well, maybe he can take some responsibility."

"Maybe he will," Quinn says.

Robbie waits, thinking Quinn might ask something about him losing his job, but he doesn't. Robbie's spent the afternoon looking at job listings, and maybe he feels a bit more hopeful. He'll find something, he thinks. And with that uncertainty, he conjures back a long-ago feeling, the butterflies of competition, the flutter on the brink of stepping up and having to prove yourself. It was such a long time gone. He might even be excited, waiting for what comes next.

"So I don't need a ride," Quinn says, a stranger now.

"Have it your way," Robbie says. "You always did."

Robbie can see his little punch has scored, but Quinn shakes it off. "You can go first," he says. "I'm going to hang here for a few minutes."

"Just like that . . ."

Quinn gathers himself, clearly about to say something he'd rather not.

"Look," he finally says. "We're both free. Don't you understand that? Can't you embrace that? That we can all really be free?"

In his car, as Robbie turns the ignition, the sports talk comes back on. Long harangues about the pitching rotation for next year's Red Sox. Men at microphones, shouting at each other, so sure of their beliefs. Raising their voices like these things are sacred, when in any true scale they are not and never were.

He eases the car out of the parking space and Quinn stands there with his hands in the pockets of his hoodie. Robbie has the urge to roll down the window and shout for him to just get in, but he knows it would only be one more rebuff. His brother, the ever-stubborn.

He turns onto the service road and can't help looking in the mirror. His brother, not looking at him as he recedes. Robbie gets to the stop sign and makes his right turn. His brother, once again lost in the ether. His brother, whom he once loved.

37.

SO THEN CHRISTINE HEARS QUINN IS GONE. GINA HAS the cash and the way she sees it, the money is paying her backward. As if Christine was only her endless burden.

A few weeks later, Christine moves back in with Robbie, because he has offered and Jean has already been too generous. But he also tells her he had an interview for a new job, a very different job, in Binghamton, New York. He said if he gets it, which he thinks he will, there will always be a place for her there. He says he expects Sarah would come summer vacations and school vacations. Christine doesn't see herself living in a place she's never even heard of, but maybe that would change in time. But she's also got a degree to complete, and her own life to begin.

Nick hadn't kept his mouth shut about their night together. Christine had gotten her period then spent a month convincing people she wasn't pregnant, and another month convincing them she hadn't gone and had an abortion. Nick's mother had called Gina, screaming at her; Gina had run her mouth on a barstool, and Buddy said the customers were "aware." But again he didn't fire her, so she kept working. She was nearing the finish of Year One of the community college, halfway to her associate's in nursing degree. She just needed to hang on, and she'd have something nearly solid.

Christine feels badly for Jean. She and Robbie split without ever seeming to sort out what had happened. But, of course, who was to know what really went on? Robbie stuck to his story of going off on a search based on a scant tip, and Quinn had stuck to his tale of lost memory. There could have been alternate versions. Jean got very quiet in those weeks Christine stayed with her; she said that taking care of her daughter, and working hard to do so, was all that really mattered. Christine had apologized for thinking Robbie had gone off with Dawn, but Jean had waved her off, saying, "It went a lot deeper than that. It's hard to believe Robbie didn't know things he denies knowing."

And so Christine went into mourning again. Her father was gone, what felt like for good, and this time at his clear volition. He'd told the court he'd be sending money. She would only know him by a return address.

That first night, on which Robbie had come and told her Quinn's boat was missing, had been one filled with memory dreams. The images in her head flickered like the old VHS tapes, those half-hearted efforts Gina made to record the birthday parties and holidays. The actual footage was mostly filled with Gina's bar friends jammed onto the couch with their mixed drinks and cigarettes, and Christine smiling toothlessly, oblivious, blowing out candles, and Heather at the edge of the frame, the teenager already plotting her own escape. But Christine didn't have a lot of memories of her father, so she took what she had and embellished them, or maybe just extended them through speculation. In the dream videos, he was there, and smiling, and her father in the way she thought fathers were supposed to be.

But the dreams she had for weeks after the disappearance of the *Christine II* were of rough seas, of pitching vessels and men underwater. She'd come up from a pillow in the middle of the night, gasping. Most of her grieving for him, the abstracted Quinn Boyle who never truly existed in her life, was in the quietest hours of the night, before morning and the way life pushed you on to the next thing. But in those first months, the feeling was physically painful, the sharp blade of all the regret she felt. Maybe the regret wasn't for what anyone could have done, but for what was so easily missed. In school, later on, the reading in psychology class covered the Seven Stages of Grief. Her classmates slogged through the reading as they did most else, dry text that had nothing to do with them, just another dose of "material" to be thrown back at them on a test. Christine, conversely, couldn't stop rereading it, both comforted by it but a little horrified, too, that the things we go through as humans can follow such straightforward scripts. We all think our own story is painfully, and singularly, personal.

When she had first met Nick, they had sat in the snack bar at the community college and she'd told him a little about herself. Introductions are always an exercise in self-definition: Who am I? She told him about her parents and she told him about the *Christine II*, out there somewhere, named after her, broken apart. Having failed to protect its sailors from the overwhelming powers of the natural world. After she finished, she'd felt conflicted. She wondered if she was laying it on thick to connect with a boy, even as she kept most of her own agony held in. She felt as if showing off, but she wasn't even giving him anything real.

"How can you possibly feel bad about someone being gone, when you hardly knew him?" Nick said.

"Because of all the things that didn't happen, and that can never happen now," she said, and began to shed real tears that she worried he'd think were for drama's sake.

"Sorry, I just don't get it," he said.

Gina seemed unmoved by any of it. But then again, Christine now saw so little of her. Maybe she held things from Christine, as Christine did from her.

So she walked around with this sick feeling for months and months, and a year passed, and then one day her father had somehow risen from the dead.

It was an amazing day. Amazing how she found out, really. No one who should have called her actually did. She was doing a shift in the restaurant and Bob, the cop, had come in for lunch. She could see him looking at her, checking. She couldn't figure out what she had done this time. She didn't have his table, either; the new girl, Val, did. But then Val came to her and said, "That guy wants to talk with you."

She went to him as he sat reading the paper.

"Yes?" Christine said, in too defensive a defensive tone.

"I think what your father did was pretty awful," he said.

Of course, she's thinking, *My dead father, who's been gone for more than a year?*

"Yeah, well you're pretty awful," Christine said.

He looked like she hit him.

"I meant that in a sympathetic way," he said.

"Sympathy for who?"

"For you."

"I have no idea what you're talking about."

Bob looked at her as if she were trying to mess with his head.

"You do know that your father's been found alive, right?"

She stared at him for a long time, and the blood must have been fleeing her brain and pumping adrenalin. She felt as if levitating from the floor, right until she hit it.

They propped Christine up on a nearby chair. Val brought water.

"I can't believe no one told you," Bob said. "I should have kept my mouth shut. I'm really sorry."

But she wanted to know, and he told what he could. Buddy let Christine go for the rest of day.

So on this day of sudden news, Christine stayed in bed for hours, feeling awful. She'd determined, very young, that people are basically shitty. As she got older and retroactively put the pieces together, she truly saw how bad people could be. *What the hell?* she thought, of a childhood spent in the midst of Gina's endless party, of her father's invisibility, of the endless parade of men sitting on the living-room couch, drunk, and them being there in the morning snoring from her bed. *What the hell?*

Then, well, she had to pee. She thought, *You need to do that.* Not a great or deep philosophy, but meaning: you get up, do what you have to, you deal with it. She would deal with life without a father, or a mother. She accepted that they had been caught in something so young they never had the chance to be whatever it was they might have been. She tried to feel charity, and forgiveness. She even tried to feel love. The kind where you feel forsaken, and where it's you doing all the giving, with nothing expected back. Thinking that, she felt better than she had in a long time.

A few days later, she was holding an envelope full of cash. Not exactly the love she wanted so badly, but a sign that something had been there. And Nick, misguided as he was, trying to do something on her account. And Jean, who didn't need to do a thing for her, but did.

So there she was, just trying to feel thankful. The world so full of damaged people and at least being thankful for what small things they might do. Christine thought it would be nice to be a nurse someday, to do small acts that might be remembered, even if so small that she might not remember them at all when she punched out at the end of another day.

PART SEVEN

38.

THE BUS PULLS OUT OF PROVIDENCE ON AN EARLY EVE-
ning in which the fading sky has gone deep red. Quinn looks at
the legal papers in his lap as the bus crunches into a higher gear
and strains up the ramp to Interstate 95 South. The bus ticket,
his traveling itinerary, says $283, 5 transfers, 3 days, 3 hours, 56
minutes. He's on his way out. He'll pass through New York City
at eleven tonight. He'll see Chicago late tomorrow morning. He
can be back in his room in Seattle two days after that. Quinn
thinks of his running shoes, and of his cut-foam mattress. He's
tired, so deathly tired, and wants nothing now but solitude.

He has no driver's license, and no credit cards. He has some of
the remaining pay from the *Arctic Star* (less his next scheduled
child-support payment), stuffed in the pack on the rack above
his seat. He has his release papers, and by virtue of those, he has
his name back. Quinn Boyle, something he thought he'd perma-
nently retired. It's his to use again, but he's not completely sure
he ever will. Better to disappear before they have another reason
to come after you. And Ken Doyle, in the end, has turned out to
be a simpler and maybe more contented man.

Freedom, not only from another prison, but out from the
low ceiling of his hidden life. His life of shame and apology and

275

defense. For once, he feels truly free, and for once the accounts are settled. And that kind of freedom is unsettling, no notion of where to go, or what to do, or whom to be. The bus is his capsule for three days more. He relaxes into it, the sky fading through the trees.

He tries not to think about his brother, of all of the loyalty Robbie had unquestioningly given and all the trouble he endured, by virtue of being the brother. Quinn knows that to Robbie he has become an unsolvable riddle, and Quinn can do absolutely nothing about that. And in this, Quinn feels the first knot of emotion he's let himself feel in years, as he tries to fix his eyes on the horizon and let himself settle as one would to fight off a seasickness.

The sun is gone, as he is now.

He has no joy in having fooled them. He said he couldn't remember what had happened, in part because he wanted desperately not to. But the memory always came back, unbidden.

They had come out of port that morning into a rising sun, riding high and unburdened on lights seas. Quinn had been feeling a small hope, that the catch might even better the last one. He always believed he had honed a gut instinct about what the seas had to offer, and this one already felt rich. He watched the far horizon, only Ireland out there past the chop, as Dad used to say. But Santoro, at the stern, kept his eyes shoreward, first as town faded back, and even as that western horizon came as blank as the one at their bow.

Two hours out of port Quinn began to prep the bait, to Santoro's sluggish match. True, much was just busy work, but they were at work now. Quinn was afoot with things as Santoro only sat.

"You can get to it any time now," Quinn had shouted from his place, to little effect. Santoro was just sitting at his bait, looking dark and anxious. Quinn would not give in so easily; he didn't want to concede his mistake so early, of heading into a bad trip in rich waters. He said nothing. He knew Santoro's mood, waiting to go to prison. Quinn's own last days before his sentence had been a lurching between a manic need to blot the mind through physical effort, and the crash into prostrate melancholy, thinking of all the stupid mistakes, and all the ignored warnings. He'd been there, for sure, so this now was revealing itself as a new mistake, to not have understood that. Santoro in the bar was a man fueled by newfound shame and entrapment. For that, finally, Quinn had decided to be charitable, even after all the history. The man had imagined one last flight to sea could pull him from his gloom. And now it was not. Santoro was showing no signs of pulling himself into the work. Quinn, alone, wouldn't be able to counter that. One man could not bring in the catch they both needed.

But Quinn had allowed so much, in so many ways. Santoro had always been his main supplier. Quinn's needs had forged an odd alliance that was never truly friendship. Robbie had no idea how many bags Santoro had handed Quinn over so many years. The ones Quinn had been caught with had been bought in bulk, to ford a long season. When Quinn was crazed with the need for a fix, Santoro came in like a savior. In his own time in prison, Quinn had, after a month of being clean, raged silently at the thought of Santoro, who had so easily helped him into his addiction. But by the middle of the bit, Quinn had turned his rage only at himself. He was the only one accountable. And by the time the gate opened and he walked back into his version of freedom, he'd gone a long way toward forgiving himself, and Santoro, for their many shared sins.

He'd have turned the boat around right then, but for his own false economies. He thought of what he'd just paid for the bait. He couldn't bear wasting it. Another stupid mistake. He detected no duplicity in Santoro's sudden slumping, only the simple loss of hope. The man had gotten on the boat back at the harbor with a gym bag and barely a word to Quinn, who really never had much of a word for him.

So Quinn went to the wheelhouse. He busied himself with the radio, listening for what other boats were getting up ahead. Three hours out, and his mind caught up in bugs a hundred miles ahead, was when the first blow hit him.

He'd never heard Santoro come up on him. And when he took the impact, along the neck close the base of the skull, he didn't know who or what it was. He dropped to the wet deck, hard, stunned at first and then nearly blinded with pain. He felt Santoro's boots up against him. He went fetal, all reflex now and no conscious thought. Here was the second blow. He was hit across the ribs, and then on the hip, and he knew now he would die if he just laid there. Now Quinn came out of his tail-fisted cinch and kicked out, hard, and then leg-whipped again, and on one of those thrashings he got Santoro flush on the side of the leg, folding the knee sideways, unnaturally, and making Santoro bray in a truly surprised agony. He dragged himself back, and then went onto his knees.

They both rose to their feet, both now infused with great suffering, two men on the tiny expanse of the aft deck, surrounded by opposite walls of wire pots leading to the open stern. The deck was now a cage in which they held opposite corners. He saw that Santoro had in his hand an aluminum baseball bat. The shark bat. Quinn's head was all but rendered to incapacity, but the brainless instincts were intact: survival, and the will to fight, and the flame of vengeance.

Santoro, swinging the bat like the bad ballplayer he always was, had botched his one chance. It must have been intended to be a clear and killing blow. But he'd missed, maybe an inch too low—a margin misplayed enough to be a foul ball, a missed tackle, a free throw clanging off the rim.

Quinn's neck burned furiously. He could feel his right arm going numb. The engines churned on, carrying them to deeper seas, and he saw now how Santoro was himself in stunned pain, and scared now.

There were no words to speak. The sound of the ocean and the engine had disappeared. Only the hoarse breathing inside their own ears, the gasping of men in a final fight. Quinn was hunched, struggling for balance. Santoro had the bat, and now gripped it more tightly, raising it high, not preparing to take a baseball swing but rather a hard and downward chop, an axe onto wood. Santoro lurched forward, the one leg nearly useless.

The muscle memory of so many forgotten afternoons on muddy football fields. The unending whistle, the muddy ocean of cleat marks as they all listened to their breathing inside their helmets and again leaned into their stances as the coaches roared. Quinn was working on only the scant reflex of endless repetitions, so many years ago. He knew this was a last chance.

He hunched, and sprung, coming at Santoro low, as Santoro never did learn to do, despite all the coaches' exhortations. Quinn was uncoiling, driven by sweet fluid memory, hitting Santoro at the pointers of his hips. The perfection of well-executed movement. Santoro had only begun his downward swing. The barrel of the bat came down hard now near Quinn's tailbone, setting a new fire that shot down his legs as he took Santoro off his feet, and up, and over. The tumble and thump, and then quiet. And then Santoro was gone.

Quinn lay face-down on the deck for a long time, trying to regain the movement in his legs. He faded in and out of the light. For long moments the sensation was of paralysis, but he willed his toes to move and then, miraculously, they did. The engine churned beneath him, and it was some time more before he pulled himself to his knees. He moved, crabbing, to the wheelhouse, and cut the engine. The boat, coasting, made no sound. The bat lay on the deck. He pushed himself up until he could see over the transom. He looked through the high stacks of traps. He saw only water, endlessly behind him.

The *Christine II* drifted, for what must have been hours. He'd struggled into the cabin and onto his bunk, through-shot with pain. He was continuing his physical inventory, trying to guess what might come back and what might not. In time, everything was moving, if painfully; he knew the damage would heal. He also knew that even this agony was masked with adrenalin, and when it abated he would truly suffer.

On that first try, Santoro had missed his chosen spot by a couple of inches, the difference of life and death for both of them. Had the bat hit the base of his skull, had it crushed that small bump where the neck rose up under the edges of his hair, he'd have been instantly prone. Instead, the barrel of the bat hit him along the thick of the lower neck in a way that had spared him. He guessed he might have reflexively turned when he heard, or sensed, the sound of Santoro beginning his swing. The hard-earned straps of muscle along his neck, from the years on the traps, had been able to sustain the blow.

When he finally had gathered himself to form a clear thought, it was only of how he could ever get past this. No one was going to believe him, even as Santoro clearly had his motivation to escape. Quinn had no guilt about what he had done. It had all been survival. He felt no sympathy for Santoro, as he never had. The only question was if this would bring him to his own end.

Quinn stood finally, grimacing, and stared at the reaches of sea, as he had those years before, when Botelho had simply been there one moment, and gone the next. Quinn was not a murderer then, nor did he feel he was now. But he was only four hours out of a port to which he could not return in a way he once had. He had nowhere to go that wouldn't bring him ruin.

It was only ten in the morning. He was realizing why Santoro had attacked so quickly. Close to shore, relatively, for a man who would have had to pilot a boat back himself. Enough fuel to take the Christine II somewhere else, a place where he might escape. And better than two full days before anyone would fail to notice they had not returned. Longer, maybe.

Quinn had no such clarity at this moment. He lay in the cabin with the same forty-eight hours left for plots and contingencies, but utterly without design. This was the life he knew best, far from shore. He rocked in it now, sheltered for the brief time that he could be.

He heard the other boat as one hears a train by listening with an ear close to the track, the subsonic hum that courses through the hull and the bunk. Since he'd been hit, the ears had been chiming steadily; the urgent pitch reminded him of the sanctus bells at a high moment of consecration, reverberating in an altar boy's hand but never quite dying. Someone was coming straight at him, not passing from a distance. He heard the engine grow closer, and then closer, and then cut.

He lay very still.

"Santoro?" a voice called from far off.

The new surge of adrenaline stanched his pain better than any shot of heroin ever had. He rolled himself over, silently, and moved along the floor and snuck a look out the edge of the hatch. The man standing in the boat was no one he'd ever seen. He was dressed plainly but carrying a short-barreled assault rifle with a long and curving clip that reminded Quinn, incongruously, of the centerboard of the old wooden catboat in which Dad had taught him and Robbie to sail. The boat was unmarked, thirty feet, built for pleasure cruising. Quinn saw no markings or numbers, just bone-white hull. Not a cop or a fishing inspector, and too far out at sea to be observing any protocol. And he'd never seen a cop carrying iron like this guy was.

"Santoro, you done?" he called from the other boat.

Quinn waited.

The silence of the doldrums; the gentle rock of placid seas. The *Christine II* undulated on easy water. Then he could hear the other boat bumping up against his own.

Quinn was low now, a bug in its bedroom, trapped and ready for a fight. Under the bunk, he slid out the box with the tools and the lines and under it all, that sawed-off shotgun. He'd bought it back then out of fear, when he was buying too many drugs and realizing that it was a dangerous pastime. He'd spent a skein of shaky months when he couldn't pay up, with this weapon by his side, ready for their attempt. One of those had been Santoro, who'd fed him those bags of heroin in endless, easy procession. Payments, in time, were made. The fear had abated, finally; the odd dilemma had become that of how to dispose of a gun. So he simply had not.

He slid under the bunk in the space where the box had been, and waited. He had the stubbed barrel trained from the shadow on the three steps down from the work deck. He felt himself shaking. When the boots came one step down, and then another, and he saw them abruptly pivot his way, he brought the barrel up and fired.

The blast in that small cabin cut out his hearing, but then the assault rifle was going off in the shot man's hand, the death grip, the holes penetrating the hull. The roar was so overwhelming

282

and unimpeded that Quinn didn't register the body hitting the floor, but he felt the boat shudder. He saw the face then, staring back at him, the mouth open in postmortem surprise. A face he'd never seen. It hadn't been a head shot, Quinn's aim lower to be sure he hit his target, but the man was clearly, instantly, dead. The blood was pooling from the chest, in what he expected was a gaping wound.

Quinn couldn't hear anything now, and he didn't know who else was coming. He tried to reach for the semiautomatic, but it had fallen on the far side of the body. It was an instant in which one has a premonition of his own death, but then nothing happened. His ears began to return, the altar boy's bells more insistent, and slowly the sound of the ocean began to rise above the clamoring chime.

He crawled out from under the bunk. The body was facedown, the head turned to where he had been. He studied the face.

"Who *are* you?" he said aloud, and aware of his own voice cracking. He felt along the pants. No wallet, no papers, nothing. A man who had made a plan. The holes in the hull were at the waterline, pulsing seawater into the cabin.

Now he had the semi-automatic, still hot at the barrel, a machine far beyond his capabilities. He located the safety but then left it open. He slowly edged his way onto the deck and looked to see who else was in the unmarked boat. But it was gone off, soundlessly. He came up higher onto deck and he could see it now, adrift a quarter mile away, empty, a ghost ship moving in its own currents. He went to the wheelhouse and turned the engine over.

How did this guy find me?

This was big ocean out here and this was no coincidence. After Quinn had sided up on the boat and tied it on to his own, it occurred to him to search Santoro's gym bag. Water was ankle-deep now in the cabin. The *Christine* had taken on a starboard list. Inside the bag he found a driver's license with Santoro's face and an unfamiliar name, and a half-dozen prepaid debit cards with no name and no clear balance, and a zipped bank depository bag with five thousand in cash, all in hundreds. And at the bottom of the bag, below the changes of clothes and scant toiletries, there it was. He took the device out and turned it in his hand. White, domed like a smooth-shelled clam, cold plastic inscribed *Nav Tracker 1.0.*

He threw it from the unmarked boat as if it had a stinger, watching it hit the water and float. The he used the gaffer to pull it back, used Santoro's bat to smash it to small bits, pulled the battery, and threw the pieces back in. Now he flung the bat out, watching it helicopter and then slash the water. He didn't care if it floated, but it didn't.

The anonymous body lay in his cabin and he would not touch it. He went onto the other boat, searching furiously. He found the tracker, and smashed it against the gunwale, likewise dumping its candy-wired guts on the water. He kept looking, frantic, for devices. He threw the distress beacon over, and clambered back onto the *Christine II* and dumped his own. In that instant, he felt naked. He was far to sea, with two men dead and no clear exit.

Now he went into the cabin and took his own gear, and Santoro's. He had the semiautomatic and he went back over onto the white boat. He had no clue if this would work. But he untied, and when he'd drifted off ten yards, he leveled the gun at the waterline of the *Christine II*. His fiberglass boat. His flimsy tub. He'd been, with the last of his money, reduced to that refitted weekender, a sport fisher in disguise. He'd felt the shame of it. Even in his ancient wooden warhorse, he'd felt like a captain, and he'd imagined himself someday in a vessel of steel, the true worth. It was a ship when it was steel. He'd often noted how around him, in the harbor, was an iron fleet. A lot of them were nearly rusted through; didn't matter. He'd thought to be in fiberglass—to be in a plastic boat—had merely been the latest of so many shames.

The trigger took more strength than he expected, but then the gun went off. The power of it was overwhelming; he fought it as the rounds, dozens in an instant, blew the side of the boat apart. He stopped, and watched. The *Christine II* listed more now, first slowly, then in geometric speed. It was taking on water steadily but he realized he needed to open the hold tank to let the boat fully sink. He turned the white boat back toward his own, roped to the languidly-sinking boat, and hurdled over. The cabin was already underwater, the anonymous body submerged. Quinn went to the empty hold and opened the valves and the water flooded in. He jumped back onto the other boat and when he hit, the legs seared with the returning pain. He was still in his orange rubber pants. He pulled them off and flung them toward his own boat. The pants, shed, stayed afloat, a bright flag on dark water.

The Christine II went down quickly then. For a few minutes he waited for the bob of its return, some upward push to stay above. But there was no return. He had three hundred feet of water under him.

The semiautomatic lay on the deck, but all his fight was gone. He picked it up, feeling the heat on the cooked-off barrel, and dropped it over the side. It fell into the blue, and slick in its blackness it might have seemed a fish, in that instant before it was gone.

Toward evening, moving south, he tried not to think, but his head was scrambled. His legs and arms were searing. His neck was tightened up and hard to move. The sun was dropping fast and the cold was with him, and just before the horizon faded into dark he shouted out at the water.

"Santoro, you fucking idiot, the guy would have killed you anyway!"

The sun set over a dark day. The dark night seemed oddly bright. He navigated by long-familiar stars, dead-reckoning all the way southwest until he saw the Montauk Point Light and went northwest into Long Island Sound. He followed the coast by its landed constellations, the light's throw from distant civilization, running off into imprecise distances. At dawn he turned toward shore. He was somewhere along southern Connecticut. He saw beach houses and the steeple beyond, what must have been a town. He made his way down the shore and into a marshy inlet with high grass and no buildings in sight.

He stepped off the boat into knee-deep water, and pushed it back off by the bow, turning it, watching it slowly recede with the tide. To someone looking at it from shore, at a boat out there on the water, it would seem only the vessel of a lazy day of fishing. By the time the tide would deliver it back, empty and unmarked, he'd have a full day on that news, and two more on the disappearance of the *Christine II*.

It was early, the air only beginning to warm. He limped out of the cold water with the dawn sun behind him. The waves brushed the shore, only the hint of undertow that would presume to pull him back. He moved despite the pain, up the beach and through the reeds and then along a quiet road, his shadow in front long and etched. He carried one bag, all he needed; the rest was strewn along miles of ocean. There was no going back and no need for remembering. He would push all this from his mind and wipe it clean. He would willfully forget. *I don't remember. I do not remember.* The rhythm of the phrase began to merge with his footsteps, a mile and then another, a town and then another, and then an early-morning bus stop. And then, by that night, a cross-country bus on which he would bear his searing pain sitting upright and cramped. And then onward to a life, healed and without expectation, and freed of a lifetime of shame.

But right then came that singular pang of doubt, of walking away from all he had known. The comfort of a hostile place, but one of familiarity. Grief beset him, in a choked moment. To never know those people again, nor they him. As clean as a death. But he was a man with no choices now, except this one.

By night's cover, he'd followed the stars, to this terminal point on a rocky shore. Now, with the warmth on his back from behind him, he would watch the day rise, and follow him, and overtake him and move ahead, toward other places. Now, with nothing else left, he would follow the sun.